I0634742

# Saved by The Bull

Book 1
In the *Al Sharika* series

By

## Richard Sexton

Saved by the Bull

Book 1 in the *Al Sharika* series

Copyright 2024 Richard Sexton who has asserted his right to be identified under the Copyright, Designs and Patents Act, 1988 as the author of this work.

ISBN 978-1-7385-680-0-0

This novel is based on true events, but certain details, characters and timelines have been altered for dramatic purposes. While inspired by real events, this work is ultimately a fictionalized interpretation of those events. Certain long-standing institutions, agencies, public figures and public offices are mentioned, but the characters involved are wholly imaginary. Any resemblance to actual persons, living or dead, or actual events is purely coincidental.

"They suck you in until you cross the line. Then, they've got you – for life – or death."

*Sir Christopher Sherrif, KCMG OBE*

# Contents

# Chapter 1

## Travel

"She needs her bottom cleaned."

Patrick Field blinked at John, his Australian companion and owner of the Lucky Sue. It was early evening in the middle of June, 1980. Lucky Sue was a twin masted 80 foot long schooner. She was scudding along on a starboard reach headed north past the Islands of Malekula to the west and Ambrym to the east. Waves from the gentle swell slapped against her leeward bow.

"I just thought that we'd be making better way than this," Patrick grumbled. "The wind is nice and steady – it's, what? Force 3 or 4? Why aren't we going faster?"

"Speed isn't important to 'Yachties'," countered John. "I thought you realised - we roam the Pacific, stopping off to top up the stores – or when we run out of beer!" John switched his weather-beaten gaze from the tops of the sails to peer at Patrick. "We hadn't

1

been in to Port Vila for months and I quite missed the place. Anyway – keep your hair on. We'll get there soon enough. Look at that sunset - it's going to be a cracker tonight."

Patrick wasn't any happier.

Port Vila is the main town and harbour on the island of Efate. It's one of a group known then as the New Hebrides.

"Cheer up, Mate. It's a bit of a bonus dropping in to the Royal Counties Bank to collect our stores money and getting involved in this caper. I like some excitement for a change."

Unmollified, Patrick cast his mind back. He first met John at the local Sailing Club, which was out of town but sold cheap Australian beer. Patrick was a keen dinghy sailor but knew little about craft as large as the Lucky Sue. But he persisted with his concerns at their slow progress.

"If that's Malekula over there, how long is it going to take us to get to Santo? I'm worried that the wind will drop away and leave us motoring into Luganville Port. With that noise, we won't exactly be sneaking past Malo."

He'd hoped to bypass the small outer island of Malo guarding the creek entrance to the port while it was still dark. Then they could ghost as far inland as the reducing water depth and fading wind strength would permit. "I don't mean to go on about it, but if the wind drops and we motor for the final mile or so, anyone watching on shore will hear us."

-----//-----

Patrick Field had never been abroad before (except to the Isle of Wight, if that counts). But early the previous year and at the tender age of 21, he was sent by Royal Counties Bank, London to the South West Pacific for a 2-year posting.

He visited his local library to find out about the region. His parents' collection of National Geographic magazines and their set of Chambers Encyclopaedia gave him more details. This research suggested that the islands enjoyed a tropical climate but that malaria and Denge fever were common.

"Denim jeans and T-shirts would likely not be suitable. Nor would your London suits," said the Personnel Manager of Royal Counties Bank Staff Department. He'd arched an amused eyebrow at the end of Patrick's pre-embarkation briefing. Then pushed across a thick wad of airline tickets. "Buy your lightweight clothing from 'Tropiccadilly'". The man rose from his seat, indicating the short briefing was now over. That meant nothing to Patrick. He must have looked quizzical, so the Personnel Manager threw over his shoulder on his way out of the door, "It's the London branch of Airey & Wheeler. They supply clothes for hot or tropical weather."

When Patrick had gone home afterwards, he'd pulled out a map of the world and traced the route his flight would take. He would board a British Airways jet bound for Bangkok via Bahrain *en route* for Hong Kong. Then to Manila in the Philippines, Noumea in New Caledonia and finally to Port Vila in the New Hebrides.

Turning up at Heathrow airport, he shivered as he got out of the taxi. He had dressed in light clothes for his ultimate destination. But it was a very chilly morning, and he found himself doing jumping jacks while waiting in the queue at check-in.

The journey took over 50 hours because of all the stop-overs. Patrick's main recollection was one of horror when the door opened at the first stop, Bahrain airport, allowing a wall of wet heat to blast into the cabin. In fact, the Bahrain climate only varies from the high teens to around 40 degrees C.

4

But Patrick was used to United Kingdom summer highs of mid 20s and much less humidity. His second thought was relief that he had left his jeans behind and donned one of his expensive but lightweight cotton outfits for the journey. The chilly start at Heathrow was worth it. After Bahrain would be three more stops before the New Hebrides with increasing temperatures at each one.

He walked out of the air-conditioned departure lounge at La Tontouta International Airport at Noumea for the final leg of the journey, following the passengers in front. The aeroplanes used for each successive leg of the journey had become smaller and smaller as the available runway length reduced. He creased his eyes against the sun blazing down from a clear blue sky and worried that his feet would burn, even through the soles of his shoes as he stood on the baking tarmac.

A Spike Milligan parody of a poem by Felicia Hemans ('Casabianca') popped into his head:

> 'The Boy stood on the burning deck
> Whence all but he had fled -
> Twit!'

The line snaked towards the very smallest aeroplane in front of the concourse. It was a Fokker Friendship, resplendent in Air Melanesia livery of white with a sandy stripe kicking up at the tail - the airline's tiki emblem. For days, Patrick had endured little sleep, poor food and worry about boarding connecting flights. Now he watched with mounting dismay as the 30 or so passengers ahead of him jostled for position up the step ladder. Each bore several large items of luggage, wrapped tightly in sheets of bright material tied with cords. Some were so bulky they barely squeezed through the hatchway. This was going to be like the aeronautical equivalent of those daft 'How many people can you cram into a Mini' competitions, he thought.

As he shuffled closer to the bottom step, he was relieved to spot his own hold luggage in a pile of cases and bags beneath the belly of the plane. Would there be room for him on board? If there were more than 2 dozen people ahead and roughly the same number behind, how could they all fit in along with so much 'hand luggage'? He prepared himself mentally to be turned away at the door, despite the boarding pass in his hand.

Nobody else had any particular concerns, though, and there was lots of good-natured chatter going on. Maybe it was always like this. He began to realise there was an art to 'socially-acceptable' jostling. Apparently, it was ok to press your neighbour sideways gently as if you yourself were being shoved by others and could do nothing about it. Yet as he secured a foothold on the first step, English reserve compelled him to make way for a small and slightly bent older woman. She dived into the tiny gap with unexpected athleticism. Her package of belongings knocked Patrick's head sideways and blocked further movement for a short time. It was seized by a bulky Australian crewmember who wouldn't have noticed if he was lifting the old woman too. The package was squeezed through the doorway and Patrick's way was open at last.

"G'Day, Sir," greeted the airman. Patrick put down his own luggage for a moment and retrieved the boarding pass from his mouth.

"17-A, I believe," he volunteered. The man smiled and replied with a faintly amused expression and a nod towards the interior of the cabin.

"Riiight …it's back there, Mate," as though to say, 'You haven't flown with us before, have you? We don't go in for that seat numbering malarkey'.

It crossed Patrick's mind as he fastened his seat belt that the human and soft cargo filling in the fuselage was so packed, the risk of actual injury in the event of a crash was minimal, even if no belt was worn. He rested his head on the plexiglass window and watched the engine sputter into life. It coughed and belched blue smoke for a second or two but then settled into a smooth rhythm. The other engine echoed the procedure and the aeroplane began taxiing. People were still moving down the aisle, treading on each other and the bags and packages between the seats.

In the larger aircraft, there had been cabin service, of a sort. Even the occasional odd-smelling blanket in case he wanted to sleep. But in here, such luxury was non-existent. The incessant talking amongst the passengers was more akin to indecipherable yelling, because the engine noise and vibration drowned anything less than a shout. Patrick tried to look out of the window to take in the scenery. Even the window was shaking and blurring his vision - or it was his eyeballs vibrating...

About five minutes after they levelled off, the general hubbub increased in pitch. The Navigator had risen from his seat and was lobbing full cartons of juice down the aisle, it being impossible to walk to the rear of the 'plane.

Patrick was thirsty. He put aside his English reserve and called, "Could we have some more back here please?" When a precious carton arrived at row 17, he debated whether to pass it further back. His upbringing suggested this would be fair. He compromised by not drinking the one he held but promised himself that the next one he'd send rearwards. He saw that the Navigator was sitting down again and so called. loudly, "We still need juice back here, please."

The man didn't budge, but raised a laconic hand to indicate that the supplies had all been dispensed. Passengers could sort it out among themselves. Another lesson learned, Patrick told himself. He levered the bevelled mini-straw off the wax carton.

Looking out of the window, he watched the smooth disc of the spinning propellor and let his mind wander. The light blue sky tended towards white as he peered up. There was a sharp dividing line to a darker blue of the sea as he looked down. The water didn't appear so far away. From time to time, he could make out ships with their wake streaming behind and there were other cigar-shapes which left no wake. Not boats or yachts – unless they were at anchor – or maybe large fish?

And then he spotted land on the horizon. A slim black line to begin with, but it developed in thickness and was no longer so straight as they flew closer. Was this Efate or another island? It was lost to view as the pilot banked and started the descent. Now there were fishing canoes and, as the pilot lined up for his final approach, the coast reappeared and there were children playing in the water. The plane was put down very hard, brakes applied and without using much of the runway, they swerved onto the apron and drew up to the airport building.

Everybody around Patrick had cheered as the wheels touched the tarmac. They became subdued and quiet as the 'plane halted with a slight jerk, engines winding down. Patrick undid his seat belt, feeling guilty in case he was supposed to keep it fastened. Would there be a loud instruction from the cockpit for 'The Passenger in Seat 17a to please refasten his safety belt'? Realisation dawned a few seconds later. Nobody else even wore a seatbelt, so the usual clickety click of seat belt buckles like photojournalists' motor drives at a press conference was absent from this landing procedure.

Patrick waited. The side door aft of the cockpit opened and one of the ground staff came in, exchanged a few words with the pilot and began making his way towards the tail. In his crossed hands, he held aloft two spray cans and made it to Row 10 by stepping over legs and bags. At that point, he gave up, fearing that he'd fall over and aimed the cans down the 'plane, misting with a phytosanitary spray. To his dismay, Patrick ended up with a face-full and sneezed and spluttered for a few seconds. It made his eyes water, too.

The member of ground staff retreated and that was the signal for everyone to struggle towards the doorway at the same time. "Thank you for flying with Air Melanesia," roared the Navigator. "Fly with us again." Patrick waited until the queue had almost gone before extracting himself and his hand luggage.

"Thank you very much," he murmured, as he stepped past the grinning crew.

"No worries, Mate."

Now, where were his hold bags?

## Chapter 2
# Arrival

The pile of bags in the shadow of the aeroplane grew as two ground workers leaned into its belly and heaved them out. They weren't trying to set out the bags so passengers could identify their possessions. To them it was a motley pile of cargo to be deposited more or less clear of the wheels, so the plane could move off. Every so often, one of the passengers milling around would dart forward to snatch something they recognised.

"*Olgeta stap long ere*," tried another member of the ground staff as he sought to keep order, but soon gave up. 'Like herding cats', thought Patrick, smiling despite his travel tiredness. At last, all the ground staff had had enough. They abandoned the pile and the ensuing scrum peeled away layers of baggage, finally revealing Patrick's three items. This time he didn't hesitate to dive forward.

Looking on, behind the faded white rickety fence with a sign proclaiming

'Immigration', were two sun-tanned white men, one nearing fifty years of age, the other barely thirty. Patrick struggled towards them with his bags, one hung on each shoulder and a large and heavy hold-all in his left hand. He held out his passport to the Immigration officer at the gate.

"Move on, please," the man beckoned, not even glancing at the open pages of Patrick's passport. In the New Hebrides, it was enough that he had a passport.

"You must be Patrick," said the younger white man, stepping forward. "Welcome to Vila - here, give me that" and he reached for Patrick's heaviest bag. "I'm Joe. I'm the accountant and this is Andrew Cutlass, our Chief Manager."

"Thanks," Patrick said, relinquishing the bag with gratitude. "How do you do?"

"What news?" murmured Cutlass. "Good flight?" And he grasped Patrick's proffered hand with little enthusiasm.

"Yes, thanks – although they all rather merged together, I'm afraid. This last one was quite an eye-opener."

A student of body language might have taken the weak handshake as an initial indicator of character. Patrick's later rueful reflection was that some experiences have to be undergone to drive home their meaning. The process was sometimes painful.

"Are you hungry?" asked Joe. Without pausing, he went on, "We thought Royal Counties Bank might stand you a dinner as it's your first night."

As a matter of fact, Patrick was hungry. His diet for the last three days had been poor quality, over-salted or deep-fried airport food. All was eaten at speed while listening for airport announcements. Not conducive to a relaxed digestive process. He realised that he was also dehydrated, being unused to the sweltering heat. He'd have loved a shower or a bath as well, as his clothes were beginning to stick to him, but that nicety would have to wait.

They walked towards a beige-coloured and very shiny Peugeot 504. It gleamed in the late afternoon sunshine. An overweight New Hebridean man leaning on the bonnet straightened up when he saw them approaching. He trotted around to open the rear passenger door. Andrew Cutlass led the way by climbing in, leaving Joe and Patrick to stand by the boot. The driver opened it and reached for one of Patrick's bags.

"Thank you," said Patrick, hefting the second one off his shoulder.

Joe introduced the man. "This is John," he said, "Andrew's driver."

John was all smiles, bobbing his head and he shook hands. "*Mefala yufala welkam tumus.*"

Picking up the gist, Patrick said, "I'm very pleased to meet you, too." John opened the other rear door for Patrick while Joe slid into the front passenger seat.

"The Rossi, John," instructed Cutlass. "And turn on the A/C."

The tarmacked airport approach soon degraded to a dirt road as they headed towards town. 'Crushed coral', Joe explained, seeing Patrick turn around and stare at the clouds of dust in their wake. "We thought you could do with a bite to eat and something to drink and then we'll drop you at the flats. I'll nip back to the branch tonight and cable London to say you've arrived. They will telephone your family."

"Righto – that sounds good. Thank you," said Patrick. Cutlass, beside him at the back, wasn't in a mood for idle chatter and remained silent. Joe kept his gaze to the front, so Patrick was content to watch the scenery. There were coconut groves and banana plantations on both sides as they sped along. He had never been in a Peugeot 504 before. But being something of a motor car nut, he was impressed by the way its supple suspension soaked up the ruts in the road. He was sure that the wheels were hammering up and down, but little of this transmitted to the interior.

There were more shacks, now, and the occasional lean-to shop or market stall. These gave way to more formal, low-rise concrete buildings - offices, shops, a garage or workshop or two. Then they turned into a tarmacked parking area in front of the Rossi Hotel.

Joe and Patrick hopped out, while Cutlass waited for John to open his door. Leaving the bags in the boot of the car, the three men headed for the hotel's double doors.

"This is also the Vila Branch," Joe nodded at the building on their right as they walked. "The Royal Counties Bank sign is on the other side, at the front. We call the Rossi our 'other branch'." Patrick and Joe smiled at one another but he noted that Cutlass didn't

17

share the joke. Perhaps he considered himself above such frivolity.

As Joe held open one of the doors for him, Patrick looked forward and exclaimed, "There's the sea." The Rossi had an enviable position, right at the water's edge, looking out into the bay. Its bar area made the most of this view, with tables scattered about, each with two or three chairs angled seawards. The sun was heading for the horizon, pretty much between the points of land on either side. It bathed the hotel with a welcoming warm light.

"Beer, Andrew?" asked Joe. "Patrick? What'll you have? I recommend a Zombie, as this is your first time here."

"Fosters," said Cutlass, curtly, scraping back his chair.

"What on earth is a Zombie?" Patrick enquired. Joe smiled and didn't respond, so he went on, "Oh, ok. 'In for a penny' and all that." He picked up the menu from the table.

"There's not much to choose from," intoned Cutlass. Turning to Joe, behind them at the bar, he called, "I'll have a Club Sandwich."

Joe called back, "Patrick?"

Patrick had spotted a burger he liked the sound of and so replied, "Hideaway Burger, please, and can I have salad instead of fries?" Joe passed along the orders to the barman. He returned with two beers and an enormous brandy balloon glass filled with a layered, multi-coloured liquid, topped with vegetation and a tiny parasol.

"That ...is a Zombie! Welcome to Port Vila – cheers."

They clinked glasses and Patrick sorted through the green sprigs to find a straw. After an exploratory sip, he pronounced it, "Refreshing. Pineapple juice, I guess, but how they achieve all these colours is beyond me." He took several deeper drafts from the glass and prodded it with the straw. It wasn't as sweet as he'd expected. It was quite good, actually.

"What do you know about Trade Finance?" asked Cutlass, not being one for small talk.

"Only what I learned in 'Finance of Foreign Trade' as part of the AIB exams."

"Oh, yes. I forgot you passed your exams. Congratulations, by the way." Patrick dipped his head in acknowledgement.

"I expect the actual practical aspects are a little different, are they?" Patrick asked, feeling the need to be humble.

"Like much in banking, a big proportion of our work is tedious," began Joe, "But every so often it gets a bit exciting."

"We don't like excitement, though, do we, Joe?" Cutlass scowled at his accountant. "We like steady and predictable." Joe flushed with embarrassment, underneath his tan.

"It's different from London, out here," amended Joe. "I'll go through the basics in the morning. Do you want another?"

"Mmmm. Yes, please," Patrick responded, draining the final drops of the Zombie. He pushed the glass towards Joe. "I could get used to this."

Cutlass snorted. "Give them a hurry up, would you? I don't want to spend all night here. I'll have another Fosters." Joe scurried away. "You'll learn to keep the local staff in their place. Look weak and they'll walk all over you."

Patrick furrowed his brow. He had not worked in a culture different from his own before – hell, he hadn't even gone abroad before, so had no idea what to expect.

"I'm not sure what you mean, Andrew."

"It's quite simple. Give them straightforward instructions, don't take 'no' for an answer and check what they have done. Then check it again."

Joe came back carrying their drinks. The waiter was two steps behind, bringing the food. Patrick admired his burger. It consisted of several layers of meat, cheese, onion and tomato. A skewer with a larger parasol held it all together on top of an attractive salad. There was lettuce and other leaves mixed with shredded carrot and dressed with vinegary oil and crushed nuts. Quite a work of art.

They all bit hungrily into their food. Cutlass finished first. He wiped his mouth and got up to leave. "I'll have John put your bags behind the bar. Joe will take you to the flats. See you at eight sharp in the morning. Good night."

Never what you might describe as a 'slow eater', Patrick was amazed that the man had outpaced him by so much. He pushed back his chair and half rose to say good night, but was still chewing. By the time he'd swallowed, the Chief Manager was striding out past the bar.

"Don't worry about him," Joe said. "You'll get used to his little ways. Those are good, aren't they?" glancing at Patrick's plate.

"I was in need of something other than deep fried Mystery Meals." Patrick speared more of the salad. "That was all that was available on aeroplanes and at the air ports. The food and the Zombies are beginning to work their magic – I'll sleep well today – tonight – or whatever it is now."

Joe checked his watch. "It's 6:30 in the evening. Better set an alarm for 7 tomorrow. I'll send John to pick you up at 7:45. Okay?"

# Chapter 3
## Trade Finance

Patrick did indeed sleep solidly that first night. On waking, though, he discovered he was soaked in perspiration. For a moment he pondered, 'Where am I?' But he walked to the bathroom, figured out the control and turned the shower to maximum volume. Pretty soon, the streaming cool water blew away the fog in his head. Much refreshed, he dressed in his new tropical clothes, hoping the slight creases wouldn't matter. Next stop - the kitchenette for something to eat. "Hope you like cereal," Joe had said, cheerily, handing over a carrier bag of basic foodstuffs when he dropped Patrick off last night. "There's bread and milk and tea as well."

He paused for a prolonged stretch to ease his back, still cramped from all the flights and made worse by the thin mattress on his bed. But then he faced the next puzzle of the day. He stared, blinking at the shelves in the refrigerator. Why was his passport in there with his wallet?!

'Gee. I was so tired…', he thought. But he found a bowl for cereal and boiled water for tea.

He hadn't quite finished when there was a bang on the flyscreen. "Mr Patrick? Hello? *Me stap long car blong takim yufala long bank.*"

Patrick scooped the last of the cereal from his breakfast bowl and looked ruefully at his not yet brewed tea. "I'll be right there, John – one minute." Thinking they'd be safer on Bank premises than in his flat, Patrick picked up his cold passport and wallet and hunted around for the door key.

There was a scraping noise on the door. "*Hemi wunfala key,*" called John – waving the errant item in his gnarly hand. Yet more evidence of his tiredness - Patrick had left the key in the lock all night.

"Oh – righto. Thanks…" He shook his head and began to go red in the face, and not only from the morning's heat billowing in through the open door. "Off we go then."

John left the car windows rolled down for their journey. The gentle breeze through the swaying palm trees at the side as they bounced along the tracks towards town was welcome. "What a lovely smell from the sea,"

Patrick said, sharing his genuine delight. The tang of salt in the air was almost more refreshing than his morning shower had been. John smiled. He couldn't understand why the Chief Manager, Andrew Cutlass, always insisted on using the A/C when they drove. Perhaps this man Patrick was different from the other ex-pats.

Joe, the accountant, was in his office near the front door when Patrick tapped on it. The branch was not yet open for customers and a member of local staff looked to Joe for permission to admit him. Joe nodded assent and called him over once the big glass door was locked closed again.

"Here are a pile of letter of credit requests and last night's post, probably with bills of exchange and other payments to make. Come with me round to your department; I'll introduce you and you can dig straight in."

The stack of folders pressed on Patrick's chest causing his still-cold passport to make a damp patch on his shirt. He extracted it. "Should I put this in the safe?" he asked.

"Better give it to me – my secretary will make a copy and then we'll file it in the safe with everyone else's."

He couldn't help noticing that Joe was all business this morning; there was none of last night's easy pleasantry. "Sara? This is Patrick. Sara will be your secretary; that's Jean-Marc and …where's Luke?"

Jean-Marc piped up, "*Hemi long wunfala store cupboard*." Joe nodded.

"Tell him to come and see me." And then he left Patrick standing awkwardly beside what he guessed would be his desk. Patrick added the folders he'd been given to one of the piles beside the telephone.

"Shall we go through those together?" asked Sara. She kept her eyes down, as though shy, but she looked up eagerly when Patrick replied.

"That would be helpful, thanks." He was no linguist, but was beginning to catch on to the language structure used around him. All the same, he was grateful that Sara spoke in clear English rather than the local Bislama language. He feared making an expensive mistake if he tried giving instructions in a language in which he wasn't fluent. "Who does the foreign exchange payments?"

Sara inclined her head. "Mr Gilles. 'E ees Frennnch," she said, rolling her eyes and elongating the words with a faux-French accent.

Despite himself, Patrick grinned. He knew right away that Sara was going to be a valuable asset. She must have taken to him immediately if she was prepared so soon to make gentle fun of another member of staff – moreover, an *ex-pat* member of staff.

"Could we go to say 'hello'?"

Sara scraped back her chair. "*Oui - bien sur, Monsieur Pierre.*"

Around the back of the store cupboard they went and towards a floppy-haired but tanned and well-built man scrawling on some papers.

"*Veuillez m'excuser, Monsieur Gilles, puis-je vous presenter Mr Pierre.*"

Patrick stepped forward. "*Attend, attend,*" Gilles said, raising his hand to stop them. He stabbed at his desk calculator and wrote the answer at the bottom of a column of figures. Then he focussed on them, all smiles. "*Bienvenue* …you are English, yes?"

Patrick beamed in reply. "Sara says you do the foreign exchange – I expect I will be calling on you for help quite often."

"At least once per month – Pay Day – to send home the Staff Sterling payments. But if

27

you are Mister Trade Finance now, it will be more frequent, yes. *Parlez-vous Français?"*

Patrick tried to recall his schoolboy French. *"Er, oui – un peu. Si vous parlez lentement – je comprends."*

"Bravo," applauded Gilles. "But you and I have work to do, I think." His phone rang and he turned away to snatch it from its cradle.

"Let's go through those L/Cs," Sara said.

-----//-----

Patrick spent time in the Outward Collections department of Royal Counties Bank in London before joining the bank's Management Development Programme. His posting to Port Vila branch was part of that. It had given him real practical experience of letters of credit, bills for collection and negotiation, basic foreign exchange contracts and promissory notes. He soon felt confident of the tasks ahead of him, and he settled in well. The local staff sensed this confidence as the days passed and felt able to ask him questions and learn more about trade finance. Together, they chewed through the work as it came in.

Now and again, Patrick came into contact with some of the other bankers in town. He'd take shipping documents around to the banks to present them for payment and so stopped sometimes for a short chat. He was always astonished that the staff in the branches of Australian and New Zealand banks wore shorts. Royal Counties Bank dress code demanded long trousers. Moreover, they'd often have an open beer can on their desks – Patrick wouldn't dream of drinking anything other than coffee, tea or water at work. There was one French bank, which he rarely visited. The only real point of difference he observed was that it closed for two hours at lunchtime. The French, he determined, took lunch very seriously. There were no other British banks.

One Friday, a large New Zealander named Scottie suggested that Patrick might like to drive out to Erakor Lagoon that night to join their weekly dinner at La Hotte restaurant.

"There'll be bulk tinnies, CDMs and FCs and the tucker's alright, mate." Patrick accepted on the spot, feeling that a night out, letting his hair down, so to speak, would be great. He wasn't entirely sure what Scottie had meant, but reckoned all would become clear after he got there.

"Joe?" he asked during that afternoon. "I've been invited along to the Aussie bankers' end of week dinner." He was about to ask for directions, but Joe interrupted.

"I know it: at La Hotte." Patrick nodded. "I went a couple of times but Sharon doesn't like me coming home drunk and waking the kid, so I haven't been out there for months. You'll have a good time, but watch out for the liqueurs." Patrick looked askance, so he explained: "Marcel – he's one of the owners - brews his own liqueurs from various fruits – the apricot is deadly." The corner of Joe's mouth turned up in rueful remembrance.

"Where is the Erakor Lagoon?" asked Patrick. Joe gave him directions.

So it was that at 7:15 that evening, Patrick turned right at the roundabout in Numba Tu district and headed south through thick jungle. He drove on the main dirt track for a couple of kilometres, sometimes catching glimpses of land on the other side of the lagoon, but kicking up a dust cloud all the way. It was no surprise, then, that all the trees and bushes right next to the road had a uniform beige colour. Other than an occasional track winding off to the side, which he guessed led to a small settlement, nothing resembled a restaurant. At last, though, he spotted the large, painted sign with a copper-coloured wooden facsimile of an oven hood – the literal meaning of the name 'La Hotte'. There were a few other cars in the car park already, so at least he wasn't the first to arrive. He backed into a handy space near the entrance. The building itself, of local hardwood, was very dark with age. It was a couple of storeys high with a steeply-pitched roof of wooden shingles to resist the monsoon-like rains when they came.

The windows were tiny and out of proportion to the bulk of the building itself. He approached the almost medieval wooden door, guarded either side by two enormous tiki statues. Local *Kastom* believers carved these from Ferntree plants to ward off evil spirits. He lifted the latch and pulled. A theatrical squeal of protest from the hinges announced his arrival to those sitting around the bar. "Look out, lads: the Poms are here!" called one of the Australians.

"It's only me," soothed Patrick. "No need to panic. Now - whose beer is empty?" knowing the fastest way to the Antipodean heart was pouring them cold beer. The cavernous inside of the building was as dark as the outside. Artful lighting by concealed spotlights focussed onto war masks mounted on the walls. The effect was unnerving for guests who were sober and would be positively scary once they were drunk.

There was a chorus of jeering and shouts of 'Yes, Mate'. Scottie, puffed up with self-importance, stepped away from the crowd. They were all bellied up to the bar surrounding the cooking area. But the tall and wide copper hood, which gave the restaurant its name, dwarfed everything. "Swan Lager for me and Frosties for this lot – 'cept Carl down there, who's a banana bender from way back. Give 'im Barbed Wire."

Sometimes Patrick felt it was harder translating 'Okker than the local Bislama. Swan lager was a straightforward order. 'Frosties' meant Fosters lager and 'Barbed Wire' denoted the brand of Four X lager.

To Patrick's relief, the small, swarthy ex-pat behind the bar smiled and said, "Don't worry – I've got it."

"And a Fosters for me, please." Patrick took out his wallet to pay.

Seeing this, the barman said, "Paul down there will settle up for everyone at the end of the night."

Patrick turned to Scottie. "Which one is Paul? This is very generous of him." He intended to go and say thank you right away.

"No worries, Mate. You'll pay next week. See: Paul's bank pays tonight and then draws a bill on Royal Counties Bank which you settle up – otherwise we go 'round Joe's house and rough him up. Got it?"

"I think so." Questions swirled in Patrick's head: who counted how many beers he would have? Supposing he wanted pudding after the meal? But at that point, the barman pushed their beer order across the bar and Patrick was drawn into the banter. He'd 'go with the flow' – it was Friday night, after all.

The menu had been pre-ordered. A salad of shrimp was followed by steaks, fries and a pile of quite delicious shredded cabbage and onion, which the restaurant owner, Antoine, flambéed in a spectacular manner. When flames reached high up into the copper hood, they could all feel the rush of heat on their faces. Patrick's enquiries about how to prepare this dish were rebuffed, so it remained a mystery. Instead of puddings or cheese, as Patrick expected, the group then moved on to more serious alcohol.

"Hey, Scottie – you told me to expect 'CDMs and FCs' – are you going to tell me what they are?" Patrick shouted above the chatter.

Scottie had been knocking back bottles of Swan lager like it was going out of fashion. Owing to his undeniable size and that he'd eaten heartily, he had remained tolerably sober. "They're coming right up, Mate." And then, turning to the bar, "Oi, Marcel – we're ready for Afters."

Marcel was already fiddling with something on the working surface behind the bar. Soon he lifted a tray of small brandy balloons filled with green liquid. As the tray reached the end of their table, Patrick saw the glasses were full of crushed ice over which the liquid had been poured. Another tray of a larger size of blue Fosters cans joined the brandy balloons and people began taking one of each before passing the trays along.

"There you are: Crème de Menthe and Fosters Chasers – 'CDMs and FCs'" exclaimed Scottie with great delight. Joe's cautionary words earlier about taking care with Marcel's liqueurs crept into Patrick's head. Except this was more like commercially-made Crème de Menthe.

Patrick sipped and found the minty taste to his liking, its sweetness toned down by the crushed ice. "Crack a tube, Mate – you gotta 'ave 'em together," advised his Kiwi self-appointed alcohol consultant. So Patrick did.

The combination was a bit of a revelation, he had to admit. Mad, but boy, it was good.

Patrick scraped back his chair, stood and shouted for a bit of hush. "I'd like to say thanks for inviting me to your Friday night dinner – it's been great. And the food has been delicious." He turned towards Antoine and Marcel at the bar. "I'd like to propose a toast to our hosts, Antoine and Marcel." He raised his Crème de Menthe towards them. "La Hotte."

Everyone repeated the toast and the noise level again rose to loud chattering. Patrick sat down, feeling giddy. Scottie and a couple of others clapped him on the back and went to sit at the bar to settle in for what they later referred to as a 'serious session'.

He checked his watch: 10:30 already? "I gotta go, guys." He stood up again. "Do you know why the sun never set on the British Empire? God didn't trust the Poms after dark. Thanks again, fellas. It's been er…bonza."

Hoots of good-natured but raucous laughter greeted this clumsy attempt at colloquial Australian. Patrick downed his remaining drinks, rose to his feet and headed for the door. Scottie waved and shouted after him, "See you at the Barbie on Sunday."

Difficulty finding the door latch was a potent reminder to drive home with care on the unfamiliar dirt road in the dark.

As he pulled the heavy door closed, Patrick saw two men standing with their heads close together in the shadows beside his car. He went towards them. One was Roger Hammerson, who ran the Price Waterhouse accounting office in town. To an outside observer, the two might have been exchanging a few last words before leaving for home after having dinner together. But he was pretty sure there had not been any other diners in the restaurant while he was in there with the Aussies. He did not think he was mistaken. Hammerson's companion was small and swarthy with curly black hair - he appeared Arabian. Patrick didn't know him. "'Evening, Roger", he said, fumbling for his car keys.

"Who's that? Oh, yes – Patrick. Hello. We're just talking". The two men pulled apart.

'Well, obviously,' Patrick thought. 'What an odd reply'. But he said, "Well, good night, then."

Hammerson nodded but seemed uncomfortable and said nothing more. The other man glared at him and remained silent.

The New Hebrides was a tax haven. Patrick was aware that this made it attractive to large corporations, but also to criminals. Some financial jurisdictions had rather loose regulations. Money laundering activities flourished in such places. Few bankers there questioned the origin of incoming funds. The London headquarters of Price Waterhouse enjoyed a well-earned high reputation. Patrick had naturally assumed that Roger Hammerson possessed the same integrity. But something about the man's reaction shouted guilt at being caught out. Patrick tried to convince himself that he may have happened upon two friends meeting. But they looked too furtive to be friends – no, this was a business discussion. So why conduct it in the late night shadows of a restaurant car park, far from the centre of town?

As he settled into the driver's seat, a stab of discomfort at what he believed he'd seen sobered him up. The haze of happiness brought on by food and alcohol had peaked as he closed the restaurant door. It now fought to resist the cold whiff of criminality.

He tried to centre his mind and concentrate on driving home without crashing. But couldn't forget the curious conversation and Hammerson's shifty reply.

# Chapter 4

# The Independence Election

Saturday morning dawned far too early for Patrick. He had remembered to draw the curtains across his full height bedroom window. But they weren't lined and did little to keep out the South Pacific sunshine. They were also a hideous orange pattern and lit up the room with an other-worldly glow.

Blinking, Patrick tried to focus his eyes on the wall cupboard and his brain on where he was and what time it might be. It was only when he heard rhythmic chopping outside, he figured it must be Tom Charlie, the gardener. The boy would be trimming some unsuspecting plant life. Thus, it must be Saturday morning. 'Phew. Panic off. No work', he thought. As he lay, summoning up the will to head for a reviving shower, little blips of memory from last night popped into his head.

He hoped he hadn't made too much of a fool of himself in front of his new friends. Patrick's upbringing in England had been rather sheltered. He had never attended a dinner party where the main aim was downing as much alcohol as possible. Despite his junior status within the bank, he had attended several formal dinners in London, some for which he had hired a dinner jacket, no less. On these occasions, he blessed his parents' insistence upon knowing how to set a table with successive knives and forks and spoons. Also, how to eat pudding (not 'dessert') with a spoon and fork and other niceties of etiquette. These habits were ingrained and meant he could concentrate upon conversation with nearby guests without accidentally offending anyone's sensibilities, no matter how old and stuffy they might be.

He hadn't detected any wariness on the part of his dining companions last night – indeed, he felt they were genuine in their delight at meeting him. Their conversation might be what his mother would term 'rough', but they were lots of fun and didn't take themselves seriously. He was sure that whatever jibes they levelled at him for his accent or country of origin or table manners, it was intended in good fun. On occasion, he recalled he'd fired back with some verbal riposte and it was received with roars of approval and laughter.

Yes, all in all, a great evening. Hang on… Hadn't Scottie said something about a Barbie? Did he dream it?

By now, banging the shower curtain to knock off the night's cockroaches had become another ingrained habit. He boiled the kettle for coffee while the skittering of escaping insects abated. He had never before paired the experiences of drinking strong, black coffee with standing beneath a lukewarm shower, but then, lately, he found himself doing several things he hadn't done before. 'Like CDMs and FCs', Patrick smiled to himself. And he discovered that drinking coffee while a shower hammered on the back of his neck was pretty good too.

His head wasn't quite so muzzy afterwards. The 'fridge gave up some cold meats, bread for toasting and the last of his prized jar of Branston Pickle. This very British delicacy was a rare arrival in Port Vila as most of the imported food leaned towards French palates. Patrick was grateful for that, and was becoming an enthusiastic seeker of more European flavours. He still hankered for an occasional pickled onion with his cheese or a spoon of Branston pickle. When he could no longer scrape even the tiniest morsel of

41

pickled vegetable from the jar, he sighed, rinsed it and set it on the draining board. It might come in handy for small change or something.

Going back into the bedroom, he drew the curtains. There was Tom Charlie, still hacking at a palm tree. A pile of fronds grew behind him, evidencing his morning's efforts. Spotting the movement of the curtains, Tom favoured Patrick with his most toothy grin. Patrick waved back. He pulled open the sliding door to let in some fresh air and stepped out to check on the progress of his pineapple. Whether it was self-seeded or Tom Charlie had planted it, Patrick didn't know. But this small pineapple plant right outside the bedroom was, to Patrick's delight, producing a fruit. Still small and very green, but one day, it would be a pineapple. It would be perfect for a refreshing pudding one evening soon. Around the front of the flats were some tall banana plants, but they hadn't fruited yet. He was fast reaching the conclusion that one only had to push a stick into the ground in this country for it to grow roots and flourish.

Going back into the flat, he eyed with distaste his pile of clothes needing washing. 'Later, I think', as his desire for some fresh air overcame any hint of domestic guilt. He decided to head for the sailing club. A couple of the ex-pats who visited the bank during the week owned sailing dinghies. Without exception they'd told him to just turn up at the club at any time: "We are always in need of crews," one had said.

So he sorted out his flip-flops, swimming trunks, shorts and a T-shirt and towel and started his car.

Dave, one of the Aussi bankers from last night was there already. He was busy rigging his Laser, but straight away introduced Patrick to the engineer for Vila Base Hospital who owned a 2-person catamaran. "Sven? This is Patrick who tells me he's done some sailing in the past. Do you need a crew today?"

They shook hands. Sven was a stocky man of few words, but his tanned, leathery face broke into a smile. "Sure I do. I'm fed up trying to sail this by myself. Have you used a trapeze before?"

"No, but I came close! I sailed an Enterprise every week for a couple of years when I was a teenager. I had a couple of outings on a Fireball, without needing the trapeze and raced an FJ for a while. But I'd love to try."

"Right. You're hired. I'll show you what to do when we're afloat. First, you need this harness." Sven handed over what looked like a pair of padded underpants with a hook on the front. There were several straps and buckles to adjust. After a deal of wriggling, he achieved a reasonable amount of comfort. "Take your time: you'll be hanging your whole weight off that," warned Sven.

Patrick tightened the jib halyard and made sure the sheets ran easily through the jamming blocks while he familiarised himself with the catamaran. Sven squinted at his flip-flops. "Those won't do. Do you have tennis shoes or plimsols?"

He shook his head. Sven went over to his Suzuki van and rummaged for a bit, emerging with a battered pair of tennis shoes. "Here. Try those. Even if you can't lace them up, they'll give better grip on the side than bare feet."

It was true. He did have larger feet than Sven and the shoes cramped his toes, but he hoped a few minutes in cold water would shrink his feet enough. And so started their successful racing partnership. Now Sven had an agile and strong crew who (after some practice) could hang out on the trapeze keeping the windward hull of the cat kissing the surface of the water as they sped along. Catamarans do not point very high up into the wind and are hopelessly slow on a run directly down wind. All the monohulls would point fully 20 degrees higher. But the speed Sven and Patrick could achieve on close and broad reaches outweighed this advantage. They would often be derigging the craft in the boat park by the time the second-placed boat crossed the finish line. Even on handicap, they won many races.

After that first race, Patrick slid over the windward hull into the water as they neared the beach. He hauled the craft up out of reach of the waves and trotted off to fetch the launching trolley.

"Do you fancy a beer?" he asked when the cat's sails and rigging had been tidied away and secured against storms.

"Sure."

He bought beers and, in view of the man's patience with him needing quite literally to learn the ropes, Patrick treated them both to burgers. They tucked in with appetites sharpened by exercise.

"Christ: you inhaled that," mumbled Sven, still working on his burger.

"Breakfast was ages ago," protested Patrick. "And it's hard work, bouncing in and out on the trapeze." Sven smiled at the implied insult that he, as helmsman, did little work.

"Ah, but a young fit bloke like you shouldn't even notice that gentle cruise round the buoys." In fact, their race had been a long way removed from a 'cruise round the buoys'. There had been plenty of wind. Most awkward, though, was the choppy sea. The leeward hull sometimes buried itself, slowing their progress and threatening to swing Patrick forwards around the forestay.

"I guess so." They had been gazing out to sea all the time and Patrick shaded his eyes from the glare. "Can you see whose Laser that is?" As they watched, Dave planed in and rounded up into the wind, dismounting into the shallows with aplomb. "I'll fetch his trolley."

He wanted to say thanks to Dave for the introduction. He pushed the man's trolley into the water.

"Thanks, Mate." Dave looked exhausted under his tan. Up close, Patrick saw that he was rather older than the others he'd met last night. It crossed his mind that the man might have been overdoing it in today's fresh winds. "…Wish I'd never introduced you to Sven! Now we'll never catch the bastard."

"I'm afraid I may have slowed him down," countered Patrick. "I made lots of mistakes and we were close to going over at one point. Are you ok?"

"You can buy me a beer to make me feel better."

Sven refused the offer of a second beer with Dave as he had to get away. He said to hang on to the shoes and asked if he could crew again next Saturday. "Beers on me next time – provided we win."

As Patrick turned towards the bar again, he saw Sven pausing to talk to a very attractive girl beside another Laser dinghy. When he came out with a couple of cold ones, Sven was fiddling with something around the end of the dinghy's boom.

"You spotted Jessica," observed Dave, arching one eyebrow and accepting his beer.

Patrick was guilty. "Um …yes. Is she a member here too?"

"She's the doctor at Vila Base, so knows Sven, as the hospital's engineer, can fix anything. You won't get anywhere, there, Mate."

"Sorry?"

"She's off limits – unavailable – never mixes, keeps herself apart. Guess she has to – you know, as the doctor."

Patrick frowned. Wasn't Jessica too young to be a doctor? Maybe she worked too hard to have much of a social life. But then he remembered Scottie's comment as he was leaving La Hotte the previous evening. "Scottie said last night, 'See you at the Barbie'. Do you know what he meant?"

"Sure. Scottie yaps about lots of things, but Sundays are regular, so even he gets that right. We fire up the Barbie at the Mess on Sundays around 6:30. You bring your own steak, the girls prepare some salads and you mark down the beers you take and settle up the next week. Wanna come?"

"I'd love to."

"A word of warning, though: Scottie always forgets to defrost his steak in time. He tries to sneak someone else's off the grill." That sounded like the dopey Scottie he was getting to know. Patrick loved steak, particularly rib-eye, known in the supermarket in town as 'entrecôte' or 'côte de bœuf' if on the bone. He'd visit Bon Plats on the way home and buy one. He thought it unlikely that anyone else would want their meat with bones in and he determined to keep a close eye on it.

-----//-----

"That's not a steak, Mate: that's a bloody lump of cow"!

"It reeks – is that garlic?"

"Give it a slap and that'd be mooing."

These were three of the comments made when Patrick revealed the thick entrecôte he'd marinated for two hours in garlic, pepper and olive oil. He had developed a liking for especially rare beef. The French term for this is 'saignant'. He'd often nibble some of the uncooked meat before cooking to assess its quality.

Sure enough, nobody wanted their meat on the barbeque anywhere near his overly fragrant steak, although one of the girls asked to try some after he'd cooked it. Patrick was pleased to oblige but was unsure about her conclusion that it 'didn't taste as bad as it smelled'.

To go with the steaks, there were salad bowls of rice, potato and lettuce and, of course, inexhaustible supplies of beer -

Fosters, Tooheys, Victoria Bitter and XXXX in the Mess's enormous 'fridge. Patrick went home very full and very happy that night.

The next morning, Andrew Cutlass called all the ex-pat members of staff into his office.

"As some of you may know, if you have been paying attention, there is to be an election next month to select members of the new parliament when the New Hebrides becomes independent. The authorities may ask some of you to act as Presiding Officers. This means you will conduct elections in the different districts. You will have time off to do so. This is a great honour. I expect you all to uphold the highest standards of the Royal Counties Bank and conduct yourselves with dignity, probity and utter fairness. I will tell those of you who have been selected.

Additionally, I have been asked to coordinate with the Central Bank to name a new currency. The New Hebridean Franc will have a new name after Independence. I am the only banker in these islands with a banking qualification, so I will be giving my suggestions next week. That is all."

Patrick put up his hand. "Er, Andrew? I have a banking qualification too: I passed my A.I.B. before flying out here."

There was a moment's silence as Cutlass paused. He'd forgotten that and been caught 'on the hop'. "Oh yes. Quite so. Quite so. I shall consider that. Back to work, everyone."

"Good man," murmured Joe, as they left Andrew's office and descended the staircase back to the banking hall. "I forgot you had said that. Well done."

"Thanks," said Patrick. "I hope it didn't put his nose out of joint. I regretted saying it as soon as I'd opened my mouth."

For a moment, Joe's face betrayed his expectation that the lad would pay for what he'd said, sooner or later. "Probably. You'll find out…"

Patrick's fears of being left out on purpose proved to be groundless. One Tuesday afternoon, after work, Cutlass said he should attend the briefing for all who were to act as Presiding Officers.

He went along to one of the government buildings where the briefing was scheduled. An official handed out bamboo poles and a roll of canvas to make a polling booth.

Another one consulted a list, found his name and selected a wad of voting slips with pictures of the four candidates for the Pele Island constituency. Finally, someone directed him to the stack of padlocked, wooden ballot boxes with slots to accept completed papers. He was made to sign for all these while an officious little man from the Finance Ministry recited the oath in a rapid monotone. Patrick noted with amusement and mild interest that the recitation was generating a build-up of spittle at the sides of the man's lips. He barely stopped for breath and managed to give dual impressions of being bored silly while frothing at the mouth. Not so surprising as he'd given the speech more than a dozen times already to the people ahead in the queue, knew it by heart now and had lost interest.

Patrick was hoping the oath would come to an end soon, as his arms were full and the ballot box was quite heavy. At long last, the monologue ended ('praise be'). He saw the official's glazed expression change to mild irritation and a raised eyebrow.

"Well? Do you?"

Patrick blinked. "Sorry? Do I what?"

"Swear…?"

"Oh, yes. Naturally." The official jabbed a stubby finger at a paper on the desk. This was for Patrick to sign. He complied with an unaccustomed flourish. Not his usual Bank signature, which he scrawled a hundred times daily to authorise various things, but instead the one he reserved for writing personal cheques or important documents. He remembered to stop himself in time from adding his Bank signature number – F 416. That would have been very silly.

And so it was that early the next morning, Wednesday, the 14th of November, 1979, Patrick boarded a motor cruiser moored at the quayside of Port Vila. It would take him around to Pele island, a little way north of Efate, to conduct the national election. His companion for the day and to help with translation was Hone, a young New Hebridean from the Mech Room of the Branch.

The boat picked up speed as the pilot opened the throttles once clear of the other moored craft. Patrick could feel the beginnings of the swell of the sea. He looked to his left as they drew level with Iririki Island, the location of the British Ambassador's house. He wondered idly if the British

Ambassador's daughter, Florence, was up and awake yet.

A few nights ago, they had both been sitting around with friends after a visit to a restaurant. She confessed to a fondness for early morning swims before breakfast. Although only 19 years old, she had fallen for a lawyer named Alan, some 12 years her senior. Patrick was sure he was not a good sort. He based his conclusion on absolutely no objective evidence at all, but merely a strong feeling. Patrick kept telling himself it was more likely jealousy on his part. Alan earned quite a lot and drove a brand new, 2nd generation 1,500cc Honda Civic with a 5-speed gearbox (the first on the island). His smart/casual dress code appeared carefully tailored to fit him and Alan consigned Patrick's preference for Australian lager firmly into the social shade with a refined wine habit. It was many months later that Patrick and a couple of friends would venture for the first time into La Cave du Gourmets. He learned that the French never go anywhere without a ready supply of decent quality wine. Thus began his own vinous education in earnest. For the time being, though, Fosters, Tooheys or Castlemaine's XXXX were his party tipple of choice.

Patrick reckoned himself to be more of a friend to Florence than a mere cocktail party acquaintance. He surprised himself by admitting he felt quite protective towards the girl. She was a lovely person and Patrick could see only unhappiness ahead for her with this Alan. He'd never dared have that sort of discussion with her, though, and told himself it was probably all in his head and none of his business anyway. Still…

There was no sign of life on shore. No give-away pile of clothes or towel on the landing stage. So, for the fourth time, he checked the pile of election impedimenta behind him in the well of the cockpit. Of course, it was all there, with Hone perched on the Ballot Box with his feet on the canvas. Patrick began to feel the weight of responsibility for what he was about to do. He had donned his best light blue tropical suit and polished his shoes until their gleam would have satisfied even his ex-Army father. Here he was, at the tender age of 22, being chauffeured in a smart motor boat to act as Presiding Officer in an important national election. This would determine how the New

Hebrides would run as an independent republic after 73 years as a British / French Condominium. Ex-pat wags nicknamed it 'Pandemonium' because of the constipated administrative processes forced by English and French Law systems running in parallel.

He passed the time by trying to identify landmarks on shore to estimate how far around the west coast of Efate they had come. Pretty soon he could see Pele ahead, if he shielded his eyes against the rising sun. It was going to be hot today.

As they drew closer, the pilot slowed the boat, his gaze alternating between the depth finder and checking the wave patterns. There were marvellous coral reefs all around this area. They were a joy to swim over and to dive upon but could be disastrous for any sea-going craft trying to pass across. They slowed to bare tickover and the V-hulled boat rolled uncomfortably with the waves. Ahead, Patrick spotted a gathering of locals on the beach. More were joining the group as news of the boat's arrival spread. Hone waved at the little crowd. Patrick realised there must be a girl he recognised – one had covered her face and run away while others laughed and giggled at her embarrassment. He raised an eyebrow at Hone who just grinned and shrugged his shoulders in answer.

"I'll touch the bow on the beach; you hop out and I'll back away," called the pilot. Patrick nodded and then remembered his polished shoes. A dousing in seawater would ruin them. Should he take them off and paddle? Not very dignified. He couldn't carry them as his arms were going to be fully occupied with the ballot box, papers and canvas and sticks.

As though in answer, four of the biggest men stepped forward into the shallows. Arms outstretched, they motioned for him to jump. Patrick was borne clear of the final waves and put down onto the dry beach. Two others reached into the boat and took his gear as Hone handed it over the bow.

Another, older, thick-set man stepped forward of the main group. His legs bowed but his posture was upright and proud. Twin curled boars' tusks emphasised the heavy muscles on his chest and his arms had leaves tied above the biceps. There was a wide grin on his broad face, framed by bushy, white beard and hair. Patrick concluded he must be the Chief.

"*Mi glad tumas blong visitim yufela*," offered Patrick, and stuck out his hand. The Chief strode up to him and grasped it.

"*Yufela welkam tumas*," laughed the Chief, nodding and raising his eyebrows at Hone to include him in the greeting. "*Kam, kam.*" He waved an encouraging arm. Still holding Patrick's hand, he headed back up the beach, over the coral sand and towards some low huts beyond the treeline. They left Hone to supervise the safe landing of their election kit by some of the villagers.

As they tramped along, Patrick and Chief Tamatoa introduced themselves to each other. They came through the curtain of trees at the top of the beach to a clearing where the village was set out. Here were all the huts of wood and leaves. A larger hut sat in the middle of the clearing. It boasted corrugated iron siding painted in sun-faded primary colours. Patrick surmised it was for village gatherings. Chief Tamatoa had ordered the villagers to clear it and to sweep the dust floor in readiness. The cool shade inside was welcoming. It was the start of the New Hebridean wet season, when temperatures would rise to more than 25 degrees Centigrade. Humidity, which was greatest in these northern islands, could make this very uncomfortable. To Patrick's relief, the day was free of rain. A gentle breeze off the sea wafted through the open wooden shutters.

"Hone? Give me a hand, would you?" asked Patrick. Together they stretched out the canvas, laid the bamboo sticks on it at intervals and laced them together. But how would they stand the makeshift screen upright on the packed-earth floor? Patrick doubted they'd be popular if they dug up the ground, even if they could press the sticks into it without breaking them. He turned to the chief, who was watching proceedings with much interest.

"*Yu save wanem bucket*?" Momentary puzzlement flashed across the man's face but then he saw what they intended. A single bucket would not be enough – they'd need a bucket of sand per bamboo pole. The chief spoke to the people nearest him and four scampered away. They came back, staggering under the weight of four buckets filled to the brim with sand.

Patrick was delighted. "*Tank yu tumas*," he said, bobbing his head.

Everyone grinned. This was going really well.

Patrick explained to Hone what the procedure would be. He was afraid that, when he relayed instructions to Chief Tamatoa, he might not convey all the details. Then, in halting Bislama, Patrick said that everyone, starting with the Chief himself, should line up and take a voting slip. Next, to keep their choice secret, they should enter the booth, make a cross in the box beside their favoured candidate and fold the ballot paper. The final step would be to place it in the slot in the padlocked Ballot Box. Hone confirmed with a slight tilt of his head that his words did cover the general gist. Patrick invited the Chief to be first.

The watching villagers were agog as Chief Tamatoa stepped forward. His dignified manner suited the occasion. The Chief took his ballot paper and vanished behind the screen.

Patrick checked his watch. 11am. Pretty good going, he felt, to have travelled to Pele, set everything up and have voting underway in only four hours. There were 53 people registered to vote and, looking around, he thought every single one had crowded into the hut. The Chief took a long time. Eventually, though, he emerged, brandishing the folded paper so everyone could see what to do. There were a few claps of delight and much chattering broke out as he pushed the ballot paper through the slot. Tamatoa smacked his hand on the top of the box as though to ram home his vote and grinned at his villagers. There was some argument about who should come next, but Hone shepherded everyone into a rough line. He walked up and down, offering helpful suggestions or answering questions from voters. Patrick had brought spare blank voting slips, expecting that these first-time voters might spoil a few by accident. There were only two occasions when he needed them. One man put crosses into every box and asked if that was right. Hone explained that if he wanted to vote, he ought to choose *wun fela* candidate. Hone came to Patrick for guidance when a woman, covered in the white powder of mourning, explained that her brother had died the previous week and couldn't come in person. But she knew how he had wanted to vote, so could she have another paper, please? As politely as he could manage, Patrick said that the rules did not allow that, as unfair as it might seem. The woman accepted this but was not happy. He hoped the cause was more because of her recent bereavement than him disallowing a proxy vote. Hone told him later that covering in talcum powder was something the family of the deceased often did when in mourning for their loved one.

At length, 51 of the 52 possible legitimate votes nestled in the sealed Ballot Box. Patrick stood up and announced in a formal manner that the voting process was now complete. He explained how they would take the box back to Port Vila where Court Officials would open it and count the votes for each candidate. He thanked everyone for their participation and started packing up the kit.

Everyone clapped and started talking at once. Chief Tamatoa led Patrick and Hone outside and towards his hut. It was larger and set apart from the others. They sat by its doorway and the Chief sent one of the boys up a nearby palm tree to bring down some coconuts. Patrick watched, open-mouthed as the lad scampered up the tree, machete in his teeth. Somehow his bare feet and arms found purchase around the trunk and levered him up towards the fruit. A couple of swings with the *wan big naef* dropped three coconuts to the ground.

The lad scampered down the tree again and brought the still-green fruits over. But before handing them to Chief Tamatoa, he made three slicing cuts into the top of each coconut to allow the milk to be drunk and more cuts into each of the three facets on their sides. Patrick watched, spellbound, as this young lad, no more than nine years old, wielded the long and sharp blade with such ease and familiarity. The chief handed a coconut to Patrick and encouraged him to drink. He realised he was very thirsty but had never drunk coconut milk straight from a fruit before. To his surprise, the taste was quite delicious - delicate and almost perfumed. When everyone's coconut was empty, the lad took them back and split each into three wedges. Tamatoa showed Patrick how to tear off the slices in the skin, each of which then formed a perfect spoon to scrape the jellylike white meat from the inside of that section.

The texture was unfamiliar, as Patrick had only eaten pieces of old, dry coconuts before, from the greengrocer in England. He couldn't reconcile the taste similarity between the two with the dramatic difference in texture. He tried a little, sliding it around in his mouth. The soapy meat possessed a silkiness which was entirely absent from the mature, harder, fibrous coconut flesh of his previous experience. And the taste was lighter and fresher too - cleaner, somehow. He concluded he liked it. His face must have registered all these changes of emotion, because at this point, Chief Tamatoa laughed out loud and slapped Patrick's leg.

A man came up to the chief and muttered in his ear. Tamatoa's grin faded. He told them both that, *"Bot blong yufala, parapele blo' hem, hemi foifoi."* Patrick looked helplessly at Hone. His limited vocabulary of Bislama did not extend this far.

The lad translated: "A radio telephone message says our boat damaged a propellor on the reef as it left. It is still in Port Vila for repairs." Then, to the Chief, *"Hemi kam naanei?"*

There was discussion back and forth. Maybe it would return before dark; maybe not. Hone explained this as well in case Patrick hadn't kept up. It was still early in the day, Patrick reckoned, so there was plenty of time and no need to worry unduly. He assured Chief Tamatoa that all would be fine and asked if he might go for a stroll around the island while he waited? The chief assented right away and offered to go too.

So, the three of them set off back to the shore line, a little contingent of children and youngsters trailing behind, laughing and pointing. This was very, very pleasant, reflected Patrick. He thought of advertising images of balmy tropical islands featuring palm trees swaying in the sea breeze. They were real, after all. Ok, the sand here was not the imagined soft sands of advertisers' dreamscapes. Abrasive crushed coral from the reefs round about, deposited over scores of years could never be described like that. It was quite tough on the skin and on one's highly-polished shoes, Patrick realised, with regret. He paused to remove his socks and shoes before they had got very far along the beach. Also, the grasses through which they strode now and again were not soft and yielding by any means. No, the picturesque plants were thigh-high elephant grass with knife-like edges capable of slicing open the skin of the unwary. Even in the water, you weren't safe. If you went too close to where the waves wash back out to sea or paddled in the shallows, you'd be lucky to escape stepping on the poisonous spines of a resting stone fish. 'Tropical paradise? Ha!' thought Patrick.

Chief Tamatoa proudly pointed out where villagers prepared communal meals, where they planted yams and bananas, how large they were and especially the places where fishing was good. Indeed, Patrick had already spotted several outrigger canoes pulled up into the trees. They walked all the way along and past Turtle Beach to a promising spit of land poking towards Nguna, an uninhabited island about 300m off the NW coast of Pele. The chief came up to a small pile of coconut leaves above the tide line and stopped abruptly. "*Mifela, yufela hemi go long Piliura*," he said, meaning they should return to the village the way they had come.

Patrick's disappointment must have shown. He was hoping to round the corner, to get a look at the NE coast.

"*Hemi bad majik long plas ya*," warned Tamatoa. "*Kastom*." He spat on the coconut leaves to ward off evil spirits.

"Bad Magic?" queried Patrick. Both New Hebrideans were nodding their heads with certainty. Patrick looked to Hone for elucidation. But they resorted to Pele's local language which Patrick couldn't follow, interspersed with rapid Bislama, of which he understood a little. When they finished, Hone turned back to Patrick and reported, intriguingly, that there were two hazards which the Chief wished to avoid. One had to do with bad men mooring their ship off that NE coastline. "What's the second?" asked Patrick. Hone couldn't meet Patrick's gaze and shifted from foot to foot, very self-conscious.

"It's - you know – girls," he finished, with an embarrassed gulp. This didn't constitute much of an explanation for Patrick. It didn't make any sense. He knew that girls and women were not permitted to witness either the Kava Ceremony or the witch doctor's Island *Majik* ceremonies. All the secrecy was to shield ceremonies and activities carried out by men – not any by the women. Why would going to this place be '*Bad Majik*'? And who were these bad men with their ship? Patrick was intrigued.

There was nothing for it. He turned and followed Tamatoa and Hone along the beach. The lad was listening to something the chief wanted to impart, with his head bent towards the older man. Patrick had an idea. He dropped one sock and trod it into the sand.

After another hundred metres or so he exclaimed in feigned annoyance that he'd lost one of his socks. "It must have dropped out of my shoe when we turned around." He said he'd go back for it and encouraged the others to keep on towards the village. "I won't be long," he called over his shoulder.

When he came to the sand where he'd scuffed the sock to hide it, he checked behind him. Tamatoa and Hone in the distance were still walking away. They didn't see him bend down to retrieve the errant sock and so didn't suspect his ruse to be able to round the headland and get a glimpse of the 'Bad Magic' ship.

Soon he had gone far enough that he was out of sight of his companions and could proceed at a brisk pace. He hurried along the shoreline, past the piled-up coconut leaves and around to the north side. Sure enough, there was a pretty ordinary freighter, wind-rode at anchor. Despite standing for a few minutes and shielding his eyes from the sun, he saw no activity on board at all. No crew members scurrying about the deck doing whatever they normally might do. There were occasional streaks of rust down the sides and all appeared very ordinary, in Patrick's judgement. He often needed to visit the port in connection with his Trade Finance role at the bank. This vessel was exactly the same as all the copra boats and inter-island traders he had ever seen there. As the wind swung around in his direction, moving the ship as well, he could hear a diesel engine running on board. That would be to provide power for lights and cooking, but at least it suggested there were crew on board. Moreover, he could make out the name on the stern: '*Lali Mare*'.

He noted that in his memory. As part of his job, he received weekly timetables from the Port Authority about arrival times of particular vessels. It would be easy to keep an eye out for when the *Lali Mare* was due to dock and what she was carrying.

The wind swung around again. The regular 'put, put, put' of the diesel engine receded and a weird moaning sound replaced it. Probably wind through the trees near the shore, thought Patrick. All the same, it had an edge: almost animalistic.

Realisation dawned that whatever sound reached him was independent of the strength of the wind. In fact, during the lulls between gusts of wind, the noise was actually more pronounced. Patrick resolved to investigate. Was this more 'Bad Magic', he thought to himself?

## Chapter 5
# The Birth

Following the moaning sounds, Patrick started up the beach and into the tree line. He found a track between the trees, bordered by elephant grass. The noise of the surf soon receded as he walked deeper into the jungle. The sibilant swishing of dry vines on the palms of coconut trees as they swayed in the breeze was louder now.

Now and again, a green parrot erupted from cover, screaming annoyance at the disturbance. Patrick mopped his brow. 'Better slow down a bit', he thought. The back of his carefully-ironed shirt-jack was sticking to him.

All sorts of large plants thrust their leaves and stems across the path, narrowing it. The canopy of trees overhead reduced the sun's glare, but it doubled the humidity. There was now little or no breeze. Patrick paused. Surrounding him were little jungle sounds. Far-off bird calls, strange rustlings of unseen creatures scuttling into deeper bush and still an occasional parrot.

He hadn't heard that odd moaning sound for a while now and questioned whether he'd lost his bearings. But he pressed on, wishing he had one of those long bush knives. Progress was becoming slower and he stopped for a second to wipe sweat out of his eyes.

His heavy breathing eased. He was deep in the jungle and the silence was oppressive. There was no rustling. No wind stirring the leaves.

And then Patrick's sixth sense awoke. He listened harder than ever. The skin on the back of his neck tightened. Looking around, everything was green, green, green. But nothing moved.

His eyes dropped to his polished shoes: definitely the worse for wear. There was a piece of foliage hooked into one sock and a dried trickle of blood down the other calf, souvenir of a close encounter with the elephant grass. He waved away a fly which had settled on it.

There! Faint moaning came again. It was in the same direction as the track. But it had a human quality. What was he going to find? Should he retrace his steps to the beach, apologise to Chief Tamatoa and leave as soon as the boat could get in? Despite the tropical heat, he shivered. But braced his shoulders and stepped forward.

Very soon, the track was clearer. The plants beside it had been regularly swiped and a nearby tree had many cuts where villagers had trimmed new growth. The moans were weak and ended with a whimpering noise. It must be somebody hurt or injured! Patrick remembered that his election count of 51 revealed that 2 people were absent. He knew 1 had died so might this be the missing person?

Without warning, he found himself at the edge of a clearing. There was a hut in the middle.

"Oh, cripes," he said out loud. Now it was clear. This place must be the *Bad Majik* having something to do with girls that Hone had been so reluctant to talk about. It was the Womens' hut.

"Hello?" Patrick called, softly at first. Then louder. "Is anyone there? Er …*wunfela e stap longplas eer*?"

The wailing started again, a little lower in pitch this time. Patrick approached the darkened doorway of the hut. "Hello in there. *Wunem blo' yufela*?" His eyes adjusted from the bright sunlight to the darkened interior. There was a platform on one side with a small figure sprawled on it.

Straight away he realised the lumpen shape was a young and very pregnant girl. The tattered remains of her cotton shift were pulled up to her armpits and there were some bloody and soiled towels wadded around her hips. Horrified at what he saw, Patrick asked, "*Wunem blo' yufela*?" Her plight appalled but fascinated him at the same time, drawing him inexorably towards the unfortunate girl. The hut was like an oven and Patrick tried hard to moderate his breathing and ignore the stale odour.

He went closer. The girl's eyes were glazed and unfocussed, not even following the movements of his hand when he waved it. He felt her neck for a pulse. Unsure whether he'd found one or was feeling his own pulse, he tried pressing two fingers across her inner wrist. Nothing. Wait – are you supposed to find the pulse on the inner or outer wrist? He checked by feeling for his own. Ok – inner. He tried again …there was a weak fluttering there. But it was inconclusive. Was she breathing? He bent towards her face but couldn't tell. He had no shiny surface to hold

74

near her mouth or nose which might fog up with even gentle breathing. She must be breathing if she could moan and if she had any sort of pulse, but was in so much trouble, he knew.

The urgency of the situation overcame his natural reticence and he felt under her left breast. Yes! Her heart beat was feeble but now he was sure she was still alive, though barely. That settled it. But he would need help.

Straightening, Patrick smoothed the girl's brow and said, "*Mefela fetchim yufela help.*" He didn't know if she would understand that attempt at Bislama, or even whether she could hear him as there was no reaction. He could only hope.

He backed out of the hut and returned along the track towards the beach as fast as he could manage, bushes and leaves tugging at his clothes as he went.

He emerged onto the beach as Hone was tracking his foot prints. They met at the treeline. Tamatoa had sent the lad back to recover the wayward white man. "Hone!" exclaimed Patrick. "There's a girl in a hut back there who needs urgent medical attention. We need the Chief's radio telephone."

"*Hemi Kastom,*" replied the wide-eyed New Hebridean, shaking his head. Patrick's tousled appearance was as alarming as his transgression beyond the *Kastom* barrier of coconut leaves.

"Sorry? '*Kastom*'?"

"*Hemi Badfela Majik.*"

"Yes, yes. But she's dying, man. I need to call Vila Base Hospital."

But Hone looked down at the sand and shook his head. 'What was the matter with him'? wondered Patrick. 'Even if the villagers couldn't help the girl, they could at least try to save the child'.

"Come with me, please." Patrick turned and plunged forward down to the water's edge where the sand was firmer. There it would be easier to jog the short distance towards Piliura village.

Arriving at Chief Tamatoa's hut, Patrick couldn't speak for a second or two. The chief and two warriors gazed out at him impassively.

"*Chif… Chif, mefela wanem toktok long …Vila Base. Wanem toktok long olecollim 'telefon. Plis.*" Would the Chief give permission for Patrick to use their radio telephone?

Tamatoa gazed at Patrick, expressionless for a space of time, turning over the request in his mind. If he agreed, would this man's interference with *Kastom Majik* offend the spirits? Probably. Would they exact revenge? Again, probably ...but likely on the offending mortal rather than anyone else.

So at last he nodded, and one of the warriors went to the back of the hut and retrieved a wooden box.

From its appearance, Patrick judged it might have dated back to World War 1. He flipped the catches to open the case. The crackle black finish showed much wear. As did the pitted chromium handles, Bakelite knobs and dial surrounds. The dials themselves had once been white, but were now yellowed with age and salty air. But they were still legible. 'Did it work'? was the vital question.

"*E goodfela*?" Patrick asked, hopefully. "*Me wanem sparks blo' makem wok'*. The Chief nodded his head downwards very slightly, and only then did Patrick see the fold-out handle. It was a wind-up model so easily transportable.

The other warrior handed over a headset to plug in. Patrick studied the knobs on the front. How to tune it to the band needed? Thinking hard, he realised it was likely already set to the wavelength of the shipping office. The island would run out of staple foods now and again and would need to order more. He could start with them and ask for the hospital channel.

"*Tankyu tumas, Chif Tamatoa*"

The big man shrugged and sat back on his chair. He'd consult the medicine man later about how to appease *Kastom* spirits.

-----//-----

Still horrified at this afront to *Kastom*, Hone stood rooted to the spot as Patrick shouldered the wooden box. But when Patrick began to walk, he had a change of heart. He reasoned that looking after Patrick would be permissible. Hone ran after him with a bottle of water. What Patrick did with it was up to him.

"Thank you," said Patrick, adjusting the box on his shoulder. "You'd better wait here for me and look out for the boat. Oh, what is Bislama for 'having a baby'?"

Hone brightened with relief. He had been anxious that this crazy man would want him to do something contrary to *Kastom.* "*Faanau,*" he answered.

Before making the trek all the way to the hut in the jungle, Patrick thought it wise to make sure the telephone actually worked. He settled down in the shade of a coconut tree, donned the headset and peered at the dials as he wound the handle. There was a hissing sound which got louder as he wound faster. It died away when he stopped, but not immediately. There must be a capacitor or something holding a temporary charge, he reckoned.

When he tried this a second time, he pressed the toggle switch in the middle. The label read 'R' and 'T'. He spoke, returning the switch to the left to await a reply. Feeling distinctly odd, as though doing something he shouldn't, he kept winding the handle and trying the toggle switch. 'Like rubbing your tummy and patting your head at the same time', he thought.

"Pele Island calling. Come in please. Over." Blank hissing was his only audible reward.

He repeated the call twice more, leaving a minute between calls to listen for a reply. Then one came – a broad Australian accent.

"G'day, Pele Island. This is Don at Burns Philp. Waddya need today? And who's that? Over."

Patrick's heart leapt. At last!

"My name is Patrick Field. I'm visiting Pele Island for the *Independens* Election and there's a young girl here who is very sick. I need to contact Vila Base Hospital but don't know how to call them. I've not used a radio telephone before. Over."

"Christ, Mate. Ratshit luck. Use Channel 16 – the emergency channel. Can you get that? Over."

Patrick stared at the worn markings on the largest knob. It was hard to make out the numbers in the bright sunlight, but he reckoned he could find channel 16.

"I think so. While I try them, could you telephone and alert the radio room that I'm calling from Pele Island? Over."

There was a hissing, burping sound in answer, but the essential words came through, "No worries, Mate. Hang in there. Out."

He stopped winding, folded everything away and took a swig from the water bottle. He hefted the box for his trudge along the beach back to the hut.

Ignoring the thorns and elephant grass this time, he strode onwards through the jungle determinedly. Sweat ran into his eyes and soaked his clothing again. Once or twice, he thought he saw movement on the periphery of his vision. But looking directly revealed nothing of interest.

He ducked into the door of the hut. The girl was not comatose any more. She'd raised herself on her elbows. As his eyes readjusted to the dimness of the hut, she was staring past him through the doorway on his right. Her eyes opened very wide. Her back arched and she screamed with all her might.

Patrick whirled around, the heavy radio telephone putting him off-balance. He caught another movement in the corner of his eye as he did so - something big and dark.

Something …he didn't know what. Just – insubstantial. Somehow there but not there. As he crouched, senses on full alert, there was rhythmic pounding in the distance. It was like someone running down a deserted street at 3 o'clock in the morning. The sounds were softer and heavier than human steps, though.

He dived outside again, shielding his eyes from the fierce sun. A dust devil spun by about thirty feet away and was still. There was nothing else. The pounding receded into the distance. He listened intently as it faded, but there was nothing more. Silence.

He needed to attend to the girl.

He righted the wooden box and opened it, eyes searching for the numeral 16 on the channel knob. There was a low stool inside the doorway. The girl watched as he moved it closer to the bed.

"*Me helpim yufela. Me toktok long docta. Ok*?" She slumped back as though accepting of her fate.

Patrick wound the handle and fiddled with the headset. He saw the charging needle move off its stop towards a central position where there was a distinct line. Was this the normal operating level of charge?

Pressing the toggle to 'T' for transmit, he began, "This is Patrick Field calling from Pele Island. I have a girl who is very sick – er, having a baby – can anyone help? Over."

He realised he had forgotten to ask to establish with whom he wanted to talk. He pressed the 'T' again. "Sorry, Patrick Field on Pele Island calling for Vila Base Hospital. Come in please. Over"

The hospital staff must monitor Channel 16 all the time as it is the emergency channel.

Or he was lucky that Don's message from Burns Philp had got through, but straight away the hospital answered, "*Hello, hemi Vila Base – wunem blo' yufela, Patrick? Over.*"

Cripes – if he was going to have to do this in the local language, it would be very hard!

"*Hemi wunfela girl – hemi 'faanau' – hemi bigfela siknis blo' bebe.*" He'd remembered Hone's word '*faanau*' for 'having a baby'. "Over."

"*Wetim smol time.*"

He sat back, leaving the machine on 'Receive'. It was important to turn the handle every time the charge needle dropped a bit.

The box crackled into life again. "This is Dr Jessica at Vila Base, Patrick. Can you hear me? Over."

Patrick was not a religious person, but he muttered a short 'Thanks' to the Almighty. Now perhaps he stood a chance. "I'm receiving you very well, doctor. There is a young girl here, roughly 17 or 18 years old, trying to give birth. But there is some problem – she is very weak, has lost blood and keeps losing consciousness. Over."

"Is she breathing? Over."

He checked again. Her pulse was now clearer than before and her chest was rising a little and falling. Her body was rigid, though. He pressed 'T' for transmit. "She is breathing better than a while back, but she is clenching her teeth and she is all rigid. Over."

"Do you have water? Over."

He told Dr Jessica how little he had – there was only about 200mls left in the bottle. She asked him to describe what he could see of her and feel. She was lying on her left side, with legs drawn up and shivered every so often, despite the oppressive heat in the hut.

At once, the girl moaned and curled herself tighter. Dr Jessica said to measure one hand's width down from her belly button and to feel for the baby with his fingertips. Rather gingerly, he moved the towels away from her hips, looking at her face for permission.

She uncurled a little but gripped the sides of the bed.

"Come on, come on" barked the radio. "Get her clothing off and outside the hut if it's soiled – now – can you feel the baby? Over." Patrick had forgotten to flip the toggle switch.

"Er, sorry. Yes, I can. Um, shouldn't I wash my hands or something? Over."

"There isn't enough water. You aren't having lunch, you are saving her baby and / or her life – preferably both. Now – tell me what you feel of the baby. Over."

He peeled the towels away from her hips completely and flicked the worst of them out of the doorway. His hand on her lower belly moved gently over her skin. "There's a hard lump on her right and …yes, the baby is kicking! Um …over."

"Roll her onto her back. Where is the kicking and how far is she dilated? Over."

'Dilated'? What …oh. Yes. This was no time for niceties, Patrick realised. It was tricky to wind the handle now and again and feel what the baby was doing. Turning the girl onto her back, he did his best to wipe up the mess between her legs using the last of the towels. He spotted a tiny foot!

He reported this to the doctor but had to check again as she asked if it was the left or the right foot and was he positive it wasn't a hand?

It was the left foot. Definitely. And the hard lump low down on her right side had moved.

"We'll take a chance that's the head. You have to push the foot back inside and turn the baby. Use some of the water, clean it as best you can, then spit on it and push it back. Can you do that? Over."

Do what? He moved his hand to press the Transmit button, but thought better of saying anything. What chance did the girl have if he couldn't help her? What further damage could he possibly do?

At last he did push the button and croaked, "OK – over."

There were no more towels in a decent enough state. He took off his shirt. It was not exactly laundry fresh, but better than any alternative.

Later, he reflected how oddly the human brain works in such situations. His head was clear. He thought to tear the shirt into strips and put some to one side to clean the baby when he or she emerged. "*Wunem water blo' you..?*" he asked the girl softly, holding the bottle to her lips. She swallowed a trickle of the water, to Patrick's delight. He splashed a little more onto the tiny, delicate foot and wiped it with a piece of the shirt. It felt soft; almost boneless. How could he push it back inside her?

He smoothed her brow and massaged her hand. "*E gud – quicktime – mefela promis. E gud… Yufela restin wuntime. Sleep longplas 'eer. E gud. E gud.*"

He turned his attention back to the foot. He spat on it, as instructed, and pushed with his left hand. The girl's muscles were so exhausted that there was very little resistance. The heel slipped back - now the toes. Patrick's head swam with the enormity of what he was doing. But then the baby kicked him – it really did! He knew he was helping a small person, not an inanimate foot.

'What next'? he thought. 'How far do I push the foot'?

He gave the machine another quick winding and pressed the Transmit button. "Ok, I've got the foot back – the baby kicked me – how far should I push? Over."

"Good. Where's the head now? Try to move it around to your left hand. Over."

All at once, Patrick had a strong sense that this was a boy. Mathematically, there was a fifty/fifty chance of being right, but he knew. The lump under the girl's skin moved with the pressure of his hand and there was a little fluttering he could feel beside it. A hand, maybe? A little further …more …more. There. The head was central now. "What next, doctor?" Oh, yes. The switch. "The head is central, doctor. What next, please? Over."

"Good. Can the girl push? If not, you'll have to get the baby out yourself – just mind the eyes. Keep talking to me. Over."

One glance at the girl's face made him doubtful. He was not even certain whether she was conscious now. Her jaw hung open, but her chest was rising and falling, so she was still breathing.

"Please try to push for me. Er, *plis, yufela pushim wuntime*." Patrick smoothed his hand down her belly, over and over to encourage the movement needed. "*Pushim wuntime …e gud. Yufela pushim.*"

The baby's head moved. Patrick's index finger suddenly hooked into something – his eye? The doctor's warning flooded through his mind. But how to tell? Then he felt pressure on the other side of his finger. It must be his mouth: the baby was biting him!

Reaching behind him with his right hand, he wound the radio telephone's handle and the charge needle recovered to its central position. He passed along the news of this latest development. Dr Jessica instructed Patrick to try to get his fingers under the child's jawbone, behind the ear. He felt the mother push and …here was the top of the baby's head.

"Here he comes! *Pushim wuntime; pushim*…"

The whole head was out now. The girl gave an agonised gasp and her chest heaved as she fought for air.

"Doctor? The whole head is out now. Should I pull? Over."

"Give the mother more water. Wipe off the baby's eyes and mouth, then pull some more – get one shoulder at a time. Over."

The flies were back with a vengeance. He swatted at them with his bloodied left hand, trying to keep them away from the tiny head. This time, when he tipped the almost empty water bottle between the girl's lips, there was a convulsive swallowing motion. "*E clos up finis; yufela pushim wuntime more.*"

And she did, bless her.

He wiped the scrunched-up little face and out came one shoulder. He got a finger under it and pulled. Inch by inch and then with a rush, like a champagne cork, out he came. Someone said, "Aaaah." Maybe it was Patrick; maybe the girl, but her eyes had focussed on Patrick. "It's a boy," he told her. "*Hemi wun boyfela.*"

89

He didn't need to hold the baby aloft and slap it like they do in movies. With an almighty gurgle, the boy opened his mouth wide and bellowed, "Nnnaaaaaagh. Naaaagh. Naaagh. Naagh, naagh, naagh."

Oh yes. The umbilical cord. He'd better ask the doctor what to do. He pressed 'T' on the radiotelephone. "What should I do with the umbilical cord? Over."

As he flipped the switch back, he heard muffled cheering at the other end. Dr Jessica said to tie a half hitch knot as close to the child's tummy as possible. Did he have a knife or scissors or something he could cut with?

Patrick's trusty Swiss Army knife would do just fine. He prided himself on keeping it razor-sharp, but the cord was remarkably tough. It gave way eventually and the baby bawled lustily as Patrick poured the last of his water onto its face. It was very small and sat easily on his left hand.

But he felt awkward, as though his big hands might hurt the child. He passed it to the girl and laid it on her chest. "Here. *Wunfela boy blo' yu.*"

Was that a little smile on her face?

The radio was asking for an update. "What's happening, Patrick? How is the mother? Over."

"I've tied the cord and cut it, but the mother is so weak, she can't hold the child – and I haven't any water left. Over."

Dr Jessica told Patrick to prop the girl as upright as possible with a box or bag or something under her elbows. Then to lay the child onto her chest, face down, while he dealt with the afterbirth.

'Afterbirth'? Oh yes. The placenta. Hours spent in biology lessons at school examining line drawings in textbooks hadn't prepared him for this. He had even produced drawings for exam papers. The reality of bringing a child into the world bore little similarity to those soulless drawings. There was nothing in the hut suitable as a backrest, so Patrick rose and stepped to the doorway to fetch something.

Ducking his head to get outside, he lifted his gaze to survey the clearing. It was no longer deserted. A silent group of villagers watched him, some sixty feet away. One or two lifted their hands to their faces in shock. Patrick was bare-chested and streaked with blood from his efforts. A low murmuring broke out in the little crowd as this shocking apparition in human form stood before them.

Chief Tamatoa was in the centre, surrounded by his largest warriors, one step in front of the group. But ahead of them all, a tiny, wizened man clad in strips of cloth and feathers began to prance and leap around. He carried a staff with things tied around it which rattled. He brandished this, challenging his enemy as with a spear. His leaping became little runs towards Patrick. He stamped and brushed the ground to make the dust fly before retreating and swerving away, only to repeat the process. Little by little, he moved closer, perhaps hoping to drive this Devil Man back to wherever he had come from. This was the village's medicine man, whose counsel Tamatoa had sought in case the *Kastom* Gods needed appeasement.

When the man came to within five feet of Patrick he stopped quite still. He wasn't out of breath or even sweating. Patrick knew his shoulders ought to have been heaving with the effort of all that dancing, given the heat and humidity. They locked eyes. Everything was still. The medicine man was peering into Patrick's very soul. Without warning, he erupted into whirling, blurred movement. He twisted round and around, jerking, hollering and shrieking to the sky, waving his staff. The dust rose more and more, the faster he spun around. A cold puff of wind blew in from the sea, peppering Patrick's face with dust so that some got into his eyes. Blinking furiously, he pawed at his face but that only made it worse.

He started towards the group, trying to sidestep the whirling medicine man, hoping to plead for help. "*Chief Tamatoa, wunfela girl long plas 'ya, hemi needim fud and wota – hemi sik tumas – wunfela boy blo' her; 'e well tumas.*"

The wind gusted strongly now. Patrick struggled to walk against it. And then almost fell forward himself as the wind stopped as suddenly as it had started. With a jolt, he realised the onlookers had gone. He cast around, looking left and right and left again. The clearing was utterly empty. Rubbing his gritty eyes did not reveal anybody at all. No medicine man, not Chief Tamatoa or his warriors and no villagers either. The trees and plants on the edge of the clearing were still, none betraying passage of a person, far less a group of them.

"Naaaaarrrgh."

The baby's angry cry brought Patrick back to reality with a bump. Clasping his head, he tried to reassure himself that he still existed and was not dreaming. He still hadn't found anything to prop up the poor girl in the hut.

'Must be heat exposure. I'm seeing things. I need to drink more water myself'.

Around the hut were piles of palm fronds and creeper. He bundled some together, wrapping the fronds with strands of liana so they formed pillows. That would have to do. He returned to the battleground and wedged them behind the girl's back and under her forearm. While he'd been outside, the baby had latched onto one breast and was feeding eagerly, if inaccurately. No doubt the recent cry was him registering displeasure that his source of nourishment had disappeared. The girl had somehow found strength to hold him. She gazed at the child, stroking his head, examining every part of him. It was as though she couldn't believe that this little human had been inside her only minutes before. The child opened and closed his miniature hands rhythmically and hung on to his mother's finger when he found it.

The charge in the radio telephone had long since dissipated. Patrick wound the handle again and the set crackled into life.

"Hello, Vila Base. This is Patrick Field – I'm still here. Um, over."

"Patrick, it's Doctor Jessica here. Give us an update on the baby: how is he? Over."

"Oh, he's fine – he's sucking away madly, although I can't tell if she has any milk; he's well. Lively. He shouted pretty loudly when he came out and has lots of toes and fingers and things ...well, not too many, but ...it's exciting, isn't it? Oh yes – over."

"All right, calm down, Patrick. You've done very well. Can you get the mother some water and something small to eat? Clean her up as best you can. You can tell me all about it when you get back to Vila. Over."

Saying a temporary farewell to the girl, he thought this bit would be easy. If he could deliver babies, surely he could find water and food! Patrick folded away the radio telephone and hoisted it onto his shoulder. Still slick with sweat and blood, he walked across the clearing to the track, feeling that he was on a cloud.

Grinning broadly, he lifted his eyes upwards, into the broiling sun and laughed out loud. This was something more valuable than anything he had ever done before.

Back at the village, Chief Tamatoa ordered a fresh coconut and a pineapple be prepared for Patrick. He drank a little but straightaway ferried them back to the hut. The girl had made herself more comfortable while he was away. She thanked him for the food and drink and for the extra palm leaves he fetched for cleaning herself and the baby. Now feeling awkward, he said he had to go back to Port Vila. She smiled and nodded and they shook hands, in an oddly formal farewell.

Back at the village again, Hone was waiting for him at the dock. He too had a silly grin on his face, although it was intriguing that Patrick had mislaid his shirt-jack. He probably thought that his boss had spent the afternoon like he had: with one of the village girls. In a way, Patrick had. If possible, his grin became wider than ever. Unable to believe his luck that he was not about to be reprimanded, Hone chanced a conspiratorial clap on Patrick's bare back. It was his shorthand for 'girls are really HOT on Pele Island, aren't they'?

They both laughed and boarded the return boat for Vila.

96

# Chapter 6

## Dr Jessica

The next day, Patrick had recovered physically but was still bubbling with excitement. He didn't sleep well but was in the bank at his usual 7:30am.

"What's the matter with you?" demanded Joe from his little glass box to the right of the door – always Joe was the earliest riser of any of them. "Why the silly grin?"

"Nothing, Joe. What a smashing morning it is," replied Patrick.

"Did everything go alright yesterday? Where is the Ballot box you were given?"

"Handed back last night. Don't worry. Everybody voted who was able to do so."

Joe grunted and returned his attention to his diary cards spread about on his desk. There were so many things for the accountant to remember, to chase up, to be responsible for preparing. He had resolved some time ago to do the minimum of actual work himself. Little else would happen if he buried himself in some task or other. Instead, he'd parcel out the jobs to those most able to do them and only step in himself at the very last moment to avert disaster – and the inevitable dressing down by Andrew Cutlass. His view of New Hebrideans was that they are a lovely, kind, well-meaning people, by and large. But they had the memory span of a puppy for Royal Counties Bank tasks. They'd remember national holidays, family celebrations and harvest times without fail. But by Monday, the cashiers would have forgotten how they cashed up the tills on Friday, and someone would need to show them how – again!

No doubt Joe had a diary card to remind Patrick to hand back his Ballot box. He wouldn't tear it up until a third party had confirmed that Patrick Field had, indeed, returned the box safe and sound. He wrote a new 'Do By' date on the card and put it back in his card box.

Patrick went to find Sara to go over what were the most urgent things to do today. He had a vague recollection there were some ships due into port today or tomorrow. He might have to go down to the dock with some Letter of Credit paperwork. He found her hiding in the store cupboard with two other women.

"There you are! Good morning, Sara, and May, Heilani – *Olgeta gud tumas*?"

They all smiled and giggled shyly. Sara rose, smoothing her Mother Hubbard dress. She left them and went to her desk and typewriter and beloved telex machine in its lockable housing. "*E gud, tumas*, Patrick." And then, in English, "We heard your boat could not return to fetch you. What happened?"

Patrick considered telling her the entirety of his adventures, but thought better of it at the last moment.

"We arrived fine, but then later received a radio message that the boat damaged one propellor on the reef as it left Pele Island. It was repaired, though and came back again shortly before dusk, so everything was alright. You should ask Hone how he got on." Patrick raised one eyebrow and grinned at her.

Sara snorted in a most unladylike manner. She knew all about Hone's reputation with girls. "No need, Patrick. He is in trouble of two kinds right now: he is late so Joe wants him and...." She moved her head closer to him and lowered her voice. "Someone said he has been going with one of the girls on Pele Island." She sat back with a meaningful expression on her face.

"Is that …a bad thing?" Patrick queried, not following her drift. Why might this be undesirable?

"He's from Malekula, silly."

Patrick was still none the wiser and it must have shown on his face.

"He didn't ask the chief's permission before – you know – and her father might go to the Medicine Man."

Patrick remembered the strange, wizened old man who had leaped and pranced in front of him, and shuddered at the thought.

"*Kastom* is a serious thing, Patrick."

"I am sure; I can see that. Perhaps Hone should go to apologise and set things straight."

Sara shook her head and lowered her gaze.

"Ah, well. I'm sure he'll work it out. What do we have for today, then? I wanted to drop by Vila Base to meet someone, so if I need to go to the port, I could combine the two things."

They sorted through yesterday's In Tray and the post which May brought around. At

8am, it was time to unlock the door. A trickle of customers filed in, led by a fearsome little Vietnamese woman from the best supermarket in town, Bon Plats. This was Madame Leung, who was always charming and kind and friendly with the New Hebridean cashiers. But she had found that being angry with the ex-pat staff paid enormous dividends. If she could manufacture a complaint and demand that Andrew Cutlass sort it out, he would straightaway blame the nearest ex-pat. And would grant her whatever monetary favour she requested.

Much later, Patrick found out that the owner of Bon Plats, named Tai Nguyen, was a low-level criminal. He was suspected of gun-running, had recruited Cutlass somehow to be an informant and made him carry out money laundering for Nguyen's bosses. These were military types linked to Col Muammar Ghadaffi of Libya. He never knew what was Cutlass' original weakness which Nguyen was exploiting. In fact, Cutlass paid thousands of NH francs to Nguyen every month so that it remained secret. Either he'd pay cash or had to provide information useful to the network. Nguyen would value it and discount that month's dues.

On this morning, Madame Leung strode down the banking hall, her heels tap, tap, tapping all the way to the Trade Finance counter at the end, where Patrick sat. Sara got up to receive her. They exchanged pleasantries and smiles and she handed a sheaf of flimsy papers across. These covered some goods which were due to arrive on the *Lali Mare* within a day or two.

The Bon Plats supermarket had to settle up in local currency for the value of the goods. When they had paid, Patrick would issue a permission document which Bon Plats staff could take to the dock side to claim the goods. Patrick took the documents from Sara, asking her to check today's shipping arrivals. He went around the corner to Gilles for the foreign exchange rate between US dollars and NH francs. Armed with this, he returned to his desk and calculated how much Bon Plats needed to pay.

He wrote it on a slip of paper and pushed it across the counter to Madame Leung. Her face fell.

"Ees not possible." She started. "Ees not possible to work like this." Patrick quickly realised the way this was going to go. She would work herself into a lather of fury, demand to see Andrew Cutlass, and stomp upstairs. A minute or two later, she'd trail behind him, smirking, while he descended, red in the face and roar for either Patrick or Gilles. He would then demand that whomever he considered most at fault, should apply the 'proper' rate of exchange.

So Patrick thought he'd try a shortcut.

"One moment, Madame. It may be that we can improve the rate in view of the size of the transaction." That stopped her in mid-flow. She could turn her confected anger on and off like a tap.

Patrick picked up his phone. "Andrew? Sorry to bother you. Madame Leung is unhappy with today's US dollar rate of exchange. Do you think you might agree to a 5% improvement in her favour as the transaction is quite large?" There was a slight pause.

"What does Gilles say?"

Patrick was about to explain that he thought it wise to seek managerial approval before negotiating with Gilles. "I haven't asked him yet because…" But he had to stop. He held the phone away from his ear. Cutlass was shouting questions at him asking whether he had engaged his brain this morning? Had he understood the parameters of his job? Did he not comprehend that Bon Plats was a Very Important Customer? ...And so on. Then the line went dead.

Patrick retreated around the corner to speak to Gilles again. Precious seconds went by before Gilles replaced his own telephone.

"I wanted to ask Andrew if we could improve the rate for Bon Plats by 5%, but he got too angry and I expect he will come down here." As he spoke, already Andrew's dulcet tones could be detected asking Madame Leung if 'All was well'?

"This is him, now. Can we do it, Gilles?"

"Not without removing the transaction commission. *Mai, je pense - oui – c'est possible.*"

"What news, gentlemen? Why is my customer unhappy, Patrick?"

Gilles cut in as Patrick was about to protest innocence to Andrew Cutlass. "Eef we subtract all our commission, zen ees possible to improve zee rate by 5%."

Cutlass smiled in a satisfied manner. "That was easy, wasn't it, Patrick? Well don't stand there - go and tell her." Patrick took a moment to compose himself. He'd need a couple of deep breaths before returning to the simpering Madame Leung and telling her the good news. As he arrived at the counter, Sara confirmed that the *Lali Mare* was due in that morning. Patrick instructed Jean Marc to prepare vouchers for Madame Leung to sign and pay for her goods. Then he signed the release document.

After she'd gone, Sara asked if Patrick would like a cup of tea. He accepted gratefully and elected to visit the hospital first to meet Dr Jessica to cheer himself up. He'd go to the dockside afterwards, postponing the possibility of running into men from Bon Plats.

-----//-----

He gathered the papers he needed, checked nobody in the Trade Finance section needed him for a few hours and headed for the front door.

"Where are you going?" called Joe.

"To the port – there are some shipments to be cleared."

"Don't be long. I want to start the Quarterly returns." Patrick smiled at Joe's parting shot. He knew there were weeks to go before anyone could start work marshalling the required figures. But Joe had to maintain the appearance of being 'in charge'.

He'd not visited Vila Base Hospital before. But it was close by the Royal Counties Bank office, overlooking the Erakor Lagoon and only a little out of his way to the main wharf area to the south. He parked and went inside to ask for Dr Jessica.

Conveniently, she was on a break and came out right away to meet Patrick. They shook hands.

"I'm very pleased to meet you: you did very well yesterday."

"Thank you so much for helping me – I'd have been useless without someone telling me what to do. I wanted so much to help the girl but was scared of hurting her even more."

Jessica nodded. Patrick had passed a basic medical school test: to be able to detach oneself from the blood, horrors and risks and instead to focus on what he could do to fix whatever was wrong. "Not everyone can do what you managed, Patrick. You saved her life and that of the baby. I've still got ten minutes before I'm back on duty. Do you have time for a coffee? It's made from Tanna beans…," she smiled, knowing this was a rare treat.

"Ooh, yes, please. That would be very kind."

Patrick trailed after her, past Reception. He found himself glancing downwards, admiring the way she moved. He recalled her at the sailing club talking to Sven. He had found her attractive, even though standing still, but any interest he might have developed had been dampened by Dave's comments about her being unavailable. Still – *she* had invited *him* for a coffee. Was her dating door a little bit ajar?

One of the senior nurses kindly fetched two fresh coffees for them. Patrick refused milk, preferring his strong and black and without sugar. He felt those would mask the true subtlety of a coffee and said so. Jessica pouted: "I need extra sugar – I was On-Call overnight. Tell me - is there any news of the child yet?"

Patrick shook his head. "I only hope the girl is accepted back into her village. I couldn't tell from Chief Tamatoa's reaction. And…" He tailed off.

"What?" she encouraged.

"While I was at the hut, I had the weirdest experience."

"More weird than delivering a baby for the first time?"

Jessica was lovely when she smiled, he thought. He focussed on his knees to help him reimagine the scene when he emerged from the hut.

"Yes. When I came out of the hut, the chief and his villagers were all waiting for me outside in the sun. There was this old man – a medicine man, I think – who danced around waving some sort of ceremonial stick." Patrick looked up at her. "But the first thing that was especially strange: despite all his energetic dancing, he didn't sweat."

Jessica cocked one eyebrow.

"And he raised a strong wind and a dust storm which blinded me for a bit. When it cleared, there was nobody there."

"That does sound pretty weird, Patrick. How much did you have to drink?"

Patrick immediately thought she was accusing him of having too much beer. "Nothing, honestly."

"No, not alcohol – I mean water: how much water had you drunk since morning?"

"Oh – a little on the boat. And some coconut water which the chief got for me after the election was over. But that's all."

Jessica was nodding. "You may have been dehydrated and in the excitement of delivering a baby, your brain imagined these things." She saw his shoulders droop. "It's not unusual – the human body is capable of amazing feats of endurance, but it cannot go for long without hydration."

Patrick saw from the corner of his eye that the nurse who had brought them coffee had reappeared. Jessica saw too. "Oh – my break time is up. I'm due for a ward round and I mustn't keep you, Patrick. Thank you for coming in to see me. Time to go, I'm afraid. But I'm very pleased to have met you." She stood up and extended her hand.

Swallowing hard, Patrick stood as well. "Oh, right. Yes, of course. Um …"

"Yes?"

"Er …could I take you for dinner on Friday?"

To his delight, Jessica smiled. "That would be lovely, Patrick. Can you find a restaurant which doesn't serve everything with garlic?"

"Right. Er, yes, of course. Sure… What time would suit you?"

And so it was that Patrick found himself going on a Friday night date with the supposedly 'unavailable' and 'remote' doctor. La Hotte and the local Australian bankers would have to do without him this week. It was a shame about the no-garlic rule, though: Patrick loved garlic. Still. Given the choice between Jessica and a meal laced with garlic, his choice was obvious.

He didn't remember much about the ten-minute drive to the Port area.

-----//-----

As well as needing to check some of the other shipments, he had got wind that a ship docking there may have a consignment of jars of pickled onions, an English delicacy which he missed desperately. While he was queuing on the dockside to bid for the pickles, he saw the '*Lali Mare*' moored further down. Men were unloading boxes onto a Toyota pickup. When it drove past, he saw there were no markings on the particularly hefty wooden boxes.

Later on, he called in on the Harbour Master, Lionel Brasted, to say 'hello'.

"Morning, Captain Brasted. How are you today?"

Brasted sported a neatly-trimmed, full set beard and looked every inch the former naval officer – which he was. "Patrick! Dear boy. I'm right as rain and twice as soft." He chuckled at his little joke. "What can I do you for?"

"I signed off some goods for Bon Plats this morning – meat and vegetables it was, with washing powder, if you please. What a mixture, eh? But down here, I saw the Bon Plats truck driving off the dock with some large and unlabelled wooden boxes. Even the washing powder wouldn't be shipped in them. Could I have a quick peek at the manifest to see what other freight was aboard the vessel?"

The captain shuffled through the papers under his right hand and extracted one. "Ah yes. Here we are. The *Lali Mare*, you said?" Patrick nodded. "Yes… Foods; Electrical goods …soft furnishings," he glanced up. "Some for your Chief Manager, Andrew Cutlass, actually and …rough-cut Whitewood from Santo." He ran his finger further down the page. "That's all for Bon Plats."

Patrick knew that none of these declared cargo items would be transported in such boxes. "I recognised the pickup as belonging to the Bon Plats supermarket. It often parks outside the bank when Madame Leung visits to conduct her foreign trade business." He saw the captain shudder at the mention of

Madame Leung. It was obvious he'd been on the receiving end of one of her tirades. "I'd love to know what was in those boxes."

The captain stroked his beard. "Bon Plats might have been doing someone else a favour by transporting their goods?"

Patrick hadn't thought of that. He was curious and was trying to find out if another bank was doing business with the supermarket. He hadn't thought of this innocent natural explanation, though.

"Oh yes; maybe. I hadn't considered that. But they don't come across as the 'doing favours' types, I have to say! Thanks very much and do give my regards to Mrs Brasted." Patrick turned and left, still puzzling over what he'd seen.

-----//-----

Patrick drove slowly, following the directions Dr Jessica has given him. He pulled up outside a bungalow so surrounded by trees and foliage that he could not, at first, identify that it was the correct house. He checked his watch. Five minutes early. Would she mind if he was early? Better that than late, surely?

Or he could be 'on time'. Yes. That was best. In fact, such exactitude might even appeal to her scientific side. Should he keep his shirt sleeves buttoned or fold them up once and leave them loose? The latter would be more comfortable, but weren't 'him'. Not his style. Come to think of it, did he have a 'style'? Earlier that evening, he'd inspected the contents of his wardrobe after an especially long shower and careful shave. While waiting for a tiny shaving nick on his nose to clot, he had gazed helplessly at the meagre choices of outfit. Royal Counties Bank salaries for junior officers did not stretch to casual designer clothing.

Not for him the easy tailored shirt and well-fitting trousers that Alan, Florence Stuart's boyfriend could afford.

'She's going on a date with me, not my clothes', he told himself. Anyway, having few choices made selection easier, didn't it?

Before getting out of the car, Patrick gave a final exploratory dab at his nose with a handkerchief. The tiny cut exhibited a wilful intention to mess up his evening by re-bleeding several times. But, for this final check, the white tissue paper was spotless.

One minute to go. But what if this wasn't the right house? He'd be late arriving at the correct one!

He closed his car door quietly, tugged at his shirt to straighten any new creases and walked as confidently as he could through the greenery towards the front door.

As he reached it, the door swung inwards and there was Dr Jessica herself with a grin stretching from ear to ear. Patrick tried to remember if her hair had been up or down when he saw her at the hospital. It was now swirling about her shoulders, hiding and then revealing her long and shapely neck as she turned to lock the door behind her. The light blue dress seemed to move independently, hinting at the figure beneath.

He couldn't help himself. "Wow."

Her smile broadened, if that was even possible. "A girl has to make a bit of an effort. I'll let you in on a secret – this is my first date for…" She play-acted thinking hard. "I can't remember that far back."

Patrick chuckled. "I'm sure that isn't true. I've booked a table at L'Houstalet Restaurant, so it's quite close. You know the one? Near Bon Plats supermarket?"

"The French one? Isn't that very fancy?"

"Nowhere near as fancy as you."

Jessica's delighted laughter at such an obvious reply came lightly and easily. "And where, kind sir, did you park your carriage?"

"At M'Lady's garden gate."

Jessica led the way and waited while Patrick gallantly opened the car door for her.

She was still fiddling with her seatbelt when he got in. "Are you okay with that?"

It clicked into place. "Got it. I guess you don't use this side very much."

"Hmmn. Come to think of it – no. I find I can't reach the pedals quite so easily from there."

"You're bad!"

He smiled. They headed for L'Houstalet.

Jessica didn't wait for him to open her door. She sprang out of the car even before he'd killed the engine. "Come on. It smells divine."

He followed her inside.

As they waited for Clément, the maitre d'hotel to guide them to their table, Patrick wrinkled his nose. Jessica had specified that he should avoid restaurants serving food garnished with garlic. There were pungent whiffs of the stuff emanating from the kitchen area.

But she didn't say anything. They ordered beers and poulet fish for her and flying fox stew for him.

When the waiter brought their dishes, she eyed his plate with great interest. "Could I try some of that? I've never had flying fox."

"Sure." He pushed the plate towards her. "You know they aren't really foxes?"

"So what are they?"

"They're giant bats, actually – their wing span can be five feet wide. Their heads look a bit fox like, I suppose."

Jessica chewed, thoughtfully. "It makes me think of a sort of strong rabbit. Or hare, maybe."

She pushed her poulet fish towards him. "I'll never eat all this – do take some."

He obliged, eagerly. The restaurant had cooked the fish fast, with the least possible extra flavouring. It simply fell apart. It was obviously really fresh. "It's beautiful," he enthused and attacked his steaming plate of stew.

But Jessica wasn't tucking into her food. "Are you alright?" Patrick asked.

She nodded. "This is so lovely. Thank you for asking me to come. It's an enormous treat. Because of the odd hours I work, I find it a bit of a struggle to eat properly. I'm so bashed at the end of my shifts that I'm too tired to cook something decent. Even when I do try, usually I get called in to look after someone, so the food spoils."

"I didn't realise any of that. I'm lucky, then. When I come home, I'm home until the next morning. So I suppose I have that luxury. You should indulge now, while you can!"

Between mouthfuls, she told him how she'd been sent there – part of a 'rotation' – she said. And how much she wanted to heal the sick and improve the quality of life for those who couldn't be cured.

He admitted his first sighting of her at the Sailing Club and asked about her interest in the sport. Jessica's raised eyebrow and playful smile indicated she reckoned to have caught him out.

"You should have come over", she said. "Why didn't you? I was only utilising Sven's handiness with tools."

Patrick took a deep breath. Should he drop his Aussi mate into deep water by admitting what he'd said? Instead, he mumbled something about needing to say thank you to one of the Australian members for introducing him to Sven. When he had a chance to come over, she'd gone.

"Hmmn. If you say so. At first I found the constant demands of the hospital were getting on top of me. Then one of the surgeons suggested I go with him to the Club. I ended up buying his Laser when he left the island. Sailing is a way of clearing my mind of all the nagging worries about patients."

She took another bite of the fish. "You have to concentrate hard, you see. It's a sort of mental medicine."

Patrick considered. "You're right. I hadn't thought of it that way, but I agree. Come to think of it, when I was younger, I used to like fishing – sea fishing. I'd spend hours concentrating on the rod tip, waiting for a bite. I'd try to think how the bait was sitting on the bottom – how movement of the water affected it. Would it be attractive to the fish?

"Did you catch lots?"

"Never lots. Sometimes I'd do alright and my Mum would cook them that night or the next. But I began to realise that I enjoyed going fishing even when I didn't catch a thing."

Jessica began to smile. "So, what you were enjoying was the switching off from ordinary life, not necessarily the catching of fish."

"And the getting miserably cold, sitting still for hours on end on a breezy beach or pier. My fuel would be sandwiches or really bad 'mystery meat' pies from the pier café. He pantomimed, 'Pie and Cheeps – Five and Seex'."

She laughed at this memory. But then grew serious. "That's the first personal thing you've told me, Patrick. Are there any others?"

He looked down at his plate. "I'm not sure. I suppose there must be. I'd have to think about that."

"What did you like at school?"

"English. History was fascinating. Geography too. And I really liked Physics, although the mathematics floored me every time."

"What 'A' levels did you do?"

"Biology, Physics and Chemistry."

"Why not English? Or History or anything which would go with it?"

"I guess my Mum and Dad wanted me to go into medicine."

"You could have said, 'No'."

"I suppose so. I didn't think of that, though. I mean, I thought that I could do anything in arts or science. It's only that I'd have to work harder to succeed at science stuff."

She smiled again. "That's the way I feel about arts topics. I don't 'get' them. I had to revise hard and try to remember things by rote learning for History and Geography. But Biology came easily. Most of medicine was simple Physics or Chemistry and was natural to me. What I expected to be the answer usually was right."

She placed her knife and fork carefully on the side of her plate and puffed out her cheeks. "I'm stuffed. That was glorious, Patrick."

"Do you think you could manage some pudding if we wait a bit?"

Jessica rubbed her tummy with one hand. "I'm not sure there is any room, yet. Could we share one?"

"Sure. I'll ask for a menu."

Clément appeared at Patrick's shoulder even before he could turn around. *"Dessert, Monsieur et Mademoiselle?"*

They ordered hot apple tarte. The restaurant served it plain but with tiny apple slices in a precise geometric pattern around the most delicate short pastry flan, glazed with apricot jam. A waiter shuffled two espresso coffees in front of them without asking. Jessica didn't add sugar to hers this time.

When they pulled up outside Jessica's house, he turned off the engine and walked around to open her door.

She smoothed down her dress. "I'd like to ask you in for another coffee, but I'm on duty at 7am, so I need to get to sleep. I've had a lovely time, though."

"Me too."

"Can we go out again, Patrick? If you want to, of course…"

"Er, right. Yes. Yes, of course I want to."

She stretched up on her toes to kiss his cheek. It lasted for one glorious lungful of her scent, supplanting that of the oleander bushes bordering her path. The evening breeze brushed a stray hair across his face. He held her hand for a moment and then she was gone, sashaying up the path to her front door. She rewarded him with a shy smile and a half wave before the door closed.

Patrick couldn't move. Emotions flooded through him. He began to laugh with joy. He tried to restrain the laughter – 'you're making a spectacle of yourself', his father would have said – but that made it worse. After a moment, he got into his car. But then he realised that the steering wheel was on the other side, so had to get out again.

Driving home that night was really, really hard.

-----//-----

When he returned to the bank, Joe told him that another ex-pat would be arriving the next day. Could Patrick join him to fetch the man from the airport? Of course, it was not a question – more of a polite instruction. Patrick said he'd arrange his work so that he could. The man's name was Kim Appleby. He'd be the new loans officer and would also be responsible for the cashiers. Patrick felt sorry for him already. Figuring out whether to lend money to a person or a business would involve him in a great deal of interaction with Andrew Cutlass – that was the downside. But for the most part, supervision of the cashiers could be handled by one of the senior local women, Marianne. She took a matronly interest in all the girls, comforted them when they had boyfriend trouble, felt ill or when their tills didn't balance up at the end of the day. So lucky Kim would have a trusted ally on that side of things.

"Sara?" he asked, the next morning. "I have to fetch a new member of staff from the airport this afternoon. I don't think we have anything which won't wait, do we?"

"Just this customer complaint, Patrick – remember?"

He'd been avoiding dealing with it. There was a lovely couple who ran a furniture making business out in the forest. They never had enough money to buy tools, adhesive or even the raw materials for the commissions they said they had. Once or twice, Patrick had knowingly passed entries which overdrew their account in order that they could clear a load of Whitewood from the dock. He'd been lambasted by Andrew Cutlass. The man was right to do so, of course, and he ought to have obtained authorisation. The couple always turned up near closing time when Patrick was keen to escape. 'Anyway', he told himself. 'They always pay in a few days later'. This time, he hadn't been available and one of his staff had refused their request.

Andrew Cutlass' secretary, Gail, opened Cutlass' post and gave the complaint letter to Patrick rather than straight to Andrew Cutlass.

She knew it would enrage the Chief Manager. She hoped Patrick and Joe, between them, could draft a suitable reply.

"I have struggled to imagine what to say, Sara. Ok. I'll write something now and show it to Joe while we are waiting at the airport. All right?"

"I ought to type it up tomorrow for signature, Patrick," Sara said, pursing her mouth.

He set to work. It had become his habit on these occasions to set out the points to make and then rearrange them to form a logical thread. Having thought about the situation for the last couple of days, he realised his own soft-heartedness might be at fault. By allowing them to dip into unauthorised overdraft, they had developed an expectation. So, on this occasion, when a junior member of staff refused to let them overdraw, they felt the rejection keenly. But how could he write this and still end on a note which would please the customer?

He plumped for utter honesty and clarity as the best course, even if it landed him in yet more hot water with Cutlass. He wrote that he realised the customer must have concluded that an overdraft facility was in place. It was true that the Bank allowed previous debits to go through. even though they exceeded the money available in the company's account. It must have been a shock when the same allowance was not permitted on this recent occasion. Patrick went on to apologise for allowing the misapprehension to arise. He finished the draft letter by inviting the customer to visit to discuss an application for a formal overdraft facility.

Sara looked through the hand-written draft. "That is very good, Patrick," she said. "But I doubt Mr Cutlass will sign it."

"Why not, Sara?"

She hesitated, weighing up how to express what she knew to be true without being insulting. "Because the Bank is never wrong."

Patrick opened his mouth to protest, but appreciated that his challenge was not with Sara, of course.

"Even so, it is what happened, and I believe the customer will accept this letter more readily than if I write some stiff, accusatory note reminding them that they do not have an overdraft." He paused and thought for another second or two. "I would like to at least try to do the right thing; could you type this draft and I'll discuss it with Joe this afternoon?"

-----//-----

To Patrick's surprise, Joe rather approved of the letter. He agreed with Sara's judgement of its likely reception 'upstairs', though.

"Tell, you what. I'll sign it and send it and then tell Andrew they want to apply for an overdraft so could Gail make an appointment with him? Better still, as Kim Appleby hasn't yet soiled Andrew's doormat, this could be his first piece of work. How does that sound to you?"

'Straight into the frying pan for Kim' thought Patrick. "Sure. That sounds workable if Gail plays along – I'm sure she will. Ah, is this Kim's flight coming in?"

Joe shielded his eyes from the fierce sunshine. "Could be. It's a couple of minutes early if it is, but yes, it could be."

They watched as the yellow Fokker Friendship circled and lined up for the runway. Joe muttered something under his breath.

"Sorry?" Patrick asked.

"Nothing. I just said 'poor bastard'," replied Joe. "Like you when you arrived, he has no idea what he's getting into."

# Chapter 7
# Living in Bank Flats

Patrick lived in one of the 4 single-storey Bank flats located in a small clearing off a dirt track in District *Numba Tu*. They were not especially well built, providing almost no insulation from heat or sound. When one of his flat mates turned up their stereo, all the flats would be subjected to the strains of anything from the Rolling Stones to Chopin, depending which flat mate it was.

For the most part, though, only 2 of the flats had permanent occupants. The others served as temporary accommodation for staff visitors. The other regular resident would be Kim Appleby. His task would be to run the loans department and help the accountant with the branch's cashier staff. He and Patrick shared similar senses of humour and bonded over evening meals. These were often finished with glasses of Glayva liqueur for mutual consolation after some perceived unfairness by Andrew Cutlass.

They got into the habit of taking it in turns cooking for each other. Both were fond of food and found they enjoyed the process of preparing meals. It required concentration. Focussing on the task of producing a plateful of decent food was an excellent way of forgetting their travails during the day. They agreed the fairest way of dividing the cost of preparing food like this was to fund a joint 'Mess' account. Each month, on payday, they'd transfer their share into it. Both could then issue cheques whenever they bought food, beer or wine.

For social company, some of the other banks in town had young bankers too. Patrick soon invited Kim to join the Friday night evenings at La Hotte and the weekly Sunday Barbeque at the Aussi bankers' Mess. They took along their own pieces of steak or some sausages ("snags") to be cooked on the communal barbeque. For refreshment, there were beers in the group refrigerator. The Aussies operated an honour system, marking down in a book how many beers visitors had drunk. The Australian bank would then draw a bill of exchange on the Royal Counties Bank branch, which Patrick and Kim funded from their own Mess account. Some of the Aussies had semi-permanent girlfriends. They'd prepare mounds of salad and rice – the major portions of which Patrick and Kim ate, the other men not being keen on 'rabbit food'.

Both were always astonished at the sheer volume of beer the Aussies and the sole Kiwi could drink in an evening. Yet they'd show up for work the next day sounding utterly chipper. The Kiwi, Scottie, once explained this to Patrick during a Barbeque. "The secret, mate, is to put the ring-pulls on your little finger – like this." And he demonstrated. "When you can't fit any more ring-pulls on there, you've had enough. Either there isn't space or you can't find your finger!" Scottie's stomach wobbled when he chuckled.

Patrick had to admit that sounded like a workable system.

"When are you boys gonna hold a Barbie?" Scottie went on. "You've got that luverly compound right there; swimming pool, lots of parking – 'be a sin not to use it."

Patrick nodded. In truth, he had begun to feel a little guilty that they always drove down the road to the Aussi Mess on Sundays. They should reciprocate. "I have a better idea. A British idea."

"Pommy, you mean," laughed the other.

"Quite so. We'd like to invite you to dinner. Kim and I take it in turns to cook

131

meals for each other, so we could cook for you chaps instead. The following week, you cook for us. How about next Friday night instead of La Hotte?"

"I'll round up the boys," agreed Scottie with alacrity. "Make sure there are bulk tinnies – we might bring a few wines."

Patrick broke the news to Kim. The idea pleased him, but he found daunting the prospect of half a dozen thirsty blokes descending on their flats. But he straight away began suggesting the menu.

"We could start with Devils on Horseback, and then steak is an obvious main course – they all like steak." Patrick agreed those would be good choices. It kept things simple. That menu would be easiest to prepare and be less work for them as hosts. The guests had displayed pretty undemanding preferences, at least as far as food was concerned, from what he'd seen so far. But for beer, that was a different thing altogether.

"What about veggies? We'll have to rely on what's at the market on Thursday. I think there's another ship due on Wednesday, so we ought to be fine." Patrick paused. He couldn't remember the Aussies ever eating pudding or dessert of any kind. Also, Tom Charlie had snaffled the pineapple he'd planned on using earlier that week. "How about banana split? That's quick... Or – another idea, we could pop bananas on the Barbeque after the meat has cooked, then cut them open, pour in some brandy and add ice cream?"

Kim liked that idea very much. They had some on the trees in their compound and there were always bananas in the market, anyway. As the Bank's loan officer, he had met Dave Anstead. Dave was an Australian beef farmer with several hundred head of cattle. He ran them in an area of coconut plantation in the interior of Efate. Dave did his own butchering. He sold whole carcasses to restaurants and retail outlets throughout the New Hebrides. A few months before, when Kim and Patrick had opened their joint Mess account, they had driven out to meet him. There was some Bank business to discuss. After they'd finished, Patrick had broached the question of buying a carcass or some joints for themselves. The plan was to freeze and use them at leisure. Dave had then waxed lyrical about the importance of treating the cattle right. It was vital, he said, to let them feed on coconut pulp and browse the surrounding foliage before killing them humanely and quickly. It was important too to hang the meat for at least ten days, up to two weeks. All this care, he asserted, made a big difference to the texture and flavour of the meat on your plate, whichever cut you used.

Thinking these were salesmen's puffs, both lads listened patiently. Finally, Kim asked, "How much for a whole carcass?"

The figure Dave named was about what they'd usually pay for just half a dozen entrecôtes at Bons Plats. Patrick was pretty sure the surprise must have registered on his face but asked, "That's for the whole animal, yes?"

Dave smiled. "Well, not the head or hooves, eh? We can fetch one now, if you like."

Kim and Patrick looked at each other. They had driven there in Kim's car, a Toyota Starlet; like Patrick's but white instead of grey. It also didn't pong of cat pee. Their adopted dog had chased a cat around the compound one night which took refuge in Patrick's silver Starlet, spraying to mark its new territory. Even vigorous scrubbing with washing up liquid had only dulled the stink. Indeed, that was rather why Kim had insisted on driving in his car. However, he didn't much fancy cramming in the best part of a cow which would no doubt bleed over the seats and floor. They hadn't thought this through.

"The price includes butchering," Dave added, seeing their looks of alarm. Yet further surprise at the bargain they'd struck mixed with relief. The bankers finished their coffees and followed Dave through his kitchen and around to the cool shed. They watched as he selected a long-bladed knife, gave it a couple of swipes on a steel and set to work. Kim and Patrick wrapped and labelled the packages as they went and an hour later they had armfuls of choice cuts to cram into the car boot. Dave promised to use his bandsaw to separate the porterhouse, T-bones and shanks which he'd wrap and bring to the Bank the next day.

"Crikey. I hope this all fits into our little freezer" Patrick said, as his friend started the engine.

"We'll find out pretty soon," noted Kim, letting in the clutch sharply and they drove quickly back to the flats.

-----//-----

With careful packing and labelling, all the meat did fit into the freezer. They put the steaks for Friday night into their own refrigerators, and that made all the difference.

Recently, they had started visiting La Cave du Gourmets, a French-owned and run wine outlet. It was possible to sample and then buy various wines under the generous tutelage of the shop's owner. For Patrick, this was a significant, though unforeseen benefit of the posting. The Bank flats were not ideal places to keep bottles of wine for any length of time, as the internal temperature was far from steady. The flats overheated during the day and remained cooler but stickily humid at night throughout the year. So they restricted their purchases to a few bottles at a time for consumption in the near future. In truth, their funds could not have stretched to much more than that, anyway. But they learned to select better wines from those they could afford.

"What should we buy for the Aussi Dinner?" Kim asked, voicing the tricky question in Patrick's head too. "Anything halfway decent will likely be wasted on this lot."

"True. But I'm expecting they will feel most comfortable downing 'bulk tinnies' (as Scottie puts it) and will leave the wine alone. Remember Scottie promised to 'bring a few wines'? I'm guessing it's because he thought we prefer wine."

"Ok. Let's get a couple of cheapo bottles of red for them – we can use it in cooking if they don't drink it – and some better bottles for us. We'll bring those out when they aren't watching," Kim suggested.

"I'm more worried about stocking up on enough beers. We have to get Fosters, Tooheys and Four X at least. Oh, and some VB as well?"

"In your car, I think. It still possesses a certain feline bouquet, you know."

There were anxious moments at work for both Patrick and Kim during the late afternoon of the next Friday as they itched to get away to start dinner preparations. They were determined to put on a good show for the Aussies. But they knew they couldn't escape ridicule by simply pushing beer on their guests.

Two of the cashiers couldn't balance their tills. Marianne and Kim were counting and recounting the money. They checked through the account entries each had made, hoping to find where someone had switched a figure or slipped a note into the wrong pile. Patrick, meanwhile, had discovered that he had calculated a foreign exchange rate wrongly. He'd divided instead of multiplying, and so had to reverse the transaction and redo everything. It was a simple error, but one which wasted precious minutes if food was to be ready by 7:30 pm.

With a cry of relief, Kim deduced that the cashiers must have actually swapped tills for a while, and had mixed up the accounting. He always followed the maxim of the famous, fictional detective, Sherlock Holmes: 'When you have eliminated the impossible, whatever remains must be the answer, however improbable'. When Marianne put it to the distraught girls that they might have swapped tills and forgotten about it, they nodded in innocent puzzlement. Was that not allowed..?

Kim admitted afterwards to having taken a while to regain his poise and dignity when he found this solution was correct.

At last, both Kim and Patrick were speeding back to the Bank flats, a few last-minute provisions with them in the cars.

"I'll get the steaks out and start trimming them," volunteered Patrick as he got out of his car. "Can you get any more beers into your 'fridge?"

"I doubt it, but ok, I'll check. I'll fix the starters now. I'll do them under my grill and then bring them back to yours for serving," agreed Kim. "And I'll count how many beers I can cram in!"

Patrick would have liked to set his steaks out on the counter at lunchtime, to come to 'room temperature' – to avoid them becoming tough during cooking. But he knew that was an open invitation to have them devoured by cockroaches. The unpleasant memory still lurked in his head of how a fully-wrapped chicken had pretty much disappeared in this way during an afternoon. So, out they came from the 'fridge as soon as he entered his flat and he set them in a warm place, covered, just in case.

Three crates of various beers sat on the floor behind the sofa. He had crammed in a selection of about a dozen bottles and cans beside the food in the refrigerator. Was it wishful thinking to hope those would suffice for the four visitors to start with? He nipped outside to the banana plants beside the driveway. Some fruits were a bit small, but there were plenty of ripe ones. He picked off the ripest hand and set it beside the barbeque, ready for the pudding course. Then back inside for more food prepping – peeling potatoes and carrots, slicing greens and trimming those steaks. He lit the barbeque using coconut husks piled up by Tom Charlie during the previous week or so. The husks would burn with a fierce heat because of the residual oils. They worked well for barbeques, imparting a light coconut flavour to whatever food cooked in their smoke.

Soon enough, the squeal of brakes and crunch of gravel outside heralded the arrival of two of the Aussies; the others were right behind. Patrick opened his screen door, grinning.

"Welcome to Chez Moi, gents! Step right this way for limitless entertainment, food and drink"! Hoots of derision reminded Patrick that Antipodean societies did not prize affectation – even in jest. "Kim is right next door and will be in with the starters in a minute."

"Tell 'im to 'old 'is 'orses til we 'ave a few beers, mate," advised Paul. "We need to work up an appetite and I've got a thirst like a bloody camel."

"You can have beers and starters together," said Patrick. "There's no rule stopping us."

Scottie had turned left as he came in the front door and found himself in the bathroom. He emerged, zipping up his trousers. "Christ: you got a bloody four square dunny in this little flat."

"I have?"

"Yup. Never seen a dunny that large 'cept on my in-laws' farm."

Patrick took the beer orders and settled them down on chairs, choosing a Fosters for himself. At that moment, Kim rattled the screen door and brought in a tray piled with prunes wrapped in bacon, each held together with little cocktail sticks. "These are Devils on Horseback," he announced. They all set about the serious business of eating and drinking while Patrick replenished the beer stock in his 'fridge and went to check on the main course.

When the barbeque was at its very hottest, he seared all the steaks for 2 minutes each side. A couple had been marinading in garlic and these were intended for himself and for Kim. He remembered none of the guests would like that - theirs were plain, with salt and black pepper only. Into a dish they went, covered with a plate to keep warm and rest for 20 minutes. Plenty of time to get the potatoes and other veggies right. Before bringing in the steaks, he set out bananas on the rack, figuring there was enough heat left to cook them. He just needed to turn them over halfway through.

Kim had brought around some cassette tapes for background music, but nobody took any notice. There was too much chatter, joke telling and general banter.

"Kim? Could I fetch more beers from your 'fridge? These haven't been in here long enough." Patrick wanted to avoid any traditional jokes about Poms and warm beer. The only sin worse than giving an Australian a warm beer was *not* buying him a beer. 'There was no danger of that tonight', he thought.

Kim nodded. "Sure."

"Could you keep an eye on the spuds?"

The armful of 'amber nectar' came from next door just in time. Guests had drained dry the initial offerings and he noted that the ring-pulls were starting to accumulate on people's fingers. He'd barely finished one, but then, he'd been running around, cooking.

Soon it was time to serve. Kim excused himself and joined Patrick in the kitchenette.

"Mmmmm. Those steaks..." he sniffed appreciatively. "Shall I put those on top of the shredded cabbage?"

"Yup. I had forgotten how small the plates are. Here's the first – that can be for Paul."

Patrick served all the guests and then piled plates for himself and Kim. He judged it might be about time to offer some wine, too. Pulling out one of the lesser bottles of red, he proffered it around the table.

"Don't mind if I do, mate," was the typical reception. "Got any more of that?"

"As it happens, we do," said Patrick, arching an eyebrow at Kim.

Eventually, Scottie sat back in his chair, clattered his knife and fork onto the empty plate and belched. "Bloody good tucker, mate. I am stuffed."

"I hope you left room for pudding, gents," Kim replied. "We've got barbequed bananas for afters." He reached behind him to Patrick's bookshelf and found a bottle of brandy as Patrick exited through the screen door towards the barbeque. "With brandy and cream."

"Naah, mate," interrupted Scottie, pushing back his chair. "You need whisky."

"Whisky? I'm not sure the flavour…"

"Yeah, whisky is best. Here give me that bottle." Kim replaced the brandy and found some whisky on the shelf too.

"Is this alright?"

Patrick came in with a bowl of blackened bananas and put them in the kitchenette. He hunted for bowls and spoons. Kim went to join him. "Scottie is insisting we use whisky, not brandy. He may have had 1 or 2 'over the 8', as it were."

Patrick shrugged. "He can have whisky if he wants. I'm having brandy and cream. You?" Kim nodded.

They put a banana into each bowl, opened up the skin lengthwise with a sharp knife ready to accept the alcohol of choice and took the bowls out to the table.

Scottie poured very hefty quantities of whisky into most of the bowls and then looked up. "Where's me smokes?"

"Sorry?" Kim asked.

"Me smokes. I need me lighter." Realisation dawned. Bananas flambéed in whisky… Patrick found him a box of matches.

The first bowlful went up with a WHOOMP noise, the flames reaching almost to the ceiling.

That woke Paul, who had dozed off at the end. He muttered, "Bloody Hell" and then fell forward, so his face buried itself into his pudding. Lucky for him, his had not yet been lit. Patrick rescued the box of matches from Scottie and pretended not to know where they had gone.

They all sat and watched the flames licking around the already blackened banana in Scottie's bowl. It must have burned for at least five minutes, there was so much alcohol there. "I might have another tube while I'm waiting," quoth the redoubtable Scottie.

It was very late indeed when Patrick and Kim pushed and carried their guests outside. For sure, none were capable of driving in any normal sense of the word. Those who could stagger wandered off up the track towards their own Mess housing.

Kim and Patrick agreed to pile up the plates and do the washing up in the morning, and not to worry too much about the inevitable cockroach feast that night.

-----//-----

For Patrick, it was a very quiet Saturday. Even though he and Kim had consumed far less alcohol than their Friday night guests, it was still rather a heavier night than they were used to. They both stuck to domestic activities – washing and ironing in the morning and a quiet swim in the afternoon, drinking lots of water. They chatted about various work-related things of little consequence.

Then Kim asked about the Election process Patrick had conducted on Pele Island. He knew, of course, that Patrick's collection by boat had been delayed – the sound of the tyres of his friend's car announced his arrival home well after dark. Kim wanted to know more about the island itself. Patrick opted to share the details of what he had seen and done after the actual voting had finished.

"There were a couple of things which happened as well as the voting," he started.

"Ok – spill," encouraged Kim.

"Knowing the boat was damaged, Hone and I went for a walk with the Chief. Look – I haven't told anyone about this and I'm not sure I ought to, either."

"Now I'm intrigued." Kim leaned forward. "You have to tell me now – it can't be all bad - can it?"

"Well, alright. But don't say anything to anybody else. It might cause trouble of some sort."

"I promise. What happened?"

Patrick set out the events of the day. The stroll along the beach, stopping at a *Kastom* barrier beyond which even the Chief refused to go. How he tricked his companions to be able to see the *Lali Mare* hiding at anchor on the far side of Pele island, out of sight of anyone on Efate. Finally he got to the anguished moans of distress of this girl trying to give birth.

Kim's eyes grew very wide. "What did you do?"

"I fetched the village's radio telephone and the doctor at Vila Base helped me."

"That was Jessica?"

Patrick nodded.

"Wow!" said Kim. "Go on."

"I've been feeling, I don't know, ...odd ever since. Like I've interfered or something. I mean, supposing I hadn't heard her cries? I'm sure the villagers knew full well that she was struggling, but they didn't want to help her."

"I suppose their belief system is 'whatever happens is supposed to happen' – for a reason," Kim summarised.

"I don't know now whether I ought to have inflicted my belief system onto them –

because, in effect, that's what I've done, haven't I?"

Kim turned that over in his mind for a few minutes as they sat in silence. At last, he asked, "Was the girl pleased at having her baby?"

"Oh yes. But isn't that the effect of all those hormones flooding through her system after giving birth? I'll ask Jess next time we see each other. I'm a bit worried that the villagers might reject her or her baby now."

"But if the villagers believe that everything happens for a good reason, won't they realise that your act of helping the girl was supposed to happen?"

"I hadn't viewed it like that," admitted Patrick. "I hope you are right." He felt a little better after this logical counsel.

"I'm intrigued about why the *Lali Mare* would sit around the back of the island, though," Kim went on. "If the port wasn't ready to receive her, she'd wait in one of the usual anchoring spots outside the bay, surely?"

"I don't know the waters around there, but I reckon there are reefs, because it isn't far from some great diving areas. Surely anchoring in that location would be dangerous for the ship? It might break up and destroy some of the coral even if it didn't end up running aground itself."

"I doubt that bothers them," said Kim. "There's something I haven't mentioned to anyone else either." Now it was Patrick's turn to look up in surprise.

"I've been comparing the annual accounts of Bon Plats with the business turnover going through every day. It's almost time for their annual review and I can't reconcile the accounts they publish with the trade they do."

And Kim started to explain why he was so puzzled. A reputable firm of accountants prepared and audited the Annual Report and Accounts. It showed reasonable levels of sales and a modicum of profitability – enough to keep the business's owner, Tai Nguyen, in luxury. But when Kim cross-checked the foreign exchange dealings done by Royal Counties Bank alone for Bon Plats over the previous year, the total was many times greater than the reported business turnover.

"But that means the accounts, the filed accounts, are not a true representation of the business," queried Patrick.

"Right," said Kim. "It's almost as if we have been transacting deals for two businesses but booking them all in the name of one."

"I see why you haven't told Andrew, though; he'd go apeshit."

"He's going to have to be told at some time," Kim reminded him.

Then Patrick remembered his recent visit to the port. "It may be nothing to do with this accounting stuff, but when I went to the port the day before you arrived, I saw the Bon Plats truck down there. It took away two big unmarked boxes which weren't on the ship's manifest."

"How do you know they weren't?"

"I popped in to see Captain Brasted. I was trying to figure out if Bon Plats was doing business through one of the other banks. He went through the manifest for the *Lali Mare* that day. None of the goods for which we had letters of credit would have shipped in crates like that. He did say, though, that perhaps they were doing someone else a favour and transporting their boxes. In that case, they were nothing to do with the supermarket, and might even have come on a different ship."

Kim became even more serious: "Bon Plats don't do favours to people, in my opinion."

"I said exactly the same thing to Captain Brasted. Maybe they are starting a transportation business..? What are you going to do?"

"The review is due in London at the end of next month, so I've got a bit of time. I'll talk with Joe about how to broach the topic with Andrew. But first I want to study the foreign exchange deals Gilles has done for them for the past couple of years. It's a lot of work, but it may uncover an explanation."

-----//-----

When he first arrived on the island, Patrick had been introduced to a tall rangy man named Karl Day who ran the Toyota dealership for the New Hebrides. What he didn't know until later was that Karl was also the local Hash Master.

Some say ex-army businessmen formed The Hash House Harriers in Kuala Lumpur, Malaysia, before the Second World War. They realised their lifestyle of working, eating and sleeping was unhealthy. One tradition has it that they resolved to meet every week on a Monday night at 5pm in the main financial square for a non-competitive jog before returning home.

Stories now vary about how the group actually formed and took its name. One suggests that an enterprising local saw the businessmen and turned up with a large pot of corned beef hash and cold drinks and sold many bowlfuls to the hungry runners. Another, more likely story, relates to the epithet coined by members for the Selangor Club in Kuala Lumpur. 'Hash' was the army term for all food. Reportedly the food was actually very good at the Club, but the members billeted in the Selangor Club Chambers rather rudely named it the 'Hash House'. Accordingly, their running group was named using the alliterative triple Hs.

Records show that the Selangor Club group used to run on Friday nights. But in time, all the businessmen went to different countries and adopted the habit of running at 5pm on Monday nights, retaining the name 'Hash House Harriers' wherever they went. When eventually ladies were invited to join in, of course their side took the name Hen House Harriers. They had all adopted the British fondness for paper chases, in which runners follow a trail of shredded paper or flour or something similar.

Patrick quite liked the idea of a social run right after work on his least favourite day of the week. The prospect of a jolly evening with a beer or two with some running mates helped him get through the rigours and challenges of Mondays. It was also a brilliant way to visit parts of Efate Island he'd never normally get to.

He attended a few runs and found he liked it. Even the tribal war calls of 'On-On' when a leading runner found the correct marked track did not put him off. Or the faux-ceremonial awarding of prizes (good and bad) after the run for real or imagined slights upon one of the Hash Committee. Signal honours included carrying the Hash Horn, which the lucky runner would sound at intervals on the next week's run. Booby prizes included the award of the week's 'Hashit', compelling the unfortunate to perform the next run wearing a toilet seat around his neck. Moreover, he would have to perform a 'Down-Down' at the award ceremony - drinking a whole can of (often fizzy) beer without stopping. Failure to complete this resulted in a 'shampoo' – emptying the rest over his head.

One day, Karl Day called him at work. "G'day, Patrick. How's it hanging, Mate?"

"Karl! Hello. I'm very well, thanks. To what do I owe this honour? Is it time to service my car?"

"That piece of shit? No way. If it stops come and buy another! Nope, you are laying the trail for next Monday's run. I'll drop off some sacks of paper tomorrow at the Bank."

"Gosh – thanks," said Patrick, very surprised at the granting of this responsibility. He'd thought about it a couple of times, though. He puzzled how the Hares chose where to go, how they dropped paper to set false trails off to the sides and then returned to the proper route. They'd mound up a stack of sometimes coloured paper further on as a Check Point to reassure Hashers they were now on the right path. "I might have a couple of questions, if that's ok."

"Sure, Mate, sure. See you tomorrow."

The best tip Karl gave him was not to try to set the trail on a Sunday. The islands were becoming infested with Giant African Snails which had been released accidentally a few years before. These snails eat voraciously, and devastate leaves and crops, but they also ate shredded paper. Woe betides the Hash

154

Hare laying his paper trail too early. It would be destroyed or completely removed by the snails overnight and during Monday. An unclear trail for the Hashers on Monday evening would result in an immediate and indefensible award of the Hashit for the following week.

So Patrick restricted himself at the Aussie Barbie that Sunday night to just a couple of beers and donned his running shorts and shoes at 5am on Monday morning. He had roughed out a route in his head which he thought long enough to challenge the faster blokes and not too long for the slower runners. The Bank flats would be a good place for the 'On-On' – the beery gathering afterwards - as there was lots of parking available. So he set out with his sack of paper in a circular trail which included a short stretch of a beach and finished with a track up through Dave Anstead's land. It was hard going, but towards the end, he found running into the 6 am light rain and breeze very invigorating.

The breeze was not only cooling on such a humid morning but it carried delicious wafts of bacon frying. Stepping over fallen coconuts, trying not to twist an ankle, the aroma was really distracting. Dave had seen him approaching up the slope and called out, "Hey, Patrick – come and have some breakfast."

He couldn't resist. Although spattered with mud and wearing a T-shirt now soaked with sweat, Dave waved away his objections, welcomed him inside and told him to sit. Diana, his shapely girlfriend, was wearing one of Dave's over-loose shirts as she stood at the stove. "Hi, Pat – do you want some coffee too?" She brought an enormous plate for him, overflowing with six rashers of bacon, three fried eggs, a pile of mushrooms and four slices of toasted bread. Patrick checked his watch: if he was to make it home to shower and still get to the Bank by 07:30 to open at 08:00, he'd have to be quick.

"Oh, Diana – that is marvellous. You are so kind. I'm kind of short for time, so please excuse me if I eat fast." Diana laughed.

"What you can't finish, I'll wrap up as sandwiches" and she winked at him over the rim of her cup of coffee.

It wasn't far for Patrick to run home, across country, finishing the paper trail as he went. He developed a bad case of hiccoughs because he'd eaten so much too quickly.

These persisted even as he climbed into his car after showering, shaving and dressing. He hoped all the members would approve of the run that night.

## Chapter 8

# The Birth comes Home

When Patrick got back to the Bank flats that evening, one of the Hash Committee had already dropped off the Hash trailer complete with a chest freezer bolted onto it. Although the freezer was locked, he knew it would be chock full of beer and ice to keep those tinnies cold. Sensibly, the man had parked it beneath some of the overhanging banana trees, so it was in shade.

He quickly opened his flat, went in and changed into running gear. As the Hare for tonight, it would be his responsibility to follow along at the rear of the pack to make sure nobody wandered off too far and got lost and he just hoped like mad that the snails hadn't yet got down to serious munching of his paper trail.

About 10 minutes before the off, cars started to arrive. Patrick acted as parking attendant for a bit and then just gave up, since nobody was really paying any attention to what he wanted. Poor Kim, who was working a bit late, would have to park somewhere on the track outside and walk the final 50 yards or so.

At length, the Hash Religious Advisor called everyone to attention for the Hash Master's introduction. Karl stepped forward. "The hare for tonight is Patrick, here. He's a Pommy bastard, but can't help that, so nobody make fun of him." He paused for the laughter to die down. "I'd like to thank him in advance for setting tonight's trail, but that would not be wise, as it's his first one." The crowd groaned, theatrically, knowing they were being warned it might not have been set with conventional markings. "Patrick, if the Religious Advisor here deems your trail marking or route difficulty to be short of our minimum acceptable standard, you will be sentenced to a Down-Down every week for a month. Do you understand?"

"Understood, Hash Master," shouted Patrick. There were muted cheers from the crowd.

"I bloody hope so," grinned Karl. "Now, welcome everyone; I'll introduce you to Pierre, over there, who is a new member. He's the nervous-looking Frenchman hiding by the beer. If you don't like beer, Pierre, there might be a wine or two for afterwards."

160

Then he handed back to the Religious Advisor who restated the main Hash sins of dawdling at checks, trying to take short cuts or (Heaven forfend!) being competitive and, adopting a deep voice worthy of the evil villain in any pantomime, threatened dire imprecations and a variety of punishments for any transgressors. To close, he reminded everyone that his Word was final.

Karl then took charge again. "Patrick, you must speak up if there are any special hazards to be aware of. Failure to give adequate warnings will result in a report to the Religious Advisor. And you know what that means!"

"Er… nothing, really. Well… No. Nothing at all out of the ordinary."

"Very well. Where's the Hash Horn? ON-ON"!

The runner holding the Horn gave a loud blast and off they all set, looking for the start of the trail.

-----//-----

Kim was working late at the branch, making a list of all the foreign exchange transactions done by Royal Counties Bank for Bon Plats. He grew more worried as he worked, because the sums were large. All were in the hundreds of thousands of dollars and a couple exceeding one million. There was a mix of currencies too - Australian dollars, New Zealand dollars, Japanese Yen, Singapore dollars and Pounds Sterling. All were converted into US dollars. There had been many cash deposits of Australian and New Zealand dollars over the last two years; indeed, Kim himself had overseen a couple of recent such deposits of Australian cash. He couldn't see how these had been remitted elsewhere because the records had been locked away in the branch safe at closing time.

He decided not to leave his workings at the branch but to take them home. This pattern of trading with large sums of foreign currency moving from place to place didn't sound right to him and he wasn't sure how to tackle the problem. He'd talk to Patrick later.

-----//-----

A couple of the Hashers came up to Patrick after the run and congratulated him on his route. Unknowingly, he'd found fresh territory for the Hash and they particularly enjoyed dodging the coconuts as they ran through Dave Anstead's land.

"Hope you cleared it with him, Mate," said one. "I didn't see his bull out there tonight, but he's a mean bastard and runs bloody fast."

Patrick looked a bit alarmed at that. Dave had known full well where the run was to go, but hadn't said a word. Patrick hadn't given a thought to whether there might be a bull. Maybe the animal had been penned for the evening to be on the safe side. Patrick made a mental note to say thank you.

Patrick was just starting in to his second beer when the Hash Horn was sounded and the Religious Advisor shouted for a bit of hush. Patrick suddenly giggled to himself. 'Is that Hash Hush'?

"I have a few notices to read out, Gentlemen, Poms, Pierre and Patrick. First, some housekeeping: the following members are late paying their dues." No fewer than six names were read out and two of them stepped forward waving fistfuls of New Hebridean currency. "Too bloody late, Mate. Down-Downs for everyone."

The crowd jeered and raised their cans and bottles in salute. "And we've got a Virgin Frog, tonight, Pierre." Pierre started to look a little alarmed at being singled out.

163

"Do I see brand new shoes, Pierre?"

"*Er, oui. Ils sont flambant neufs*," he admitted.

"Right. Take off your left shoe."

"*Comment?*"

Patrick stepped forward. "*Il dit, 'Enlevez votre chaussure gauche'.*"

Pierre looked very puzzled, but complied. The Religious Advisor seized the shoe, filled it with wine and handed it back. All the other unfortunates sentenced to Down-Downs knew what their fate would entail and had charged their mugs and glasses appropriately.

The baying crowd then broke into a Hash song.

'Here's to the Hashers; They're all Blues.

They're all Pisspots, through and through.

Give 'em all a beer and drink it down, down, down, down…'

Pierre saw that the others were drinking their beers as fast as they could, so mimicked their actions with his wine. One of the beer drinkers had foolishly opened a fresh beer to top up his glass and the extra gassiness made it very hard to drink quickly. The rule was that when the singing stops, anyone still drinking has to empty the remains of their beer over their head. He had to pause part way through – and paid the price with a shampoo.

Everybody cheered – even Pierre, who was roundly clapped on the back for joining in so sportingly. His white socks would probably never again be white as he'd chosen red wine, but he didn't mind too much. At least his shoes were no longer new.

Members began to melt away. Cars were started and reversed out towards the track. At that point, Kim walked up and headed for his front door. Patrick saw him looking serious and broke away from listening to some awful joke. "Hey, Kim. What's the matter?"

"I think we have a serious situation – with all the foreign exchange Bon Plats has been doing."

"Ok. I'll get rid of this lot, shower and we can chat over dinner. Alright?"

Kim nodded. "Thanks."

"Hey, Patrick. What's up with your mate?" one of the Hashers called. "He looks like he lost a dollar and found a cent."

"We've got a thing at work," answered Patrick. "It's at least a two can problem." This was a reference to the amount of drinking it would take to puzzle out a solution.

"Bet it's that bloody Cutlass of yours. Bloke's gone Troppo, if you ask me," opined another.

"You are probably right there. I agree he's been in the Tropics far too long for anyone's health. Time to head home, gents – I need a shower and some dinner."

Goodbyes were said and Patrick waved off the last Hasher. The beer trailer would be picked up later in the week by Hash Words who not only wrote up the weekly report of goings on at each run but handled a lot of the admin, including billing members for the beers they'd drunk.

-----//-----

Their dinner was a very sombre affair. Kim set out in simple terms what he had discovered and how all the large movements of money bore no relation at all to the supposed business Bon Plats did with Royal Counties Bank. Patrick suggested that Kim include the foreign exchange trading in his annual appraisal, but perhaps only by saying what profit had been booked by Gilles for doing the trades, rather than totalling the enormous volume of the trades themselves.

"If we work on the assumption that Andrew knows about it, and I cannot believe he doesn't, listing the Forex profits will be truthful, Kim, but not irritating. How does that sound?"

Kim pursed his lips. "But it isn't the *whole* truth, is it? I'm worried that we are touching the edges of some very unsavoury monetary dealings. I just don't know who we can tell. I suppose there could be a perfectly legal explanation, and we'd look stupid for reporting this outside the Bank – but I cannot see how it can be right."

"Maybe you should keep your workings here, in the flat, or in your car rather than at work. And go see Gilles tomorrow to ask for the profit calculations, eh?"

Reluctantly, Kim agreed. The next morning, they went in separate directions. Kim to the branch and Patrick off to the port again. He was therefore not present when a young girl turned up at the counter with her tiny baby in a sling and asked some of the cashiers if there was a young, white man working there who had curly, blond hair.

Andrew Cutlass was in an unusually bad mood. He had just learned from Joe, the accountant, that one of the processing machines in the 'Mech Room' was not working properly and Monday's entries would all have to be run through again. The machines, made by N.C.R., were nick-named 'Jumping Jennies' and looked like complicated sewing or weaving machines. The operator needed to choose a particular rod with preset cams to place on top of it according to the type of entry to be recorded. The humidity and variable temperatures played havoc with such intricate machinery, so it was a wonder that they were as reliable as they were, usually. On top of that, one of the Mech Room operators, Hone, was absent and they hadn't heard when he might be back. The consequence was that the supervisor, Marianne herself, would need to pitch in so the quarterly reports to London weren't delayed. This meant she wasn't overseeing the cashiers – and so it went on.

Cutlass spotted all of the cashiers had left their tills and were gathered at the counter, fawning over one of the customers. Fuming, he drew closer and saw they were cooing at a new-born baby. The beaming girl, presumably its mother, was chattering away in Bislama. Cutlass opened his mouth to order the cashiers back to the stations when he half caught some of the conversation. Despite his absolute reluctance to avoid learning any of the local language and to stay aloof from 'all that sort of thing', some words and phrases had inevitably landed in his head. He thought he heard, "...*mekim wunfala bebi...*" and a cashier had said Patrick's name.

Cutlass straightaway put two and two together and concluded that young Patrick Field had taken advantage of some innocent young local girl and got her pregnant. Out of the corner of his eye, he noticed Marianne leaving the Mech Room.

"Marianne? Could I have a word?"

She looked up and came over. "Yes, Mr Cutlass?"

"Why are the cashiers not at their tills?"

"I'll find out," she promised. She joined the group at the counter and spoke rapidly to the girls. One by one they went back to their stations and the mother and baby waved goodbye and made to leave the branch.

"The girl was asking for Patrick's name as he helped her make her new baby."

169

Marianne smiled broadly. "He's a lovely little boy and smiles a lot."

That was all the confirmation Andrew Cutlass needed. "Ask her to come up to my office, please." He stomped back to Joe's office as Marianne called after the young girl. "Where is Patrick?" he demanded.

Joe checked one of his diary cards for today. "He is down at the port until lunchtime, probably. What do you need?"

"Send him up to me as soon as he returns."

-----//-----

Joe caught Patrick as he came into the branch. "Andrew wants to see you. He's on the warpath about something. Marianne might know what it is as he was talking to her when he was down here."

Patrick had been rather enjoying the day until that point. Visiting the port, smelling the sea and chatting to some of the port officials always made him happy. He went over to Marianne.

"Hello – Joe says Andrew wants to see me and is very angry about something – do you have any idea what it's about?"

Her face creased into a wide smile and she told him about the girl bringing her baby into the branch wanting to find out Patrick's name to add to the lad's Island name.

An awful feeling was creeping into Patrick's mind. "Does Andrew think I am the child's father?"

"Probably," and Marianne giggled. "She is waiting in Mr Cutlass's office upstairs."

Patrick closed his eyes. This was very bad news. "Marianne, please come with me for a moment."

He took her into one of the interview rooms and gave her a shortened version of what had happened on Pele Island. "First of all, are the girl and her boy alright? Healthy?" Marianne nodded. "What did the girl say?"

Marianne could see that the subtleties of the situation were a little difficult to express in Bislama and understood how Mr Cutlass had reached his conclusion. She thought Patrick should be very happy, though, in whatever way he was responsible for the child, whether as father or birthing assistant, and didn't really see the problem.

"I'd better go upstairs, Marianne. Thanks for listening." She smiled. It always seemed that she was sorting out other peoples' emotional or relationship messes.

Patrick trudged upstairs, past the foreign exchange desk and behind the cashiers. Sensing from his body language that something was wrong, most of them turned to watch him go. The carpeted stairs turned slightly to the left near the top and the sounds from the banking hall became muffled.

There was Gail, Andrew's secretary, an English lady of indeterminate years, possessed of a fine sense of humour and a penchant for cigars, sat at her desk on the left side of his door.

"Hello, Gail. I understand Andrew wants to see me." She was usually a happy person, full of welcoming smiles, but not today. A little coldly, she said, "Good morning, Patrick," and, pressing her intercom, "Andrew? Patrick is here to see you."

"Send him in, please."

Patrick opened the door and stepped in.

"Close the door behind you." There was a distinct edge to Cutlass's voice. He turned to the young girl who was playing with her baby on the sofa beside the door. "Is this him?"

She smiled at Patrick and cast her eyes downward, shyly. She nodded.

"What's the meaning of this?" This was directed at Patrick and the flushed neck and pulsing vein on the man's forehead did not bode well. He pressed the intercom on his desk. "Gail? Could you show the young lady out, please?"

Patrick waited while Gail did just that. Then said, "The meaning of what, Andrew?"

"I understand you are responsible for this child of one of the local girls. What do you have to say for yourself?"

"Well, not exactly, Andr…"

"You can wipe that smile off your face, laddy. Since you cannot be trusted with poor defenceless people, you will be sent back to the UK. The next flight is on Thursday. Go back to the flats and pack an overnight bag. The rest of your possessions will be returned to your parents' address by ship in due course. I shall send a telex to Staff Department now informing them of your return and they will decide if any further action is to be taken."

He glared at Patrick. "Now get out."

For a second, Patrick stood rooted to the spot. This was utterly unfair. A complete injustice. He wanted to assert his innocence,

173

but couldn't make a sound as there was a big lump in his throat. Then the tears started.

"OUT," roared Cutlass, pushing his face forwards over the desk.

Patrick jumped in alarm. Gail had opened the door for him and was waiting. This was worse; much, much worse than anything he had ever experienced.

"Oh, Patrick," Gail sniffed as he swayed past. She didn't meet his gaze.

"It's a mistake," he began. "I didn't…" But then she started to cry into her handkerchief and went to sit at her typewriter, shaking her head.

Patrick went down the stairs, wiping away his tears as best he could. Marianne was waiting for him at the bottom.

"Patrick, what happened? I heard Mr Cutlass shouting."

"He thinks I am the child's father and wants to send me back to the UK," he managed.

Marianne left him and went up to see Gail. Perhaps she could calm Cutlass down and convince him of the truth. The two women talked urgently together and hugged, Gail's sobbing turning into tears of laughter.

"What's going on out here?" demanded Andrew Cutlass, opening his office door suddenly. He was having a *very* bad day and was trying to phrase the telex to the bank's Staff Department, a difficult task made harder by the sound of the two women outside talking and laughing together.

Gail told him how Patrick had saved the young woman's life and that of her baby and how that meant, in a way, that Patrick *was* responsible for the child. But he was not its father.

"I don't believe this cock and bull story for one moment, Gail, and I'm surprised at you for being taken in so easily."

"It is easily checked, Andrew," she said. "Call Vila Base Hospital and ask if they had that radio-telephone conversation with Patrick."

Cutlass paused. And went back into his office, slamming the door. He wasn't going to let Field get away with this. Somehow the scallywag had taken in Gail and involved Marianne in his lies. It was highly likely he had primed someone at Vila Base to cover for him. The only way to find out the real truth was to report the events to Tai Nguyen. *He* would get to the bottom of things and anyway, the information might be useful to him. He might even let Andrew off some of the monthly fees he'd been paying for years.

After so long, Cutlass didn't like to think of the monthly cash payments he made to Nguyen as blackmail – he preferred to consider them as a club subscription. An expensive one, to be sure, but then, he dared not have his financial transgressions of all those years ago be revealed to London – that would end his career immediately. He reasoned that the transactions by Bon Plats he now signed for personally would benefit Royal Counties Bank in some way and anyway, one of the local institutions would be carrying them out, so why not Royal Counties Bank? Of late, there had been rather a lot of them, though. The increase in trading volume made him nervous because it might arouse suspicion from the staff, especially the new lad, Kim. He was too bright for his own good, Cutlass reckoned. He'd have to keep a sharp eye on that one. Worst of all, Cutlass knew he'd be in trouble if Head Office Inspectors made a visit, as they did every two or three years. He made a note to check in with all his spies in the local travel agents and hotels who were to give him notice if a party of people travelling from London had their bookings made by Royal Counties Bank staff department. He picked up the phone and dialled Tai Nguyen's number.

-----//-----

"Patrick?" Marianne went around to the Trade Finance department where Patrick had his head in his hands. "I think it will be alright, after all. Gail told him and he can call Vila Base if he wants to prove it."

Still feeling very upset, Patrick looked at her, gratefully. "That's true. He wasn't giving me a chance to say anything – he just leaped to the wrong conclusion and… well, you heard the result."

"*Me hapi tumas yufela stap long plas ere,*" Marianne put her hand on his arm and lapsed back into her native tongue to emphasize that she was pleased at the outcome.

"Will you …er, make sure that the others are clear on what happened?" Patrick suddenly thought about how the cashiers chatter to each other and to customers.

"Oh, yes," agreed Marianne. But her brow darkened all of a sudden. "But I'm worried about Hone."

"Hone?" queried Patrick. "He was fine when we went to Pele together. In fact, possibly *too* fine, if I am not mistaken." But he stopped smiling when he remembered what Sara had said about the possible consequences of Hone messing around with girls from a different village. "He isn't here today, is he?"

Marianne looked around to make sure she wasn't overheard. She lowered her voice. "One of the girls said he heard a cassowary after he had gone to bed one night."

"That's the big bird, isn't it? Like an emu?" Patrick had heard of cassowary birds but wasn't aware they lived in the New Hebrides.

"Medicine men change into cassowaries to run through the jungle to cast their spells. Hone thinks he has a spell put on him by a medicine man. That is very serious, Patrick."

"*Kastom,* right?" he said. She nodded assent. "Well, hiding somewhere won't put things right. Can you tell me where he lives? Maybe Kim and I can fetch him and have a talk." As he spoke, Patrick remembered the pounding sound he heard himself when helping to deliver the girl's baby on Pele Island.

Marianne looked doubtful but said, "Alright." Then louder, "Sara? *Yufela savvy hus blong Hone e stap?"*

Sara looked up from her work. "Yes."

Marianne walked over to her and they whispered together. Sara began to look shocked. She drew out a piece of paper from the copier and started to draw a map for Patrick.

He went back around to the Loans department where Kim was sitting. He thought he ought to get Kim's consent before telling Joe where they were off to. Kim was clearly distracted by some complex loan application but he did agree to come, then and there.

Patrick knocked on the glass partition around Joe's cubicle. "What do you want?" demanded Joe, without raising his eyes from a long column of figures.

"I think I know why Hone hasn't come to work today …or yesterday." Joe gave up counting and put down his pen.

"Come on, Sherlock – what's the answer – or am I supposed to guess?"

"No, no, of course not. I believe Hone has been going with a girl from another village - actually, another island, and he didn't get the Chief's permission first. So, I hear the girl's father has asked the medicine man to put a spell on him."

To Patrick's surprise, Joe leaned back in his chair and roared with laughter. Recovering himself, he opined, "I shouldn't laugh. But it's mumbo-jumbo, Patrick. Utter nonsense. Send someone to fetch him into work. I've never heard such ...crap."

"The locals won't go, Joe. As it's a *Kastom* matter, they won't go against it. But I can. I want to go to Hone's house with Kim and we'll bring him back here to the branch."

"Fine. Whatever. But don't get lost, running around in the bush."

-----//-----

Sara had told Patrick months before that when Hone was hired, the bank had to lend him money to buy a new pair of flip flops. He lived a good hour's walk from the branch and usually walked everywhere with bare feet. The story had impressed Patrick and although Hone worked in a different department in the bank, he felt that the lad had some get up and go about him. As he drove with Kim out towards Hone's village, he thought, grimly, that perhaps there was a bit too much liveliness about him.

180

He slowed the car, looking for the patch of trees Sara had said marked the track leading to the village. Over the months, Patrick had got better at distinguishing the varied flora in the New Hebrides. Everything grew vigorously and there was dense foliage everywhere, but he was looking for a particularly tall specimen of the Whitewood tree with its typical cylindrical trunk. Hah - there it was. Heavily buttressed at the base, it looked as if it could withstand anything. Patrick stopped the car and peered out of the window. It was very tall indeed; maybe thirty meters? Perhaps more.

"I think this is it," and he turned the car onto the track beside the tree. They bumped along, wishing they were in a Toyota pickup rather than a Starlet. Patrick hoped they wouldn't meet any vehicles coming towards them: someone would have to reverse all the way back the way they'd come as there wasn't room to pass side by side.

Suddenly, they emerged into the village itself; there were huts packed quite closely together near to the main track running between. Patrick looked for a space to be able to park up without blocking anyone. At length he found one. They got out and checked quickly around, hoping to ask someone where Hone lived.

It seemed that everywhere they looked, curious faces retreated into the darkness of their huts. Patrick knew they ought to find the Chief first, and cursed himself for not asking Marianne or Sara for the man's name.

He stood in the middle of the track and called out: "*Nem blo me 'Patrick'. Wun fela Chif, e' stap long way?*"

After a few seconds, an older woman emerged from her hut and pointed to some huts further along. Patrick raised his hand in thanks and realised it might be handy to know the man's name. "*Tank yu tumas. Wunem name blo hem?*"

She covered her mouth, slightly muffling the answer, but Patrick could hear clearly enough that he was looking for Chief Jon. He and Kim walked on, very conscious that the villagers had probably never been visited by white strangers before and didn't know what to make of it.

As with his recent visit to Pele Island, Patrick identified the Chief's hut because it was larger and given more prominence and open space. They stopped a dozen feet away and called as politely as they could, "*Chif*

*Jon? Nem blo me 'Patrick'. This fren blo' me – 'Kim'. Mefela stap long Royal Counties Bank long Vila. Olgeta pipl, e say wun fela olicolim 'Hone' – e sik tumas. Me wanem helpim."*

Patrick wasn't sure if his Bislama was adequate to communicate what he wanted. He paused, hoping the Chief would show himself. *"Chif Jon?"*

He heard rustling from inside and the Chief came to the doorway to his hut. He was a very big man indeed, towering over Patrick, but wore the same double boars' tusks around his neck as had Chief Tamatoa. Patrick tried not to feel intimidated.

*"Wun em blo'yufela?"* the chief rumbled.

*"Me wunem helpim Hone."* This elicited a raised eyebrow but nothing more. Patrick knew he had to be more convincing; he felt Jessica wouldn't mind if he took her name in vain and somewhat overstated the level of their relationship. *"Woman blo'me givim medicin long Hone blo' mekim well."*

The Chief thought this over. Then he jerked his head slightly to the left to indicate the direction to Hone's hut. But before letting Patrick go, he asked, *"Medicin blo'woman blo yufela – hemi Kastom?"*

Patrick shook his head. He had no idea what he was dealing with – was Hone actually sick or just work-shy? Maybe he needed a proverbial kick up the backside. But even though Patrick had lived in these islands for just a short time, he had come to realise the belief system of *Kastom majik* was a powerful force in New Hebridean society. And if what Sara and Marianne had intimated was true, Hone would need careful treatment.

The Chief shrugged and turned back into the darkness of his hut.

"Did he say, 'OK'?" asked Kim.

"Not exactly – but he won't stop us, I don't think."

They headed off in the direction Chief Jon had indicated. There were a couple of huts which might be his. Patrick went up to the first and asked, "*Hone, e stap long plas ere?*"

They were in luck. A middle-aged man came to the doorway and beckoned them inside.

"Hone? *Wunem blo'yufela?*" Patrick asked gently. He was actually quite shocked at Hone's appearance. Once inside the hut, his eyes quickly adjusted. The bouncing, happy young man of just a few days ago when they rode the boat together back to Vila from Pele had vanished. Hone now had sunken, shadowed eyes; he looked thin and even his skin had an unhealthy pallor.

"We are here to help you, Hone," Kim put in. "We all miss you at the bank."

"I think you had better come with us to Vila Base Hospital, Hone," said Patrick. "The doctor there has good medicine to make you better."

Hone's eyes seemed glazed and he may not fully have understood what was being said. But when Patrick held out his hand, the sick boy took it and allowed himself to be led outside. They walked slowly towards the car.

Patrick paused by the Chief's hut. "*Chief Jon? Mefela tekim long hospital blo mekim well – Ok?*"

This time, the Chief did not get up; he just nodded.

-----//-----

Patrick drove fast, back towards town. He turned into Vila Base Hospital's car park and together they led Hone into Reception.

He gave his name and asked the nurse there if his staff member, Hone, could be seen by the doctor as he was clearly not well. He described the rapid deterioration in the

185

lad's health and left Hone there. The two bankers drove more slowly back to work. Before going in, Patrick told Kim about the *Kastom* spell Sara and Marianne had said might have been placed on Hone.

"Is that stuff real?" asked Kim. "I've heard of 'mind over matter', but I thought it was more to do with boosting sporting performance because you believe you can do it than being sick because somebody says they've put a spell on you."

"I guess it works both ways, Kim. We'll see what Jess says."

They went inside the bank and told Joe that Hone really was very ill and not in any condition to come to work. The news didn't improve Joe's humour one jot. He too was having a stressful day.

# Chapter 9
# A Test and a Swim

After Andrew Cutlass's call, Tai Nguyen thought he would test this young Patrick Field. It was no use pursuing the truth about the lad helping some girl give birth if he was not going to be of any use in future.

Nguyen didn't have to wait long. He learned that his French contacts in Auckland needed to dispose of some New Zealand dollar cash. The route he had arranged before used Royal Counties Bank to count the money and remit it in French Francs to an account in Royal Counties Bank in Paris. He figured Royal Counties Bank did well enough out of the transaction. They charged NZ$1,000 to count the notes and then made more when they did the foreign exchange conversion. They repatriated the notes themselves to the New Zealand Central Bank as a bulk shipment and nobody was any the wiser.

Someone told Nguyen there was another new man in the branch who would oversee the counting from now onwards. He wasn't a target – 'yet', thought Nguyen. When the two French men arrived in town, he made a call to the Royal Counties Bank asking for Kim to attend a meeting at Bon Plats to go over some transaction records. The two visitors waited in the Rossi Hotel, next door to the bank.

Seeing Kim drive away, they entered the branch with their two suitcases of cash and asked to pay in.

Marianne walked down the line of cashiers towards Trade Finance Department. "Patrick? There are two men wanting to make a cash deposit to be remitted to Paris. Kim isn't here: could you receive them and oversee the counting?"

Patrick welcomed them into the interview room and began the counting with one of the cashiers. They double checked each other and banding each stack of NZ$1,000 as they went.

He wrote out a receipt for the NZ$87,000 and passed it across the table.

"Gentlemen," he began. "I assume you are aware that New Zealand currency is not supposed to leave the country, let alone in such significant amounts. Do you wish to leave it with us for safe-keeping before repatriating it?"

The two exchanged glances. "*Non, Monsieur. Nous souhaitons remettre l'argent à Paris en francs Français.*"

Patrick's colleague helped to translate so he was quite clear what they wanted. "But this transaction is not legal, I'm afraid. We can safeguard the cash until you return to New Zealand, but will not be able to accept it to fund a foreign exchange transfer."

There was a hurried and whispered conversation in rapid French. Then one sat up straighter and said, in halting English, "Your Monsieur Cutlass – 'E ees able to do for us thees thing before – many times."

Still smarting from his recent encounters with the Chief Manager, Patrick felt pressured. He had no appetite for another run-in. He decided to consult Gilles, the foreign exchange dealer. "*Excusez-moi un instant. Je vais consulter un collègue.*"

As ever, Gilles had his telephone perched on his shoulder. He stabbed at the air to help convey an important point to whoever was on the other end. At Patrick's approach, he ended the call. "*Ces gens sont stupides! Et maintenant? Puis-je vous aider?*"

"Yes, please, Gilles. Two French men want to pay in NZ$ cash and remit in French Francs to Paris. That is illegal, but they say Andrew has permitted it before. It's $87,000, so quite a lot. Can we do that?"

Gilles confirmed that similar transactions had been carried out. He suggested charging $1,000 to count the money. Checking a sheet in front of him, he worked out the rate he would apply for the conversion, adding an extra couple of percent in the bank's favour. He wrote down the exchange rate on a piece of paper and handed it to Patrick. "*Voici le taux de change.*"

"*D'accord. Merci, Gilles*," said Patrick.

Patrick was still quite positive that NZ$ cash was not permitted to leave its home country. So he set about explaining to the two men that the bank would carry out the transaction today, but this must be the last time. They shrugged. Next time they'd make sure they dealt with the new man, and if he refused as well, there were plenty of other banks in town.

About a month later, Andrew Cutlass received a hand-written personal note from the head of the bank's Paris branch. It reported that Field had been very polite but insistent that this money transfer route for New Zealand cash could no longer be used. Field had agreed to do the transaction this one final time, though.

Cutlass relayed the news to Tai Nguyen, who knew already, of course. It was irritating that one transfer avenue had closed. But Nguyen now had evidence of financial malpractice by the young man – participation in money laundering. He added this snippet to a fresh file he had opened on Patrick Field. His own handler would be interested in this useful update the next time he visited.

-----//-----

The next day, Patrick telephoned inviting Jessica to join him for a drive around the island at the weekend. His plan was to stop at a beach somewhere to snorkel, sunbathe and relax. She said that would be lovely and accepted right away. But then said, "Patrick, that boy you brought to Vila Base - Hone – I'm very concerned about him."

"Why?" Patrick asked. "I agree he was very off-colour indeed, but what is wrong with him?"

"I examined him quite carefully and we ran some blood tests and so on. The thing is, there is nothing wrong with him."

"Sorry? Nothing at all?"

"Not a thing. Some of his health markers are a little off, but when I first did the tests, they were within normal limits. His CBC was a little over 5 million…"

"Woah - what?"

"That's 'Complete Blood Count'. It should be between 5 and 6 million per microlitre, so that is fine. His haemoglobin was up at 16 g/dl - again, right where it should be for a young man. He was pretty weak and disoriented when you brought him in, so I admitted him overnight to wait for the tests to come back." She paused, wondering how to convey how helpless she felt. "Patrick, he's not able to eat or even drink much right now."

"Gosh. That's serious, I guess. What can be done?"

"He's on a drip and we can keep him alive, but it's as though the spark has gone out of him. I'm doing some research and have telexed back to the UK for some ideas."

"Hmmn. I'm very sorry to hear that. Poor Hone. Umm …it may not be anything to do with this. I don't want you to leap to any conclusions, but a couple of the local staff told me he might have had a spell put on him."

"Patrick, why didn't you say before? If the spell was a death spell, there's not much I can do."

"You believe in these things?"

"It doesn't matter what I believe. It's what Hone believes that counts." She hesitated. "I have to get him to have faith he can recover. I don't know how to do that because he isn't responsive. Look, I have to go now. See you on Saturday – around 9 am?"

"Mmmn Yes. That would be great. Oh, one other thing. Do you have any of that spray bandage stuff? I got a scratch on my leg when I went to Pele and it isn't too clever at the moment."

"Have you let it get wet? You ought to keep it dry, you know. I'll bring some antiseptic too as out here even little scratches can become fly-blown."

"Gross!" Exclaimed Patrick. Although he had to admit that word described the front of his leg very well. Still – it didn't hurt. "Let me know how Hone gets on, would you?" They said their goodbyes.

-----//-----

There was very little breeze that Saturday morning. So Patrick didn't feel too bad about dragging Jessica away from sailing. A nice flat sea, in contrast, would be perfect for snorkelling over and around some of the beautiful reefs. These could be found at intervals on the coast. Not only were the corals a variety of colours (Patrick's favourite was blue-tipped coral which was, unfortunately, poisonous if you scraped yourself) but they were teeming with every imaginable colour of fish, large and small. It was most relaxing of all if you simply lay on the surface above a reef edge. All you needed was a mask and snorkel to observe everyday life below. Of course, the lapping of the waves and any current would move the swimmer around. Small positional corrections might be needed. A couple of lazy strokes of the flippers would put things right for a little while.

Patrick packed some sandwiches, fruit, beers and water into a cold box. He collected Jessica sharp at 9am and they headed for the anti-clockwise coast road. The destination he had in mind was Eton Beach on the south east side. The beach cut in close to the road at that point. But it was almost always deserted and low bushes at the high tide mark gave privacy to anyone sunbathing or having a picnic.

Jessica had managed to switch off from her demanding job at the hospital. She relaxed more as they drove further away from the main town of Vila and she was bubbling and buoyant when Patrick pulled up at Eton Beach. She crossed her arms and peeled off her T-shirt even as she was opening the car door. "Race you," she grinned.

"Hey, hang about – I've got to hide the car keys somewhere and what about the cool box?"

But Jessica wasn't waiting. She very much wanted to swim. Wriggling out of her shorts, she ran down the beach, splashed through the shallows and dived into the next wave which came along.

"Come on, slowcoach," she jeered, waving at him when she came up for air. "It's brilliant."

As quickly as he could, Patrick put the car keys on top of a tyre and hefted the cool box out of the boot. There was no point locking the car as they'd left the windows wide open. The cool box went into the heaviest growth of bushes he could find for shade. Off came his shirt and shorts and he joined

Jessica in the sea. She could splash much more accurately than him, but he used his strength to dunk her under water. They played like this for some time, blissfully happy. The sun shone, the water was cool. Each thought the other exciting company. The frisson of sexual tension accompanied every movement or touch.

"Let's dry off," she suggested. So, holding hands, they waded through the shallows and up the beach. They kept a wary eye out for lurking stone fish and their poisonous spines. Patrick fetched towels from the car and they lay on the sand, watching the few clouds high up in the sky scudding past.

"Would you like a beer?" Patrick asked.

"Not yet – but we could share one of those paw-paws. Did you bring a knife?"

Patrick reached for his shorts. "Yup. Can you can eat a whole one?"

"I don't think so - half will do, thanks."

Patrick halved the fruit, cupped his fingers to scoop out the seeds and lobbed them into the bushes nearby. He handed one half to Jessica. "Let's play 'Cloud Racing', he proposed. "We each choose a cloud and watch as they progress across the sky. And see who wins."

"What's the prize?" she peeked up at him from under her fringe.

"I'll tell you later," Patrick teased.

"Hey," Jessica said, looking hard at his leg. "Show me that injury".

The scratch Patrick had received from some elephant grass during his visit to Pele Island had not healed. In fact, it was beginning to concern him in case it had become 'fly blown'. Jessica had warned him about that – in other words, flies had laid their eggs in the wound and prevented it healing. Their dip in the sea had softened the scab which had now fallen away leaving an unpleasant gaping hole.

"Patrick, that's bad. I remember now – you asked me to bring some spray-on antiseptic bandage." Jessica had gone back into Doctor mode. She scrambled up, fetched her tiny bag of what he'd assumed were 'feminine essentials' and extracted a small spray can.

"Right. I need to clean this out. Did you bring fresh water as well as beer?" Patrick nodded and got up to fetch the cool box. Actually, now she had drawn attention to the wound, it was beginning to hurt a little. Perhaps the salty sea water made it sting or some sand had got inside it. He delved into the box and pulled out an unopened bottle of fresh water. He settled himself down beside her.

She splashed some of the precious water onto her hands, swabbed his leg. Then, digging into the wound with some tool or other, she drenched it with yet more. Patrick clenched his teeth.

"I don't want to hear a peep out of you, Patrick Field – you should have dealt with this when it first happened," Jessica told him off. "Now it has become infected and it's almost down to the bone. You'll have to come into the hospital later and have it cleaned and dressed properly. Do you have any headaches? Dizziness? Any rashes?" He shook his head.

She put her hand on his forehead.

"That's nice," Patrick said, smiling at her, encouragingly.

"I'm checking whether you have a temperature."

"Oh. It's still nice," he subsided. Jessica dabbed at the wound with some paper towel, shielding it from the light sand blowing around them. She shook the spray can.

"This might sting a bit."

"Ok."

She was right that it would sting. But she had not forecast the scale of the stinging. It stung like mad. Patrick was determined not to complain, though. He knew he had been silly not to take care of the wound days ago. As the aerosol spray landed on his skin and especially in the wound itself, the alcohol propellant evaporated. It left an antiseptic coating in place as well as a feeling that she had stroked his leg with a rod of ice.

"Right. You are not getting that wet again until we have examined it at the hospital – no more swimming for you." She tucked the spray can away in her little bag again. Fanning the wound with her hand sped up and completed the drying process. Then she rose, bent to pick up a mask and flippers, said, "But I can!" and ran down the beach to the water again.

This was some sort of punishment. There was nothing he could do but watch her lithe body twisting and splashing in the waves. Then she all but disappeared at the reef edge about twenty metres out.

He lay back on his elbows, shading his eyes with one hand. He could play the cloud game by himself. After two attempts at that and some twenty minutes, though, he became bored …and thirsty. Jess was still circling around, watching fish darting in and out of the coral outcrops. He'd save plenty of water for her, but wanted to drink something now.

As he reached for the cool box again, he heard a truck approaching at speed. It raced past, scattering stones as it rounded the slight bend and blew up a storm of dust in its wake. The stones peppered the foliage beside Patrick. He closed his eyes so they wouldn't get grit in them.

"Wow," exclaimed Jessica, walking up the beach towards him. She balanced on each leg in turn and hopped to ease water out of her ears. "He was in a hurry. Where's the fire"?

"In his head, I imagine." Patrick said, turning back to watch Jessica reaching for a towel. She really was …lovely. "I saved you some water." he grinned, squinting as she moved sideways and he was again in full sun. "Tell me, Oh Goddess emerging from the Sea: are you hungry yet?"

That made her smile. Was he forgiven?

"I'll dry off a bit first. Do you mind if we wait for five minutes?"

"I won't mind, provided I can watch you drying off." Patrick said, cheekily. She aimed a half-hearted slap at him.

"I'll allow looking."

-----//-----

Much later, and after tentative dabs by Patrick with a dry towel to remove real and imaginary droplets of water, she amended her permission to include light kissing and application of sun lotion to difficult-to-reach places.

Then they drank beer. They ate the food and found themselves utterly relaxed in each other's company. Patrick remarked that he was glad it wasn't possible to play his Cloud Racing game owing to the complete and utter absence of clouds. She told him he was daft …but put her hand in his, even so.

They were very happy.

Eventually, Jessica sat up. "Would you take me home, now? I reckon we've had enough sun for one day". She tapped the front of one of his shoulders to show that it had become rather more pink than was healthy.

"It's not that late. But alright - I suppose we should. Did I mention how lovely you are?"

Jess beamed. "Flattery will get you everywhere. Come on, let's pack these things away."

Patrick realised as he buckled his seatbelt that Jess had been right about having had enough sun for one day. He was aware of the pressure of the belt through his T-shirt on an area of skin on the front of his shoulder and on his neck. He must have missed that when applying the sunscreen earlier.

"Next time I'll ask you to put on my sunscreen".

"Oh," she said, archly. "So there's going to be a 'next time' is there?"

"Maybe," countered Patrick. "I'll have to check with my social secretary if I'm free."

She slapped his thigh. "You're bad."

He started the engine and reversed out onto the crushed coral road. "Let's carry on the way we were going. That way we'll have gone completely around Efate." Patrick also knew that this would be a way of prolonging his time with Jessica. They'd travelled barely one third of the way around the island to reach Eton Beach.

"Ok. Was that Eton village we passed before the beach?"

"It was."

The road then cut inland a bit, but they had glimpses of fabulous views through the trees to the sea sparkling in the afternoon sun. Now and again, Patrick had to swerve the car around depressions where the road surface had washed out in heavy rain. Government road crews had not yet done repairs.

Quite soon, they spotted the remains of heavy machinery below the road level near the coast line. It was already being overtaken by creepers and other jungle plants. Jessica sat up. "What are those huge machines?"

"That was the Forari manganese mine. It closed last year. Kim told me there are plenty of recoverable deposits but the owners can't manage to balance cash outflows with profitable sales. I have a feeling we lent some money to it, but I'm not sure. I doubt we'll get that back now." He slowed the car as they went past, marvelling at how fast nature reclaimed unused land.

From his elevated observation point above the area of workings, Patrick noticed a group of vehicles. They were parked beside a pile of leftover ore. He braked to a stop and put on the handbrake. Down below, six men stood together, two of whom were waving their arms as though emphasising a point. Patrick couldn't make out what was being said as the wind was blowing their words away. But …there was the Bon Plats Toyota, loaded down with those wooden boxes he'd seen days before at the port.

"Stay here for a minute. I want to see what is going on." Jessica opened her mouth to protest but thought better of it. He left the engine running and picked his way down the slope, staying behind the piles of ore. The men were speaking French and he couldn't follow the gist of what they were saying. Several times there was a word sounding like 'foosey'. There came a creaking noise reminiscent of levering nails out of wood. Patrick couldn't resist peeking around the corner to look. One man had removed the lid of a box still on the load bed of the truck and two others had climbed up to inspect the contents. A packing cloth was rolled back and the two men reached in and brought out rifles! The word had been '*fusils*'. The 'snick, snick' sound of a bolt action came to him and the man called for '*munitions*'. 'That's ammo', thought Patrick.

Now very scared, he ducked down again behind the ore and ran back to his car, trying hard not to be seen or make any noise.

He opened the driver's door, dipped the clutch, engaged first gear and accelerated away along the road.

"What's the matter, Patrick? You look like you've seen a ghost. What was there?"

"I do believe I saw a business transaction which nobody was supposed to witness. The Bon Plats truck was there again and I wanted to see what they are up to."

"I don't follow," said Jessica, becoming alarmed. "What's all this about the Bon Plats truck?"

"Oh, sorry. I guess I hadn't filled you in on some of the odd stuff I've been seeing over the last few weeks." He glanced across at her. "It's better that I don't, either – given this latest development." He was suddenly sure that Jessica mustn't know in case it put her in danger. "Hey, do you fancy a spot of dinner? I've got plenty of food in my fridge."

"I'm on call tonight from nine o'clock, so, thank you, but I'd better not. I need a shower."

"Do you want help with that?" Patrick enquired, knowing the response he'd get.

"Hmmn. I might be able to manage by myself – and you mustn't get that leg wet, so, on balance, no help needed." But she smiled and that threw Patrick's emotions into a somersault. He had been afraid his inquisitive adventure had spoiled their day.

As they drove along, Patrick recalled a minor potential scandal from his time in Royal Counties Bank, London. An American company named Southern Cross was named as consignee of some goods subject to the letter of credit Patrick was examining. Delivery was to be to the town of 'Forari' in this place Patrick was not familiar with at the time – the New Hebrides. He remembered the name as it resembled that of his dream motor car manufacturer: 'Ferrari'. His boss at the bank had received word that Southern Cross was suspected of gun running. There was some shadowy connection to part of the American Government. So the bank should avoid becoming party to or playing any role in transactions involving Southern Cross.

He stopped the car outside Jess's house. "I have had a great time being with you today, Jess. And, sorry about …well, you know."

"Don't be silly, Patrick. I had a super time too. And *I* saw all those reef fish, don't forget! Come to the hospital tomorrow and we'll fix up your leg."

"Ok. See you tomorrow?" He leaned across and gave her a peck on the cheek.

"I want a proper kiss," she said, taking his head in her hands and doing just that.

Patrick closed his eyes. This woman was astonishing. He couldn't sort out in his mind why she above all others was so desirable. The fact was he'd not experienced such a yearning, consuming desire for a girl before. She was bright, articulate, sporty and amazingly pretty – especially when she smiled – or walked or sat or… well, all the time.

And then she was out of the car. This was when Patrick was supposed to drive away, waving goodbye. He came to with a little mental jolt. Jessica turned back and wiggled her fingers to him before putting her key in the door lock. That made him stall the car. He NEVER did that.

She gave a final wave and disappeared inside.

As he drove home, he couldn't help an enormous grin spreading across his face.

Dining with Kim was okay, but Jess would have been far superior as a dining companion.

He collected Kim back at the flats and they went shopping for something small and quick to eat for dinner. Browsing the wide selection of patés, Patrick happened to look up. That Arabian gent he'd seen chatting to Roger Hammerson outside La Hotte a while back was coming in. He was greeted by no less a person than Tai Nguyen himself. He watched as they hugged each other like very old friends.

"Kim – look. By the door," Patrick whispered. "That man with Nguyen. I saw him outside La Hotte talking with Roger Hammerson – you know, the bloke from Price Waterhouse. Hammerson was very uncomfortable about me seeing them – as if something bad was going on."

"Yeah, I've seen him before. He met with Andrew in the bank last week. What about him?"

"Do you know who he is and what he wanted?"

"No – but Andrew called Gilles upstairs right after he left. I remember because Gilles said the dollar was moving and was hopping

208

mad that he'd missed the best rates because he was in this meeting."

Patrick thought for a moment. "I know we receive many nationalities here, 'cos of all the yachties. But he doesn't dress like a yachtie – and I've not seen anyone like him here before. And …what's he scheming with Tai Nguyen?"

"Let's ask Gilles tomorrow. He'll at least tell us who he is."

"Ok. Come on - pork chops or escalopes?"

They settled on chops.

Quite a bit later, they sat outside after dinner with glasses of Glayva. The crickets starting up their nightly chirruping. Patrick broached the topic of the guns being unloaded at the mine.

"Aha – that explains why you were quiet. I assumed things hadn't gone well with Jessica this afternoon."

"No. I mean, yes, we had a great time at the beach, but she is 'on call' tonight – otherwise I might have eaten with her. I didn't tell her about the guns, but she saw I was, well, scared."

"Does 'on call' mean, 'I'm washing my hair'?"

"No! At least, I don't think so. We got on well. We are going to the beach again, really soon."

"You're in love!" Kim jeered, pushing Patrick's shoulder.

"What if I am? But what can I do about the gun trading Bon Plats is involved with?"

"My advice is to keep your head down, don't make waves. Under no circumstances tell Andrew. If these men are trading guns, they may be trading other illegal things. Such people don't negotiate with young British bankers like us. What you said about Southern Cross and not getting involved? That's what we should do. And don't forget the ferrety man you spotted at La Hotte and again tonight at Bon Plats."

"But we are involved: the foreign exchange volumes you have been examining for days now? Where has that all come from?"

That reminder made Kim rather glum again. "I don't know. But I'm scared to intervene further. Let's see what Gilles has to say." And he wouldn't be pressed any further on the matter.

Patrick retired to bed and slept fitfully, uncertain what to do. The thin curtains in his bedroom failed dismally to keep the dawn at bay. A combination of birds greeting each other and the gardener, Tom Charlie, banging and clattering about outside convinced him to abandon any hope of rest. He got up earlier than normal stubbing his toe on the leg of the bed. Almost worse, he forgot to bang the shower curtain to send lingering overnight cockroaches scurrying back to the tiny cracks in the walls. One crunched under his throbbing foot as he reached in to turn on the mixer tap.

'This must be how Jessica feels after a night on the wards, tending to the sick.' he thought.

His second cup of strong Tanna coffee inspired the brilliant idea of seeking council from the British Ambassador's daughter, Florence. They had become firm friends since Patrick arrived in Port Vila. Perhaps if he gave her a careful précis, she could mention the gist of Patrick's story to her father. He would be in the best position to advise what action Patrick could take.

He telephoned the Hospital and asked to speak with Dr Jessica. He waited while the receptionist paged her.

At last, she came to the phone. "This is Dr Jessica".

"Hi, Jess; sorry to catch you at work. I hope you are heading home soon. I know I asked to get together tonight but I've had an idea of what to do about what we saw yesterday, and I need to have a private chat with Florence instead. Sorry, but could I call you tomorrow? And I promise to come to the hospital to have someone examine my leg."

"I see. Well maybe I'm not available tomorrow. I'm busy now, I'm tired and I want to go home to catch some sleep."

And the line went dead.

'What did I say wrong?' thought Patrick. He suddenly felt flushed and ashamed as though he'd mistreated Jessica. He didn't mean to do that. Too late, he realised she must be feeling rejected – at least miffed. Should he have explained exactly why he must meet with Florence? He re-examined his protective reaction upon seeing guns at the Forari mine that he must not drag Jessica into any of that. He still felt that was the right course, although he ached to take her into his confidence. 'We only hurt the ones we love', he thought.

He fetched Kim and they went around to Gilles.

The Frenchman checked his diary. "That was Bashir Saleh. He runs the sovereign wealth fund for Libya. You know how Fr Walter Lini has been making nice to Libya as a political counter-weight to the West? Everyone says that his *Vanuaku Pati* has won the election. He's going to be the first President of the country. Well, Bashir agrees and had funds to go, and wanted to use us to do the exchanges. *Très intéressant, non*?" he said, very chuffed with himself. His monthly profit figures were climbing further and further. He was already counting how he would spend his end of year bonus.

"Did he say where the funds came from?" asked Kim.

"I told you: it's the country's sovereign wealth fund." He paged through at his diary. "The 'Libyan Africa Portfolio', it's called. Ok?"

"Yes, thanks, Gilles. Sorry to interrupt."

Patrick and Kim exchanged looks of frustration. Gilles' answers didn't tell them what they felt they needed to know. They walked back around the corner towards the Trade Finance section. Kim said, "Ok, that's the name of the principal – supposed to be the name in which we book the trades. But is this really sovereign money? And we have recorded them as trades for Bon Plats. I mean, could this Bashir person be doing some trades on the side for himself and pretending that they were for the fund he runs? And how on earth does Bon Plats fit into everything?"

"We need to find out the name of the remitter of the funds." Patrick was beginning to feel he was like a dog picking up a scent. "I have an idea how to do that: I'll ask Marianne how we file the entries and there ought to be an incoming telex or letter or something stapled to them. Luke can help me find the right box in the filing room."

"Ok. Good thinking…" agreed Kim.

"But first, I have an important telephone call to make. I'll tackle Marianne after lunch." He dialled the British Resident Commissioner's Office.

"British Commissioner's Residence. May I help you?"

"Yes, please. This is Patrick Field at the Royal Counties Bank. May I speak with Florence, if she is at home?"

"I believe she is, Mr Field. Please hold the line." Patrick waited.

"Hello, Patrick? Is that you?" Florence picked up the telephone and sounded her usual very bright self.

"Yes, good morning, Florence. There's a rather serious matter I'd like to discuss with you – could we get together tonight, after work, for a drink?"

"Ooh, that sounds exciting! 'A serious matter'! I don't believe I have discussed a 'serious matter' for some years. I'd love to come. Where shall we meet?"

Despite himself, Patrick couldn't avoid smiling at the girl's innocent happiness. "There's a little bar on a spit of land as you head north out of town and before you reach Hideaway Island. Do you know it?"

"I reckon it's the place Alan always brings me when he wants to keep away from my father."

"It's quite important that you don't tell Alan about this, Florence. I'm not sure yet of the implications, but that is why I need to speak with you alone. Is that alright?"

"Ok. I'll tell him I'm plaiting my hair or something."

Now it was Patrick's turn to laugh. Suave and urbane, Alan might have been, by local standards, but it was quite possible, in

Patrick's view, that he'd swallow that excuse without question. Even if Florence's hair was nowhere near long enough to plait.

"Well, you think about what to say, but don't let him talk you around. This is important. See you there at 7pm? Is that ok? Oh, and better park around the back."

"Patrick, you're scaring me."

"I don't mean to – see you at 7pm."

-----//-----

"...so you see, I have put all these odd events together. I'm worried that Tai Nguyen and Bon Plats are involved in gun running and maybe money laundering and who knows what else?"

"I follow," said Florence, who had become more and more serious as Patrick wove his tale. "But what can I do?"

"Could you relay this to your father? I don't feel confident to approach the Police here – would I ask the British Police or the French Police? And I cannot work out how the money transfer aspect of the thing could work unless Andrew Cutlass was somehow part of it – so I can't go to him."

Florence thought for a second but then said, "Yes, of course, Patrick. If he has an answer, is it ok if he uses me to tell you?"

"Sure. Of course, that would be fine. Now, drink up – time we were back at home. People will start to talk!"

"You mean Alan will start to talk." She said glumly. "Sometimes he's so …clingy!"

# Chapter 10

# The British Resident Commissioner

The next day, Andrew Cutlass was annoyed to learn that the British Commissioner had summoned Patrick Field to visit his office on Iririki Island. This did not make sense. He called Field in to press for details.

"Come in, Patrick. What news?"

"All is well, thank you, Andrew."

"I have received a strange request from the British Commissioner. He wants you to visit him on Iririki Island. Why do you think that might be?"

Patrick didn't think his chat with Florence would bear results so fast. "I don't know, Andrew. I have met his daughter, Florence a few times, on social occasions. There might be some simple banking service he needs for her."

"Is she pregnant too?"

"No! At least – I have no idea if she is or not." He was aghast at Cutlass's suggestion. The man's suspicions about Patrick's

219

activities outside work had not yet been allayed.

"Hmmn. Well, you'd better get moving. He wants you there at 11am sharp. Don't keep the man waiting. And report to me immediately afterwards. Clear?"

Patrick scrambled down to the quayside where the official launch was waiting to ferry him for the 2 minute trip across from Port Vila. A small open-topped Suzuki jeep arrived on the Iririki Island dock as they reached it. The grinning, uniformed driver bounced them up the slope to the rear of the official Residence. The Commissioner's flag fluttered in the breeze. They went inside.

Another smartly-dressed servant led him along the panelled corridor and tapped twice on the tall, double wooden doors at the end.

"Come".

He was ushered into the great man's presence.

Andrew Christopher Stuart, CPM CMG, the British Resident Commissioner, sat behind a large and ornate wooden desk. A stack of papers to his left spilled over his In-Tray. The Out-Tray, to his right, was empty. There were two chairs placed in front of it for visitors. Traditional trappings and symbols of faded British Empire surrounded the desk. Yet more hung on the walls. Patrick edged forward cautiously.

"Come in, dear boy. Do sit down. Florence tells me you have made certain troubling observations over the last few months."

Stuart's expression was open and welcoming and it became easier to tell the tale as Patrick went on. But the man's brow furrowed when he reached the part about watching as boxes of guns were opened out at Forari mine. The Commissioner grew more serious.

"We have been aware of some of these, ah, *nefarious* activities for a while, but have not had witness accounts such as yours. You should return to your banking duties and carry on as usual. I am grateful you have brought all this to my attention and it will be reported to London in due course. Should you happen across other activities of this nature, I urge you to avoid putting yourself in danger. Let me know what you have seen, through Florence, if that suits."

The Commissioner paused and raised one eyebrow. "As for your man, Cutlass, tell him that I should like an introduction to someone in your Private Banking division. I would like to open an offshore bank account. Make sure you say that I didn't want to bother him with such a trifling request." Patrick understood that he was being given a believable cover story to explain his visit to Iririki Island.

When Patrick returned to the branch, he went straight upstairs as had been demanded.

"Come in, come in – don't dawdle outside, Patrick. Now what did *Andrew* have to say to you?" asked Cutlass, using the Commissioner's first name to imply a greater familiarity with the man than was actually the case.

"He said he didn't want to bother you but would like to be introduced to a contact in the Private Bank: he is thinking of opening an offshore bank account."

"Very well. Leave it with me, will you? That is all." Cutlass's suspicions were somewhat mollified, although not completely removed. He still felt the boy was up to something. But he knew that such a prominent referral to the Private Bank might earn him some introductory commission. It would sit well on his own annual report.

Patrick was too inexperienced and junior to appreciate the importance of such things. He was more concerned that Jessica had a low opinion of him right now. He went back downstairs and telephoned her.

"Jess? It's me. I will visit the hospital this afternoon as I promised to have my leg cleaned up and dressed and …are you free tonight? Could we have dinner together?"

"Not tonight, Patrick. I have to revise for some exams. It's a constant part of a doctor's life, this reading, revising and taking exams. I'm hoping to get a promotion to registrar soon, so I have to do well in this latest round. So, sorry. Maybe some other time. I might see you this afternoon, though."

When Patrick checked into the hospital, Jessica did see him. The nurse who received him first was quite concerned when she saw his leg and right away fetched the doctor. Jess tutted and told him off again. "You have let this deteriorate and it's now quite serious. You see that white area? That's bone. The skin and muscle on top has been eaten away. I told you to keep it dry; did you do so?"

"Well, most of the time. I have to shower, haven't I?"

"You can put your lower leg into a plastic bag and secure it with tape. That will last while you shower. Then you can clean it by hand afterwards. This is really important: if the wound gets worse, infection might enter the bone itself and you will be in real trouble. Do you understand what that means, Patrick?"

"Um, yes. I suppose so."

"I'll give you some anti-biotics to try to stop infection. Are you allergic to any?"

"I don't think so".

She finished cleaning and dressing the now deep depression in his leg and scribbled out a prescription. "Take this to pharmacy on the way out."

The nurse had moved on to the next patient by now and they were alone. Jessica said, as he got up, "Patrick, I will have dinner with you tomorrow night, but we should be by ourselves. Not Kim as well. We need some 'us' time."

"That's fantastic," Patrick said. "I'll make something special – no garlic though – and I can now tell you why I needed to talk with Florence."

"Make sure you do. Now off you go – don't forget the prescription and keep that dressing dry!"

-----//-----

On the way home, Patrick stopped at Bon Plats and splurged on a whole leg of lamb. He planned to butterfly it, cooking it on the barbeque after marinading all night and all the next day in a mixture of herbs and olive oil. What a shame Jess didn't like garlic! That would have made it sumptuous, but '...worse things happen at sea,' he thought.

Late the next afternoon, he brought the lamb to room temperature. It was time to brown and baste it. Finally he wrapped it in silver foil on a shelf under the BBQ to rest and keep warm for two hours while the fire died down. His buried potatoes, wrapped in more silver foil, would bake in the glowing coconut husks. He knew the method was always a bit hit and miss. Some would be still too hard and underdone. Others would burn, but a few ought to be flaky and soft inside - perfect to soak up the meat juices.

A few minutes before Jess was due to arrive, he took out the lettuces he'd bought at the market to serve with a French dressing. He expected Jessica would tell him off for risking Norovirus or infection with E. Coli or salmonella poisoning from eating locally-grown fresh greens. But he also knew that the lamb and potatoes would be heavy, so hoped she would appreciate having a light salad too. He was keen to open another bottle of the medium red wine he and Kim bought from La Cave du Gourmets - a Brouilly from two years before. In short, he was making a big effort to impress her.

He was rescuing the potatoes from the Barbeque as Jessica drove up to the flats. "Mmmm – something smells divine. Have you been slaving for the whole afternoon?"

"Oh, it wasn't as quick as that – I took all night as well." She punched him, playfully, but then, to Patrick's delight, she planted a kiss on his lips.

"Can we start eating yet? I'm starving."

Patrick sat her down with a glass of the wine. "Cheers. I'll dress the salad and fetch some knives and forks. There are baked potatoes – I plan to serve them plain as everything else has lots of flavour; is that ok?"

"I'm sure it'll be lovely. Don't forget I usually survive on a hurried sandwich from the canteen – that or I visit a take-away restaurant – so a home-cooked meal is a bit of a treat."

The evening went well. Not only did Jessica put away a very substantial portion of the lamb but she asked for a second helping. She didn't mention the health risks of eating local lettuce even once. Patrick delivered a shortened and sanitised version of recent events. He noted Jessica's evident relief when he revealed the reason he needed to meet with the British Commissioner's daughter. He guessed she had feared that Florence had replaced her in Patrick's affections.

As Patrick poured her a cup of the delightful local coffee, she asked an odd question: "Do you have an alarm clock?"

"I do," he replied. "I rely on it to turf me out of bed in time to get to the bank before Andrew arrives. Did you want to borrow it?"

Jess grinned at him, wickedly. "In a manner of speaking – yes."

It took Patrick a second or two to catch up. "You mean…?"

"Come over here and sit down, silly."

Their coffees got cold and weren't drunk until the next morning. But neither of them minded.

-----//-----

The next day, Patrick and Kim drove the short distance home from the bank for lunch. Patrick went to take the remains of the leg of lamb out of the refrigerator. He wanted to slice it up for sandwiches with pickles. But he found himself peering into an almost empty space. Checking around, he realised the window above the sink had been forced open and so called for Kim to check his flat too, fearing burglary. But there was no evidence of break-in there. Patrick searched through his belongings to try to figure out what else was missing. A little money, a bottle of Fairy Washing up liquid and a blue beany hat were the only other items on the list. They ate lunch in Kim's flat and went back to work.

That evening, Patrick visited the Chief of the nearest village and alerted him to this theft. The man listened with great attention. He provided Patrick with an escort of two warriors to walk back to his flat in safety.

As he drove home the following night, Patrick kept having to slow down and steer around lots of men and women. They were milling about all over the roads, looking as though they were drunk. He had never seen anything similar before. It was alarming that several were waving their bush knives in a dangerous manner. He and Kim were very disturbed at this sudden increase in social discord. But all became clear in the morning.

"Sara? Do you have any idea what is happening? Last night, as Kim and I were driving home, there were people running about on the roads. Some were waving bush knives, others swaying around like they were drunk – what's going on?"

Sara broke away from the little gaggle of local staff by the filing room. She brought him an article from that morning's newspaper. It said Police had discovered a dismembered body on the beach in Numba Tu District, near Patrick's flat. The article quoted the local Chief as saying that his elders discovered stolen items in this man's hut. He had been summarily executed as a thief.

He looked up at her, horrified. "Crumbs. That's ...awful."

She shrugged. "It is our way."

He reread the article again. There was no mention of him. Not even any clues about the identity of the victim of this theft. It majored on the Chief's assertion that an incident of stealing had been reported and the miscreant found out and punished.

This was shocking. His action had triggered an extreme result. He realised he'd been taught a great lesson. Other societies function in a way which suits them and he

229

should not expect them to behave in an English manner. In weeks to come, he would reflect deeply on this. He came to realise that the arrival of white men, at first trying to impose Christianity on the New Hebrides in the previous century and more recently bringing their pickups, radios and alcohol, had changed New Hebridean society in profound ways for ever – and not always for the better.

## Chapter 11
# Election Results

Counting the votes from the election took many days. There were several recounts as some candidates protested that their losing was simply not possible. Votes in their favour must have been missed. But eventually a result was declared. As many people expected, the *Vanuaaku Pati*, headed by Father Walter Lini, an Anglican priest, won 25 of the 39 seats. He would lead Vanuatu's first independent government. Turnout was over 90% of the population, so Lini had a clear mandate from the people. They organised celebrations. There was feasting and dancing throughout the islands over the winter of 1979. That is, except for the largest, northern island of Espiritu Santo. Early in the spring of 1980, French and English governments drew up plans. They would end their joint Condominium government of the islands on the 30th of July that year.

Lini had long cozied up to Russia, China, Cuba and Moammar Ghadaffi of Libya.

He wanted a foil for the country's existing main relationships with the powerful western and eastern blocs. In the case of Libya, he thought it wise to link with another oil-producing country. To emphasise how independent he intended his country to be, he welcomed emissaries from Libya. They brought congratulations from Ghadaffi at the victory and promises of investment. Lini knew they'd expect certain financial favours from this now independent offshore tax haven. These official emissaries were arriving in full view. Local newspapers photographed them as they appeared at public events around Port Vila. Quite unlike the much earlier visits by Bashir Saleh! His arrival was unheralded, his stays were secret and his meetings with certain individuals furtive.

In contrast to the celebrations in Port Vila, the election result was not welcomed by certain French colonialists. The mood on the island of Espiritu Santo was grim. They had constructed their business activities around the French/English Condominium. The *status quo* allowed them to build fortunes off the land and the people. *Independens* threatened their land ownership and business activities. Some of these activities were legal, some not legal at all. A delegation of the colonialists approached Chief Jimmy Stevens, a Melanesian Big Man. He also led the francophone "*Nagriamel*" cult, part of the unsuccessful Federal party. They persuaded him to gather an army of near naked warriors and launch a rebellion to overturn the results of the election. The first part of their plan was to take over the former American Airforce base at Luganville on Santo. From there they could launch an invasion of the capital island of Efate, with Port Vila at its commercial and political centre.

Jimmy Stevens had already established a 'Republic of *Vemarana*' at his settlement in Vanafo on Espiritu Santo. He promised jeeps and refrigerators in return for wives, and word spread that he was marshalling his forces there. Roughly 350 foreigners and supporters of other political parties fled Santo in boats to Efate. They did not wait for the rebels to march the 32 Kms south to Luganville. Even though in fear for their lives, some paused long enough to send panicked radio messages to Efate. Most escaped, delivering feverish reports in person to any officials they could find in Port Vila.

Among the refugees were the ex-pat staff of the Santo sub-branch of Royal Counties Bank. They arrived safely, if badly shaken. Their departure was so hasty, everything belonging to the Bank remained behind. This included the vital books of Keys & Codes for sending telexes, the accounting records and all the Bank's money.

On the 8th of June, the Vanuatu government asked Britain and France for help. Ambassador Andrew Stuart of Britain requested 200 Royal Marines from 42 Commando to be sent. Stuart's opposite number, representing France, was Inspector-General Jean-Jacques Robert. He disagreed and maintained there was no need for British help and refused to allow the Marines to deploy. He arranged for paramilitaries from Noumea, French Caledonia to arrive first. But the French soldiers stationed on Espiritu Santo Island took no action. It was later determined that Robert was in league with the dispossessed colonialists. He was doing all he could to frustrate Fr Walter Lini's government.

But Patrick knew little of this at the time.

-----//-----

When he arrived at the branch the next morning, Patrick was still reeling from the death of the thief who had robbed his flat of a few menial possessions. Kim wasn't there yet and Joe's little glass office was empty. Looking around, he approached the counters from the customer side. None of the cashiers were at their tills in readiness to open up. But a little gaggle of local staff clustered around one of them. He asked what was going on.

"*Hello, olgeta. Wun 'em blo' yufelas*?"

Marianne was among them, her face serious. It was so unlike her. She replied, "Hemi wunfela rumour: olgeta *man, e stap long Santo – olgeta man e kum lo'Vila blo' kilim Fr Lini.*"

"What?" Patrick reacted with understandable alarm. "Did you say these men from Santo want to kill Father Lini?"

Marianne switched to English. "They say Chief Jimmy Stevens has sent his sons and their men to attack us in Vila. They have landed and are travelling along the coast roads to attack from both directions."

"Has Mr Cutlass arrived yet?"

She nodded. "He went upstairs."

"Ok. Could you pass the word that customers should not come in yet? Open the door to Kim or Joe or a member of staff whom you know, but not anyone else."

"Alright." Marianne said, turned and straight away relayed the instruction, making sure all the staff understood.

Patrick took the stairs up towards the Chief Manager's office two at a time. Seated beside Gail's desk in the waiting area were the three ex-pat members of Santo sub-branch staff.

"Hello," Patrick greeted them, with some surprise. "I'm told there is some sort of uprising in Santo – is that why you are all here?"

Andrew Cutlass, the Chief Manager, must have heard Patrick arrive. He appeared at his office door. "Come in, Patrick. Where is Kim?"

"Right here, Andrew. I'm coming." Kim replied, puffing up the stairs, having heard much the same briefing as Patrick from Marianne.

Joe was sitting beside Cutlass' desk already with Gilles. "Gentlemen." Cutlass began. "You will have seen that the ex-pat members of staff from Santo have arrived here. They tell me there are riots and fighting going on in Luganville and possibly in the surrounding areas of Santo. They made their escape by borrowing a motor boat and released the local staff with advice to come here."

He scanned the faces of his senior staff, one by one. "I am pleased that they have escaped unharmed. I am less pleased that …" he paused for effect. "They left behind the Keys and Codes."

It was one of those moments when Patrick's brain somehow viewed events happening right now almost as a third-party watcher might view them. Every branch of Royal Counties Bank throughout the world from London to the smallest and most remote sub-branch in the centre of Africa used the same Books of Codes to send messages by telex to other branches. They were vital to the daily working of the bank and mislaying even one book would have compromised the bank's security. Replacement of every single volume in the world would be mandatory. Patrick thought to himself, 'You could have heard a pin drop – except that the floor has carpet, so that's unlikely'.

He sniggered and tried to turn the noise into a cough, but didn't fool Cutlass. The man glared at him. "Is there something funny you would like to share with us, Patrick?"

"No, Andrew. This is serious."

"Indeed," Cutlass said. "We need to safeguard our branch …and our copy of the Keys and Codes. Joe will organise a rota of ex-pat staff starting immediately. You will stay up all night to guard the main branch of Royal Counties Bank here in Vila. That is all. Back to your desks. Ask the Santo staff to come in here, please."

Quite what Cutlass expected them all to do if armed, yelling rebels surrounded the branch that night was unclear. When asked, downstairs, Joe shrugged, "Raise the alarm? Tell Andrew? How should I know?"

The front door was unlocked for short periods during the day to allow customers they recognised to enter and transact their most urgent business. But they postponed requests for longer meetings for the time being. Sharp at 2:30pm, the door was locked finally behind all the staff except Patrick and John Marc. Cutlass had instructed them to keep the main safe locked and watch for suspicious people moving outside. They turned off all the lights, so from the outside the branch appeared deserted. Occasionally,

Patrick turned on a piece of electrical equipment to check the supply hadn't been cut off.

Kim and Luke relieved them at 6pm.

All through the night, naivete and enthusiasm for adventure plus frequent brews of Tanna coffee sustained them.

Early the next morning, Andrew Cutlass called everyone into his office. They had to figure out what to do about the Keys & Codes left behind in Santo sub-branch.

"You may have learned from your friends or others that rebel forces have landed on Efate already and are advancing upon us. I have made a note of those who have served the Bank by sitting watches during the night and I will report to London accordingly."

He turned his cold gaze towards the three ex-pats from Santo. "I should like to be able to report the safe arrival of the Santo staff as well as the security of the Bank's Keys & Codes. I cannot yet do that." The three miscreants shifted from foot to foot and took great interest in the way they'd laced their shoes.

"Does anyone have any ideas how we might …remedy this vital security breach?" He scanned the faces before him.

There was silence in the room for a few seconds. The accountant, Joe, then perked up. "Could Head Office issue a replacement set for Santo? It would only take a week or two to get here and I'm sure it'll be at least a fortnight before the guys can return."

Cutlass was very still. He exhaled a deep breath, examined the blotter on his desk and made a minute adjustment to the positioning of the capped fountain pen beside it. Then, in measured tones, he said, "Joe, if you thought for a little while before you opened your mouth, it would be helpful. You would realise that every branch and sub-branch of Royal Counties Bank in the whole world uses the same Keys and Codes. If there is a set missing, THE WHOLE ROYAL COUNTIES BANK COMMUNICATIONS SYSTEM IS COMPROMISED."

He brought his hand down hard onto his desk to emphasise the last word. A vein pulsed in Cutlass' temple and he was flushing with anger. Suddenly an idea dropped into Patrick's head. Without following the advice to think an idea through before airing it, he took advantage of the brief lull in the Chief Manager's storm to offer, "Andrew? We could fetch the copies in Santo."

Andrew Cutlass glared at the lad. He was still shaking with the vehemence of his outburst at Joe. A sudden vision of his whole career path falling apart flashed before him. He knew he'd never achieve high managerial status in Royal Counties Bank in the UK. But he had reckoned to be able to put aside plenty of money if he got himself onto the ex-pat circuit. It would be enough to keep his expensive wife happy and they would retire in some luxury. He had served the Bank in Africa in several places. Other than a couple of run-ins with the local mafia (as he put it), he'd ended each posting with many tens of thousands of pounds and dollars on deposit in the Channel Islands. After the posting to Vila, he was well on the way to doubling that now. But if he were to be the Chief Manager under whose watch Royal Counties Bank mislaid their most secret global communications method, he would likely be sacked. Even worse would be demotion to managing Stationery Department in Milton Keynes or wherever it was. There was no way on earth he would confess to this security lapse if he could help it.

In the few seconds it took him to respond to Patrick's blurted suggestion, his mouth opened and closed twice. The first time was his immediate reaction to roar at the stupid boy, but he held off in time. He gripped the edge of his desk to steady himself and breathed in deeply. When he believed he had control over his voice, he asked, "Anything from anyone else?"

Heads shook; eyes were downcast. Silence ruled.

"And, how exactly do you propose to achieve this feat, Patrick?"

Thinking fast, Patrick said, "I'm sure I could borrow a boat from someone at the Sailing Club. I could take a few people, including some to interpret if we should run into locals there, and then …go to the branch and remove the Keys & Codes."

"Just like that?"

"Um …I'm sure there are a few more details to think about, but …yes, basically."

Andrew Cutlass found himself in a difficult position. He had no ideas to contribute himself and was thus dependent upon his staff. Of the two suggestions thus far, one would fail immediately and obviously. He expected better of his accountant. The second was hare-brained and risky. Worse still, it was that idiot Field who had put it forward and he'd have to tell Head Office of whatever Patrick's role might be. But then Cutlass realised that if the effort failed, there was at least a chance he could blame it all on Field. He could try to avoid a complete career crash for himself. And then again, it might even work…

"Very well," he said. "Get back to me this afternoon with your plan. Back to work, everyone."

Still smarting after Cutlass' outburst, Joe murmured to Patrick to join him in his office. Raymond, the Sub-Branch manager from Santo was there too. Patrick explained they could sail up to the northern island, arriving after dark. The hope would be to make their way, unseen, into Luganville town. Raymond was too scared to volunteer to go and too shaken even to remember whether they'd locked up after themselves. As Patrick had the sailing experience and it was his idea anyway, he took charge of the recovery mission. Cyclone season had ended in April, and weather was likely to be fair until November at least.

"I can go and find John, one of the visiting 'Yachties' who came in last week and is still in port. I reckon he'd be up for a bit of adventure," Patrick said. "We'll need his boat for at least four days; perhaps five."

Joe authorised a modest sum of local currency so Patrick could bargain to hire the twin masted vessel.

"Bear in mind, Patrick, that's to include putting up any crew in the Rossi with full board. They'll have to pay for their own beers," Joe cautioned. He knew the reputation these people had for thirst.

Before putting the proposal to John, Patrick hand-picked some local staff, familiar with Luganville. They had the necessary language skills. John did not need much persuasion. So Patrick had secured his means of transport. Now he needed a few more men. He headed for the sailing club. Some folks would hang around there in the belief it was safer than being in town.

"Hey, Dave! Are you busy for a few days?"

Dave worked for an oil prospecting company and was never in his office. Instead, he worked on his tan, sailed a bit, repaired things and was more of an odd-job worker than an oil executive.

"I'll check my diary, Mate …Waddya have in mind?"

"It's a bit of an adventure - sort of 'Secret Sam' stuff and it involves sailing, so I thought of you!"

"Go on," said Dave. "Is beer involved?"

"When we get back, I'll stand you dinner at the Rossi plus all you can drink."

"And a slab for the weekend...?" Dave tried to add a dozen cans of beer to his price.

"OK." Patrick held out his hand and they shook on it. "I haven't told you everything yet, though."

Dave raised an amused eyebrow. "That's best at this stage, don't you think?" They both laughed. "If you need someone else, I'll ask Simon over there. He won the regional 470 championship last year."

Patrick only knew Simon by sight, but if Dave vouched for him, he'd be valuable. "Sure, Dave. It'll likely be for around five days."

He went back to the bank and briefed Andrew Cutlass. The man waved assent. He believed it was hare-brained, but at least it would get rid of Field for a few days while he took care of the branch.

Patrick's little band all packed a couple of changes of clothing and some provisions.

He outlined his plan on the quayside, made introductions and they boarded.

With the owner's help, Patrick topped up the water and fuel tanks of the *Lucky Sue*. They set sail for Luganville harbour, some 170 nautical miles from Efate. The journey north would likely take a day and a half each way. But they'd need some luck for wind and currents to average 5 knots. The outward journey would take a little less time; a little more for the return.

"The SE Trade wind is dependable", John told him. "We'll be able to get past the wind-shadow of Malekula before darkness."

The return journey might be harder, as they'd be beating into the wind. But John assured him that the engine was reliable and powerful if the wind wasn't strong enough. And one of the Lucky Sue's regular crewmen, Tom, was going too, so could sort any problems with the running gear.

Once the course had been set and the sails trimmed, there was little for Patrick and the others to do. They passed the time by looking out for wind direction changes and other shipping. Patrick, Dave and Simon were all keen dinghy sailors. These high-performance machines needed constant trimming of sails, rudder, centreboard and other controls to go fast for short periods of time. The lack of need for such fiddling aboard the *'Lucky Sue'* was frustrating. Patrick couldn't help glancing at his watch and the speed indicator on the cockpit coaming. This was when he'd voiced his worries to John that they might not get near enough to Luganville before the wind dropped away.

But John had said, "She needs her bottom cleaned" and reassured him that he was worrying unnecessarily. The *'Lucky Sue'* ploughed onwards.

They watched as the sun dropped in the sky. Patrick always waited for a 'hiss' as the super-heated star made contact with the cold water of the Pacific. His uncle had teased him with this pretend observation when he was younger. Little by little, the details of the distant shoreline became indistinct. It diminished to a darker line between the ocean and the softer sky. It was dark as they approached Million Dollar point. This is the headland on the south east side of Espiritu Santo where the US Military dumped millions of dollars' worth of supplies after the Second World War. The British and French authorities had elected not to pay for guns and vehicles left behind and the Americans took umbrage.

Luminescence from breaking surf flickered along the shore line.

He turned to John. "Should we turn off those riding lights?" John agreed and gave the order. They also brought down the sails. The breeze had dropped so they were making very little way and the boat was beginning to wallow. Leaving the sails up risked making them more visible to any watchers on shore. The pale white spread of canvas would catch any trace of light once the moon rose. Patrick's plan was to anchor close in to the beach on the south side, along from Million dollar point. Here, Canal Road ran close to the water. Then they'd row ashore and walk the remaining Kilometre into town. The Santo staff had said shortly after Canal Road became Main Street, the main dock would be on their left. Royal Counties Bank would be on their right, according to the map drawn out for him.

Pressing the engine 'Start' button at first produced a series of explosive coughs and puffs of evil-smelling smoke. But the diesel lump thankfully settled to an even and muffled chugging. The contrast was loud, of course, after the rhythmic slatting and creaking of the craft under sail and made Patrick wince. He was painfully aware that sound carries a long way over water. He kept telling himself that it wouldn't matter while they were still out at sea where there was a slight swell to break up the sound. The dangerous time would come as they entered the Creek. There the water was flat and calm. Soon they drew close to the beach and the harbour of Luganville itself.

The fleeing staff had told wild-eyed stories of armed locals running amok with machetes and small firearms. Hence their hurried departure. But Patrick's plan was to land in darkness and make their way into town to try to reach the branch unseen. The *Lucky Sue* crept along the coast until one of the men signalled there was a buoy indicating narrowing of the channel. Patrick knocked the engine out of gear. As the schooner lost way completely, he ordered the anchor to be dropped. It was attached to some 40 feet of chain before the main length of rope and the noise it made running out made him grimace. It was very characteristic and would make it obvious to any watchers on shore what they were doing. At last John agreed enough rope had been laid. Patrick nudged the engine into reverse for a few seconds to dig the anchor into the ground. Now, he could kill it. The immediate near silence was almost oppressive and emphasised to Patrick how noisy they had been. It took a couple of minutes for their hearing to adjust to the new level of sound. There were only water noises. Gentle surf breaking on the shore. Occasional wavelets slapping against the hull or the rudder beneath the aft counter. A halyard clacked against the main mast. John's deck hand Tom tightened it and tied off a lanyard as far above his head as he could reach to quieten the noise. All was secure. Armed with his diving knife, Patrick helped wrap rags around the oars to silence them while rowing the dinghy ashore.

Other than mild creaking and an occasional 'plash' from an oar catching the top of a wave, the men impressed him with how quiet it was possible to be. The whiff of rotted seaweed was the first sign of how close they were to the edge of the water. Soon enough, the hull ground onto the foreshore and before they pulled it up the beach a little way. Patrick asked them to rotate the craft 180 degrees: "Stern first, ready for a quick escape," he whispered.

Moving up the beach towards the blackness of the treeline, the sounds of the sea gave way to night-time insect life as cicadas and grasshoppers got to work.

"Wait here for a couple of minutes." Patrick wanted to accustom their ears to the new environment. All else was quiet and nothing moved. Their senses were on high alert, though, as New Hebrideans could move through jungle without sound, and appear or disappear at will. The same would likely be true of anyone left in town, especially as the insurrection will have made them wary of groups of men. Satisfied for the moment, Patrick continued up the beach and through the scrub by the road. He led his motley band west along the road edge. They darted from tree shadow to tree shadow, pausing to listen every so often.

Now they were separated from the Creek by a row of buildings, there was almost complete silence. The lapping noises of the water and occasional calls of birds settling for the night had receded. The air was still and humid and Patrick knew any tiny sound would be amplified. He could hear even their cautious tread along the broken sidewalks.

Here was the Royal Counties Bank branch. Patrick held his hand up to signify that they should wait. Nothing moved, although a dog barked in the far distance. He realised he was crouching. This was unnecessary and painful. Straightening up and rolling his shoulders released a little of the tension in his body. They all stared at the front of the Royal Counties Bank branch building. The front door was ajar. No need for the key, then.

Patrick turned his head to one of the Port Vila staff who came from a village on Santo. "The door is open," he whispered.

"*Hemi left quicktime*," explained Japin.

'No kidding', thought Patrick. Checking around for signs of life, he stepped forward, nodding his head at the others to come too. They moved quickly over the road and flattened themselves against the wall beside the bank. Patrick scanned the upper storeys of the buildings whose shelter they'd left, but saw nothing untoward. He peered cautiously around the door frame into the darkened banking hall. They all slipped inside.

Never having visited the Santo branch, Patrick was reliant upon a floor layout drawing done by an escaped member of staff. "*Japin?*

*Yufela go longplas back door; mekim unlock.*"
If they were caught by a passing rebel patrol, they'd need a way out. The sub-branch was much smaller than the Port Vila main office. There were only two cashier positions and some partitioned wood and glass offices for the management. The whole space was dominated by the safe, which was exactly the same model as Patrick was familiar with in Vila.

He'd memorised its combination to open the door, but had also written it on a piece of paper to be sure of getting it right. Rotating his Maglite illuminated the safe. He held it between his teeth and bent to bring his face close to the dial centred in the venerable, dark grey door. Why was his pulse pounding in his ears?

He began turning the dial, but paused, knowing that he needed to relax to enter the numbers accurately. Stiff, worried fingers moved jerkily, he knew, and might over-shoot the numbers. He'd have to start again. He flexed his fingers as best he could. It flashed through his mind that this area of the South West Pacific was subject to minor earthquakes. Tremors could play havoc with lock tumblers, shifting the pre-set codes. Thus the thing would refuse to unlock. That meant flying in a specialist from Chubb in Australia to open the safe. Not helpful! Patrick tried to empty his mind of such thoughts. He concentrated on his breathing for a moment. In – one, two, three. Out – one, two, three, four. In – one, two, three. Out – one, two, three, four.

And began to turn the dial again.

Clockwise to 23.

Anti-clockwise back to 38.

Clockwise again to 12.

And now the last number: back to 29.

Did he imagine it? Was there a slight movement of metal in the door? He stood up and pulled at the lever. He pulled harder and all the bolts shot back, swinging open the door. Japin's teeth gleamed with delight as Patrick looked round. "So far, so good," he whispered.

He pointed his torch inside the vault, aiming it at the floor. It illuminated stacked safe-deposit boxes, a few paintings leaning against the wall and the line of locked tills on jockey wheels. And up on a shelf, wedged against the Head Office Procedural Instructions Parts 1 and 2 were the leather-bound volumes of Keys & Codes! Exactly what they had come for.

He pulled them down and turned to leave. "Hey, what about all the money?" asked Dave, his sailing friend.

Patrick looked back. There were several hundred thousand N.H. francs in neat bundles visible behind some light metal mesh. Patrick's Chief Manager hadn't briefed him on what to do with the money. Cutlass had been so consumed by the threat to his own employment prospects of losing control of the Keys and Codes. Surely, it was daft not to rescue as much as they could carry, though.

Dave's eyes were very wide, Patrick saw. This was likely far more money than the lad had ever seen in his life. Patrick also saw that Dave was shrugging a back pack off his shoulders. "Sure. Why not?" Patrick agreed. "But we need to open the mesh cage…"

Dave produced a jack-knife out of his pack. Its stout marlin spike made short work of the flimsy lock and together they grabbed wads of notes, stuffing them into the bag. "We ought to count it," mumbled Patrick.

"No time," hissed Dave. "Look: there's more up there."

At last, their haul was complete. The others had been keeping watch at the front, cringing every time there was a noise from inside the branch. Patrick and Dave backed out of the strong-room, spinning the dial when the door swung shut. Japin led the way out of the front door. He leaned on the wall outside, as though pausing on his way along the main street. That position let him scan up and down the road. Satisfied, he turned and gave the 'all clear'. One by one, they filtered out to stand beside him. Patrick pulled the branch door closed until it clicked into place and locked it.

"Back to the boat," he ordered, clutching the precious books. "Come on - quietly."

They retraced their steps with growing confidence that they were actually succeeding. Once, someone kicked a stone by mistake. The noise of its bouncing along the road was so loud that anyone nearby would have heard. Patrick halted immediately and glared at the guilty man. He raised one finger to his lips. But no shouted challenge came and after a short pause to look around and ease jangled nerves, they continued.

By the time they reached the boat, they were all business-like again. Patrick and Dave boarded, carrying the Keys and Codes and backpack of money. The others shoved the craft back into the water, flip-flops scrunching on the coral beach. The two men at the bow dipped their muffled oars into the water and pulled. As the shore fell behind and the bottom dropped away, they could bring two more oars into play. They aimed at the silhouette of the schooner against the night sky.

Patrick sat in the stern, looking forward at his little crew. Their faces shone with the adrenaline rush of excitement and perspiration from the effort of rowing. "Ship oars," he said as the bulk of the larger craft loomed over them. The boat's way carried them several more yards. Japin fended off and grasped the mooring line they'd left over the side. He held the rowing boat close to the *Lucky Sue* so everyone could scramble on board.

Japin was last up over the rail and made the row boat's painter fast so it would bob about in their wake all the way back to Port Vila. There was not a breath of wind yet, so with reluctance, Patrick started the engine. They hauled anchor and John pointed the bow seaward. Glancing over their stern, Patrick watched the beach recede. There had been no sign of any life during their visit - no sign that they had been detected at all. Glancing at his wrist watch, he realised dawn would break soon and the sky would be lighter. The wind would start blowing too. He hoped they'd be well out at sea, perhaps even past Malo and out of reach of the rebels by then. At that point, they could hoist sail and look like wandering Yachties to any look-outs.

Patrick had asked Jessica, as doctor at Vila Base hospital, to alert someone in the radio room. He wanted them to keep a channel open during the very early morning to listen out for their return. Two-way radio was the only method of communication between islands, so there was nothing surprising about this. Patrick bent his head over the chart table, wishing he remembered more basic navigation. He'd attended an R.Y.A. course a couple of years earlier, but time had made the details hazy. It was all straightforward geometry, but he always confused sines with tangents and cosines. He took a bearing as they eased past Malo island heading for the east coast of Malekula. John checked his calculations.

"Not bad ...for a beginner," opined the owner of the *'Lucky Sue'*. Patrick opened the radio channel.

"*Lucky Sue* to Vila Base, come in, please."

He repeated the call. And the second time, instead of the empty hiss of static, there came an answer, "This is Vila Base, *Lucky Sue*. Where are you? Over."

Patrick gave their position and suggested they'd arrive in Efate itself late morning the next day, depending on the wind strength overnight. He requested that somebody tell Dr Jessica and Andrew Cutlass at Royal Counties Bank. Even over the poor connection, he thought the radio operator sounded startled at his mention of someone at a bank. Hospital or medical messages were the usual fare. But as a rebellion was under way, these were strange and unsettled times. He was confident that the message would get to Dr Jessica at least. She'd be sure to inform the bank.

-----//-----

Sure enough, Efate hove into view the next day. They navigated by sight alone into Mele Bay and on into the port area where *Lucky Sue* had her temporary berth. As they

259

approached, Patrick saw Andrew Cutlass waiting on the quayside. The Chief Manager had awarded himself an extended lunchbreak at the Rossi Hotel. He was using its terrific view of the bay to spot their arrival. It was also right beside the branch, so if marauding secessionists arrived in town, he could dive into his bank and lock up. Patrick knew the view well, having sunk many beers at the Rossi with his Australian and Kiwi mates. They'd watch the sun go down between the opposing spits of land with Ifira Island on the left.

John, as the boat's owner, took the helm to manoeuvre 'Lucky Sue' around to moor stern first against the dock. Dave had already positioned fenders on both sides and Japin tied off the stern lines which he'd thrown out. John was casting a swift critical eye over his craft, checking for damage. "Are you going to clean this up a bit?" He eyed the crumpled sails which hadn't yet been stowed and a paper bag lurking between the coaming and a hatch cover. No doubt it used to contain sandwiches but there was no point trying to establish the guilty party. His usual crew wouldn't dare to leave the craft like this.

"Sure," Patrick smiled weakly. "First things first, though." Cutlass was almost hopping up and down, itching for news.

"What news?"

Patrick smiled by way of answer and held up the two heavy tomes, wrapped in plastic sheeting in case of water splashes.

"And we brought out most of the cash too... Dave?" He turned back to peer down the hatchway.

Dave's head bobbed up for a second. "Hang about," he called. "I'm getting it." A moment later the backpack appeared, followed by Dave's tousled hair. The pack was handed over. "I want that back, you know."

"Don't worry, Dave," said Patrick. "I'll bring it back here this afternoon right after we've put the cash in the safe."

"How much is there?" asked Cutlass.

Despite the obvious success of the whole mission, this opening salvo put Patrick immediately on the defensive. His months in the branch taught him that Andrew Cutlass had a way of asking exactly the question you hoped he wouldn't. It didn't matter that you had completed 99 out of 100 tasks correctly. Cutlass would somehow know to ask about the 100th. Learning it was incomplete, he would fly into a rage, disproportionate to the size of the offence.

On this occasion, three things had put Patrick off balance. The first was that he recalled the backpack weighing more when stowed on board. Indeed, they'd had trouble closing the ties at the top when they'd stuffed in the money, so great were the bulges in the sides. Now, as he passed it over the stern, he saw creases from the top to the bottom and could easily lift it with one hand. The second was the stab of guilt that he had clean forgotten to count it all! He had been so bound up with the moment and the importance of escaping undetected. He meant to do the counting later, when danger had passed and there was time to do it. And the third was the misleading air of forced tranquillity about Andrew Cutlass. Experience with the man suggested this appearance was akin to chambering a shell in a gun. From this point onwards, any light pressure on the trigger would precipitate a loud bang of confected fury.

He sighed. There was no real way out of it. "I can't remember exactly, Andrew, but it's written down somewhere. I'll carry it to the branch and we can recount under dual control." He waited for the explosion of ire, but this mild stretching of the truth may have missed the trigger and averted trouble, at least for the moment.

Cutlass nodded curt thanks to John, turned and hurried towards the branch, clutching the precious books of Keys and Codes. He'd already torn a strip off the Santo staff for what he called 'dereliction of duty'. He expected to work himself into another angered frenzy prompted by relief that Field had averted disaster. There was no telephone communication abroad even before the insurrection. His choices were between an intermittent radio telephone to Australia and a chattering telex tape machine to reach anywhere else. On purpose, he omitted mention of the Keys and Codes from his hurried telexed report to Controlling Office in London. Ever since, he'd been plotting different strategies for explaining their loss. London was pressing him for updates and he hadn't yet worked out what to say.

His first telex had read:

VILA TO HO [STOP] SANTO BRANCH EVACUATED SUCCESSFULLY [STOP] EX-PAT AND SENIOR STAFF IN VILA [STOP]

OTHERS BELIEVED SAFE AND WELL [STOP] MORE FOLLOWS [ENDS]

He sent that 3 days ago. More recently, there was evidence of several attempted contacts on the branch telex machine. The ticker tape showed Head Office's identifier code when his secretary, Gail, ran it back. But the messages were incomplete, because the electricity supply to the branch had gone down. Power outages gave him a perfect excuse for not updating his earlier report, but he knew he ought not stretch the bounds of credulity too far.

Now he could send a more detailed report of the success of the expedition led by Patrick. He could say that the Keys and Codes had been recovered and were under lock and key. And the lad had brought back some of the money. Andrew's eyes narrowed. Did he bring all the cash? The Santo accountant had wilted under terse questioning. He pretty much admitted he had no clue about the total cash balance and had even started crying when Andrew yelled at him. Utterly useless…

Here was something of a quandary. If Cutlass announced that he had sanctioned this cobbled-together expedition, it might put him in a bad light. These were enthusiastic but amateur staff members and non-bank helpers. Because he had permitted them to set off to another island, bristling with armed insurrectionists, to rescue the Keys and Codes and cash, Head Office might criticise him for putting staff in harm's way. Such opprobrium would be career-limiting. What grated for him was that he would be duty-bound to speak in glowing terms about his idiot member of staff, Patrick Field. The lad had the idea in the first place and then led the whole thing. Probably the fool would receive a letter of commendation from Head Office – even a pay rise.

No, better by far to keep quiet about that. Head Office might assume the escaping staff brought the Keys and Codes down to Vila from Santo. But what to do about the cash Field had brought? When eventually the authorities said it was safe to return to the island and it was discovered that the bank cupboard was bare, he could pretend the rebels had broken in somehow and stolen it all. Yes, that was the story he should use. The Bank could claim insurance. Besides, the Chief Manager's house could do with redecorating and he needed to pay dues for the local 'security' from Tai Nguyen.

Where was the lad? Cutlass turned. "Come on; come on – we need to get that cash into the branch." Patrick trotted along behind, trying to catch up. He'd paused to ask John to look after his bag of clothes and supplies and promised to come back later to help clean the boat and return Dave's back pack. But that gave Andrew a 50 feet head start. A 'Thank you' might have been nice, Patrick thought, weariness beginning to affect him after the elation of the last few days drained away.

There were still a few members of staff tidying up as the Vila branch accountant unlocked the front door to let them in. Patrick clocked Joe's hunted expression as Andrew stomped past, not even bothering with a, "What news?"

He guessed the man had been like a bear with a sore head all the while, finding fault with everything and everyone. To Patrick's surprise, the Chief Manager turned sharp right up the stairs to his office, rather than hand the Keys and Codes to Joe. "Bring that bag," he ordered.

Patrick trailed behind, meekly, uncomfortably aware of not having showered in four days. Once upstairs, they approached Andrew's secretary, Gail. Her desk and filing cabinets were immediately outside the Chief Manager's office. "I do not want to be disturbed," barked Andrew. Gail nodded assent but smiled at Patrick.

"Are you alright, Love?" she asked, "We've all been on tenterhooks waiting for you to come back."

Patrick nodded. "Fine, thanks. A bit tired, now, I suppose, but it all went very well." He followed Andrew into the man's office.

"Shut the door," Andrew said, rather too quietly for Patrick's liking. Such forced control was another warning sign usually indicating that irritation was building in the Chief Manager's head. It would grow and grow until the anger boiled over. At that point, when his anger peaked, Andrew had been known to seize the ashtray from his desk and hurl it at the departing frightened member of staff. There were many dents on the inside of the office door bearing witness to past outbursts. Gail kept a small dustpan and brush handy at her desk to clear up the glass fragments when they occurred. Indeed, she had persuaded the accountant to indent for a whole box of Royal Counties Bank ashtrays from London. "Gifts for customers," they called it.

Patrick had mentioned this violent habit during one Sunday night Barbeque to someone from ANZ Bank. "I told you before: the bloke's gone troppo, mate," his friend observed, with the precise and dry wit so common in West Australia. "Spent too long in the tropics – now he can never leave," the man explained.

The office door was duly closed and Patrick advanced towards the Chief Manager's desk with the back pack of cash.

"Sit down," commanded Andrew Cutlass. "Well done for …getting back the Keys and Codes." Patrick sensed a certain gritting of teeth; this was not easy. "We need to have an understanding, though."

Patrick wasn't following this at all. Cutlass started again: "The important thing is that we have back the Keys and Codes." He paused, unsure of how to put into words what he wanted to say. "I will telex London immediately. The thing is…"

He tailed off. Patrick began to speculate if perhaps he was not the source of irritation, for once.

"Yes?"

"The thing is, it would be best if some of the …ah, details were kept between us, do you see?"

"Not really." Patrick frowned. He couldn't grasp why this whole episode should not be the source of a somewhat simple and joyful message back to Head Office. It had been a complete success, after all.

"It will be best if you leave all that to me. The less Head Office know about this affair, the fewer awkward questions will be asked."

Patrick shook his head. Questions? Awkward ones? This wasn't making any sense at all.

Cutlass fixed him with a hard stare. "Where is the rest of the money?"

Patrick could feel his face colouring up. It wasn't fair to be made to feel bad or guilty about what had been such an exciting adventure - daring, even. Especially when it had succeeded completely. And he felt that he was being accused of stealing when he simply hadn't.

"Sorry? I didn't …I mean, there isn't any more. We grabbed whatever we could. It was dark." He realised he was gabbling.

"Don't lie to me, boy," said Cutlass. "I know there was much more cash in Santo branch than this," brandishing the backpack aloft.

"Maybe we missed some," offered Patrick. "And we didn't open the tills. We took what was in the cage."

Andrew glowered at him. "Maybe. Let's say the Santo staff brought the Keys and Codes with them and *some* of the money." Patrick opened his mouth to object, but the other man held up his hand. "And then I'll keep your name out of the report about the money."

This all came as an unpleasant shock to Patrick. Cutlass was implying that Patrick had stolen most of the cash. Stunned at the injustice of this turn of events, he got up and retreated to the door.

"Well?" roared Cutlass. "Do you understand?"

"Yes, Andrew," Patrick managed, although there was a very solid lump in his throat. A hot tear brimmed in both eyes. He almost ran past Gail, not wanting to meet her gaze. Too late, he realised he had forgotten Dave's backpack.

He stopped at the head of the stairs, wiped his eyes furiously with the back of his hands and tried to steady his voice. Gail, bless her, was holding out a box of tissues. He accepted one, with gratitude, and blew his nose.

"Thank you, Gail. Um, I left my friend's back pack in there by mistake. Do you think you could fetch it when …well, you know?"

"Of course, I will, Patrick. Off you go, home. See you in the morning."

Patrick tried to smile. "OK. Thanks again."

He descended the stairs to the banking hall in a daze. The accountant was still fussing about trying to hurry the last of the cashiers still tilling up. He glanced at Patrick. "You look like you've seen a ghost. Guess Andrew was his usual cheery self, eh?"

Upstairs, Cutlass was thumbing through the piles of damp and salty-smelling notes. It totalled a little over 120,000 New Hebridean francs. He needed to pay 100,000 to Tai Nguyen so there would be only 20,000 for his house improvements. Nowhere near enough for what Mrs Cutlass had in mind. Still, it would have to do. He threw the back pack into the bin and put the money into his desk drawer. Locking it, he straightened his blotter and picked up his car keys.

He opened the office door and with the same forced calmness in his voice he said, "I'm going home now, Gail. See you in the morning" and breezed out with a lightness of step that belied the pressing turmoil in his head.

# Chapter 12
## Nguyen strikes

Patrick headed home for a well-earned shower and shave. But before the turn-off for *Numba Tu* district where he lived, the road was narrowed by the ever-encroaching jungle. Here, a car crash had blocked it. He guessed he was first on the scene, not that there was usually a lot of traffic. He drew closer. Three vehicles were involved. A saloon car had buried itself between the front and rear wheels of a small truck and about twenty feet beyond was the tailgate of another white pickup. As he brought his car to a halt, there were four foreign men engaged in fierce argument. He was about to get out to offer help when, without warning, one man produced a gun and shot at two of the others. One was hit and fell where he stood. The second bullet winged its target, who limped as quickly as he could for cover, clutching his leg. The third ducked behind the short wheelbase truck, and sprinted into the bush. The gunman looked around and of course saw Patrick. As the man levelled his weapon at Patrick's car, he slammed it into reverse gear and backed away fast. At maximum revs, he 'J' turned and floored the accelerator pedal to get out of the gunman's sight line around the nearby bend. There were a couple of shots but no corresponding strikes on the car. How could the man have missed? The range wasn't that great.

Patrick was horrified. His sleepy, laid-back Port Vila posting was descending into a dangerous hotbed of insurrection and criminality. He resolved to get back to his flat by another route. Navigation had never been his strongest suit, but there was a bumpy track through a village he'd found while Hash running that he could use instead. As he searched for the turn-off to the village, he remembered with a bit of a jolt that the truck half buried in the trees was a white Toyota pickup. Surely it wasn't the Bon Plats pickup? Not again? Evidence of mounting wrongdoing associated with Bon Plats lay around every corner.

It was his habit to park in the driveway beside the Bank flats. Today he drove his silver Starlet all the way into the car port in front of his flat. He dragged a tarpaulin over it in case the gunman should come searching and tapped on his neighbour's door.

"Kim? Are you here?"

Kim came to the door. "Sure am. How'd it go? I heard you had called Jessica to say you were on your way back. Um …don't take this the wrong way, but you look a bit …er, 'Wild Man of Borneo'. Is everything alright?"

Patrick realised he was starting to shake uncontrollably, because of delayed shock. "Someone shot at me."

"What?! Shot at you? With a gun? Have the men arrived already from Santo?"

"I don't think it was them. These weren't New Hebrideans – I think they were Asian - I don't know - Vietnamese or Chinese? I can't tell the difference."

"I told you not to get mixed up in that gun-running stuff. Who did you tell, other than me?"

"This was a car crash – an accident, I expect – at least… Oh, I don't know. Maybe it was done on purpose by one lot fighting against another lot. The point is that they couldn't have known I was driving down the road towards them when they all collided. I reckon I was an unlucky observer who happened upon the scene of a crash."

"So why did they shoot at you?"

Patrick tried to steady his nerves and thought for a second. "Actually, I was in my car and not very far away from the gunman. He didn't hit the car and I thought it odd that he couldn't aim well enough to hit me. Perhaps they were warning shots to make me get lost, so he shot wide."

"Brandy."

"Sorry?"

"You need a nip of brandy. It always steadies the nerves."

It must have taken Patrick almost a second to consider this proposition before he accepted. "If you say so."

Patrick extended Kim's logic to requesting a second 'nip' to steady his nerves even more. Kim agreed on condition that Patrick go next door immediately to shower and change. "You stink," he volunteered.

-----//-----

Patrick felt a little better once clean and shaved and after a night's rest. The next morning, he caught a lift into town with Kim, (whose Starlet was beige rather than the silver of Patrick's car. It was also a newer model). On the way, he related some of the events on Santo, but gave Kim more details of the crash. They took a roundabout route to try to make sure they'd avoid any of the crash participants who might have returned to the scene.

To Patrick's surprise, Kim advised him to make a Police report and also to tell Andrew Cutlass.

"I know I said to keep out of it, but someone might have seen your car at the crash. They could report it themselves to try to shape a different version of the story. Once the Police have that, you'll be in trouble. Better to file your recollection first."

"Ok. I suppose I agree, but we both suspect Andrew of being tied up in all this, somehow. Why should I tell him?"

"Because when the brown stuff hits the fan, you need him to repatriate you to the UK. He represents Royal Counties Bank, depends on them for his pension and has to take care of his staff – even if they do go on commando-style raids to neighbouring islands in the dead of night!"

Even though Kim was driving, Patrick couldn't resist poking him in the ribs. "It wasn't all like that – honestly. But …ok. I'll tell him."

They drove up to the bank and parked nearby. Patrick went straight upstairs to the

Chief Manager, although his feet didn't want to make the climb. They dragged on the bright blue carpet of each step. He expected the next five minutes to be very unpleasant.

Cutlass was at his desk, writing something. He glanced up when Patrick knocked on the open door.

"What news?" But then he saw Patrick's serious face and demanded, "What is it now?"

He listened as Patrick gave a shortened version of coming upon a road traffic accident as he neared home the previous evening. How he was shot at and retreated back around the bend in the road.

Cutlass insisted that Patrick, "Leave it with me". Later that day, a New Hebridean Police Officer came to the Bank. The man spent an hour listening to Patrick's story, writing it out laboriously into a formal statement. Eventually Patrick signed it and the officer witnessed it.

Patrick watched the officer as he walked the length of the banking hall to the door of the branch. And also watched him hand the statement to Andrew Cutlass on his way out! He was about to protest when Sara called out to ask him about a telephone enquiry she was handling. She was covering the mouthpiece with her hand to muffle conversation, so it was clear the customer was waiting. He needed to take care of the enquiry immediately.

As soon as he could get away, Patrick ran upstairs to Andrew Cutlass' office to ask what was going on. Gail stopped him. "Andrew doesn't want to be disturbed, Patrick – you know how he gets if he is interrupted."

"But he's got my Police statement in there – it ought to have gone with the Policeman, shouldn't it?"

"I believe Andrew agreed with the officer that it could be kept as a private matter."

"But, Gail, the whole point of making a statement to the Police was to pre-empt anyone else filing their version of events and setting a false narrative."

"I do understand, Patrick. But Andrew knows what is best. Anyway, he is on the phone at the moment, sorting it out for you."

-----//-----

Cutlass had straightaway gone to his office. He told Gail he wasn't to be disturbed and had actually locked the door from inside.

He picked up his telephone and dialled a number from memory.

"Tai Nguyen, please. Andrew Cutlass." There was a short pause. "I've got Field's statement. Ok – where?"

He folded the paper and tucked it into his slim document folder. He'd go shopping on his way home that afternoon.

Behind the meat counter at Bon Plats was an unassuming door marked 'Staff only'. It led to Nguyen's office. Cutlass had used it many times before. He checked around to make sure he was unobserved and pushed it open.

"Here is Field's statement as you asked. I've got some more information for you on top of that."

Nguyen held out his hand and took the papers. "Show me. What information?"

"Field went up to Santo branch and brought back money from the bank safe there. But he handed over much, much less than I know was in the safe. I believe he kept the greater part of it for himself."

"So – he stole cash as well as making a local girl pregnant and helping with illegal money transfers? Very interesting. It is well that my man saw him at the crash site. I will make sure he keeps his mouth shut."

"You won't do anything ...terminal will you?" Cutlass became alarmed.

"Not this time. The boy might be useful. Do you think he will ever achieve promotion in the bank?"

"Pah!" Cutlass scoffed at the idea of such a foolish lad ever assuming a position of authority in Royal Counties Bank. But then he realised conveying that hopelessness to Nguyen would likely sign the boy's death warrant. "Um. We have a saying in the bank. People like Field 'rise to one level above their competence'. So, yes, I expect the bank will promote him to some middle management role, probably in Head Office."

"Excellent. The boy does have promise then. I hope it does not take too long – for his sake. I trust you can assist with that progress? Keep me informed. And, Andrew? In view of this, you need not make this month's payment."

"Most generous, thank you. Thank you. I'll ...erm, leave you in peace."

Nguyen waved his hand in dismissal and Cutlass backed out of the room. When he was alone, Bon Plats' owner made another series of careful notations in his file on Patrick.

He pushed his chair over to the photocopier and typewriter. Using an ink eraser, a Biro and a soft pencil, he began making judicious amendments to a copy of Patrick's statement. At length he sat back and reread it. He wasn't happy with a couple of the pen strokes he'd made, trying to alter words to their opposite meaning, but perhaps if he smudged them with some ink and made a copy of the copy..? Or he could retype it? Yes. That would be best and it would appear more official.

-----//-----

Patrick didn't have a chance to tackle Andrew Cutlass about the matter the next morning as Cutlass was late into the bank. As soon as the branch opened, three New Hebrideans in the uniform of British Policemen came in and asked Patrick to go with them.

"Am I under arrest?" he asked, as they told him to step into the customer area.

"Mr Field, you are accused of causing an accident and running two trucks off the road in *Numba Tu* district. You are not obliged to say anything, but anything you do say will be written down and may be given in evidence against you. It may harm your defence if you do not mention, when questioned, something that you later rely on in Court."

The Policeman continued, "We have taken note of your signed confession. It has been accepted and you will appear before a judge in a couple of days' time."

"My 'signed confession'? What 'signed confession'? I made a statement to a Policeman yesterday about what I saw as I drove around a corner on the way home. I didn't *confess* to anything."

"Come with us to the Police Station, please – now." One Policeman jangled the handcuffs on his belt meaningfully, so Patrick went along with them.

Seated at the back of a Police car, Patrick noted that the internal door handles had been removed. He wrinkled his nose at the lingering stench of vomit which the open windows did little to clear. He told himself that the journey would have been far worse had the windows been shut.

They arrived at the roundabout beside the 'British' prison. He'd driven by it in the past, but had no occasion to enter, of course. There were no gates, but there was a sentry box at the side. The armed guard didn't bother to cover his mouth to stifle a yawn. His mates were driving the Police car so he didn't even rise from his shaded seat. A lazy handwave acknowledged their arrival. 'This wasn't exactly high security', thought Patrick. He peered ahead at the low, painted concrete building. Its appearance was benign. It could have been anything from a school to an office building. Not that Patrick had much idea how a prison was supposed to look. There were bars on the windows, though …ah - and no glass. Ok, that's one major difference.

The Policemen opened his door and led him up the steps and inside. One strolled around the back of the desk at Reception to book him in. "Name?"

"You know this!" Patrick replied. "You arrested me ten minutes ago. My name is Patrick Field."

"Age?"

Further questions included his place of birth, place of work and his home address. He considered giving his parents' address in the UK, but thought better of it and gave the bank flats address. He handed over the contents of his pockets.

When he had been shown into a cell and the door clanged shut and locked, he asked for a copy of this 'confession'. While he waited for it, he examined his new and (he hoped) temporary accommodation. The concrete walls on two sides were bare. He reasoned his cell must therefore be in the corner of the main building. Floor to ceiling bars closed in the third and fourth sides. The dirt floor was clean, at least. Evidently, someone had brushed it recently. A single unglazed but barred opening high up on one wall brought in light, some gentle breeze 'and mosquitos at night', thought Patrick. He tried to ignore the bucket in the corner, beside a wooden bench.

After some time, a thin folder was handed to him through the bars. It contained a typewritten, false version of his statement, which had been none too carefully reworded. The document finished with a photocopy of his real signature at the bottom. It was so obviously a fabrication it was dumbfounding that anyone in an official capacity would believe it. The Police notes attached to the statement described his attempt to conceal his vehicle beneath a tarpaulin as 'clumsy' and 'evidence of his guilt'.

Having read the material in the folder and thought for a bit, he banged on the bars and called for a guard.

"Excuse me? Could I make a telephone call, please?"

"No."

"May I speak with a lawyer?"

"No."

"Could I have a drink of water at least?"

The guard puffed out his cheeks to show what an unreasonable demand this was of such a busy man as himself and slouched off to fetch a cup. He returned shortly with a tin cup half filled with tepid water and placed it on the floor outside the bars.

"Water." The guard said, unnecessarily.

"*Tank yu tumas*," said Patrick. Establishing some sort of relationship with the man was going to be tough going, but might be important later on. As his Mum had always said, 'politeness didn't cost anything.' Then he was alone with his thoughts. There were no other prisoners.

If he couldn't make a call or speak with anyone who might be in a position to tell him how the legal system functioned, what could he do? The Policemen hadn't said exactly when he would go in front of a judge other than suggesting it would be a 'couple of days' time'. He doubted the guard would have any clue either.

Thinking about it, who knew where he was? The branch staff will have seen him frog-marched outside and into a Police car, but would not know his destination. How could he communicate with the outside world? At length he had an idea - he would feign illness. He waited for twenty minutes or so and then positioned himself on the floor and started rolling around and groaning. It took a good ten minutes' worth of this play-acting for the dopey guard to rouse himself even to enquire what was the matter.

"*Wun em blo' yufela*?" demanded the guard.

"*Wunfela pain long paloolapa blo'me*" Patrick reckoned that sounded plausible. A stomach pain might indicate anything ranging from the harmless to the very serious. He hoped the guard wouldn't want to be responsible for an ex-pat dying while he was on duty. The man stiffened noticeably and with uncharacteristic haste, telephoned Vila Base Hospital to send a doctor.

When Dr Jessica arrived to treat the patient, the guard led her to the cell. She could easily have followed the loud moaning noises by herself.

"Patrick!" she said. "What on earth...? Why? What are you doing here?"

He groaned again, play-acting, and winked at her to try to convey that his illness wasn't serious. He needed her to play along too. Fortunately, she was a particularly observant doctor and caught on right away. She made a show of palpating his stomach and pretending to force him to lie still while she examined him.

Use of the stethoscope cemented her command of the situation in the mind of the guard. When she demanded, "Bring cold water right away" there was no resistance offered. The guard scuttled off to fulfil his mission. Patrick kept up his occasional moaning and groaning as they whispered together.

"What the hell is going on, Patrick?" she asked.

"I don't mean to sound like a bad American cop show, but I have been framed." he said.

"To be clear, there is really nothing wrong with you?"

"Nothing at all that a good night's sleep won't cure. But I have touched a nerve with somebody powerful - somebody bad. Driving back from the bank after I returned from Santo, I happened upon a car crash. There were a couple of trucks and four men; one started shooting at the others…"

"Patrick!"

"Anyway, I drove home a different way and hid my car under a tarpaulin. Kim suggested I make a Police report of what I'd seen. I did that but Andrew Cutlass took my signed statement off the Policeman and next morning – today – the Police arrested me. They said I'd signed a confession to causing the crash."

"Why did Cutlass do that?" she asked.

"It's unclear, Jess. Kim and I suspect he is bound up in some money-laundering scheme, but we can't prove it – yet. Look - the guard will be back soon. Could you tell all this to Florence Stuart? She needs to tell her father. I trust him and she is my conduit."

Returning footsteps cut short their discussion. Jessica planted a most un-doctorly kiss on Patrick's lips and stood up, tucking her stethoscope away. "Make sure you drink plenty of fluids. Guard? Bring this man a drink every hour during the day, please."

The guard nodded. "Yes, Doctor. *Hemi wunfela ok*?"

"He will be. But remember - one drink every hour." This time it was Jessica's turn to wink at Patrick as she turned away. He struggled to hide the beginnings of a smile. His current situation remained uncomfortable, but now he'd seen Jess, he felt much better about his prospects for release.

-----//-----

Prison rules permitted occasional visitors. Florence came that evening, as Patrick was picking through the mysterious contents of his dinner. There were a couple of ingredients he couldn't identify and one he was sure he didn't *want* to identify. So it wasn't hard to put the tray to one side to receive the girl. She said her father believed his story, backed up by her visit to the bank flats to note that there were no marks at all on Patrick's car.

The Commissioner had said that he cannot be seen to interfere in local Justice. He could, though, arrange for the British Government to put up bail money if required.

"That would be brilliant," Patrick said, "But does that mean I have to stay at home, or somewhere on Efate? And how would I pay it back, if I have to?"

Florence didn't know, but squeezed his hand to give him confidence that all would be alright in the end. "You did say you wanted to talk about something serious, didn't you, back then? I didn't realise that you meant ...well, this serious."

The next morning, at 7:30am, Patrick was alerted by noises of movement elsewhere in the prison. There was some sort of disturbance with occasional raised voices. A new guard appeared.

"*Visit blo' yufela.*"

Before Patrick could ask who it was, Tai Nguyen strode through into the cell area. His mouth was smiling but his face had no expression. Nguyen dismissed the guard, who hurried away, uneasy in his company.

"Good morning," offered Patrick, through the bars.

"Do you know why you are here?"

Patrick thought before replying. Pretending innocence would be a waste of time. Yet a sharp but truthful retort might irritate the man further and prolong his prison stay ...or worse. So he opted for something he hoped was innocuous.

"I appear to be a victim of circumstances."

"You…" Nguyen stabbed the air with his finger. "You need to keep your nose out of other peoples' business."

"I'm sorry you feel that way," began Patrick.

"If you mess with things which aren't your concern, you will suffer. Do you understand?"

"You have been very clear, thank you."

"I have a network of helpers who will tell me if you interfere again. How do you think you came to be here?" The man didn't wait for an answer, turned on his heel and left.

-----//-----

Patrick's request for a bath or shower later on that day was turned down. So he spent the day and another uncomfortable night in the same clothes on the wooden bench, varying his position as best he could. He tried lying on his back with his legs dangling over the end. That was no good. Then, he discovered lying on one side with his legs drawn up in a foetal position was superior. He ran the risk of rolling off onto the floor once he had fallen into a disturbed sleep, but it was worth trying.

In one dream, he later recalled, the guard banged on the bars and said he was free to go because bail had been deposited. He rolled back to face the bars and saw the guard opening the door.

"*Yu go long outside*" the guard instructed, holding the door open.

"Really? Now?" Patrick queried. 'This is where I pinch myself to check if I am still asleep,' he said to himself – and he did. It hurt, too. So – not a dream, then.

"*Quicktime*", the guard said. The man straightened up to his full height of intimidation in case of trouble. He eyed the prisoner stretching to relieve stiffness in his back and legs and wished that they were not so slow sometimes. He didn't want to have to manhandle the white man.

"Is this for exercise?" Patrick was beginning to gather his wits.

"No. You go!"

At the Reception desk, Patrick recovered his watch and car keys and penknife, signed a receipt and stepped out into the early morning sunshine.

He stood for a moment, watching the traffic navigating the roundabout outside the prison. He wasn't really seeing them, though.

The cars were convenient things for his eyes to rest upon while he thought about events of the last forty eight hours. If Tai Nguyen had the power to arrange for him to be locked up, presumably his word was all that was required to release Patrick too. Had someone got word to Andrew Cutlass about his incarceration? He must know – the local staff will have told Joe or him that Mr Patrick had been marched summarily out of the branch. But what did Cutlass know about the other parts of the story? And was Cutlass aware he had now been set free? Had it needed bail to be posted? If so – by whom and how much?

Too many questions to answer at once. Patrick contemplated returning to the prison to try to telephone the branch to ask someone to collect him, but thought better of it. After a spell confined to a small cell, he decided that was the last place he wanted to be. Anyway, a long walk would do him good. He set off in the direction of town, through which he'd have to pass to reach the bank flats at *Numba Tu* district. Maybe Kim could give him a lift home from the branch.

And that was exactly what transpired. Kim was eager for details, of course, and gladly ferried Patrick home, on the understanding that he leave all the car windows open.

"I expect you'd 'niff a bit if you had been sleeping on a wooden bench in a prison cell with a dirt floor," complained Patrick. "It wasn't at all pleasant, as you can imagine. But it does show that Tai Nguyen is up to something pretty bad and is dangerous and powerful. And I'm worried how involved Andrew is."

Kim clearly agreed, but didn't say anything at first.

After a bit, he said, "While you were having your 'holiday' (he fended off Patrick's arm swiping at him) I have researched all these large foreign exchange transactions. There are many more than I had thought at first and the money is going not just to Paris, but Frankfurt; New York; London, of course, Singapore and Tokyo. In other words, all the major money centres in the world. The other significant destination is the Cayman Islands. And it's Royal Counties Bank's operation in the Caymans too. Remember where Andrew served before coming here?"

Patrick knew at once. "The Cayman Islands! Of course: he was Chief Manager there too."

Kim went on. "Our bank features in all the money centre remittances, but the transfers are split with other big international banks as well. I'm considering bundling all these papers together and sending them to Inspection department in the UK with an explanatory note. What do you think?"

Patrick blinked. "Gee. That's a big step. I'm not saying it isn't the right thing to do, but …you'd need to make sure you were safe in the UK before all Hell broke loose. I have an awful feeling Nguyen is powerful here but also part of some global network of criminality, so you'd need to factor in your personal safety. Could you do it anonymously?"

"It wouldn't be hard for Andrew to figure out it was me. I'm the one writing the annual review of the Bon Plats account and calculating its profitability to the bank. Ok, others have access to the figures and records, but who, other than me, would assemble them all in one place to view them as a whole?"

Patrick thought for a second. "Every month, Gilles tots up his FX earnings and losses and reports the figures for his personal annual report. Except, that doesn't mean he would have informed Inspection – quite the reverse. He has every reason to keep the volumes going."

They drove the rest of the way in silence, lost in their own thoughts.

As Kim parked the car, Patrick pulled the tarpaulin off his own Starlet. His effort at concealment hadn't worked and Florence hadn't put the cover back completely, anyway. He bundled it up and tucked it beside the dustbins near the door.

Kim started to unlock his own front door. "Oh," he said. "I clean forgot to tell you: Hone died."

"What?"

"Jessica telephoned and spoke with Gail yesterday. Gail said there was nothing wrong with him, but he had simply lost the will to live – so he died."

Patrick, for once, was speechless. How could such a lively young fella …give up living? He shook his head. "I need a shower, some clean clothes and a large steak. And wine. Do we have any of Dave's beef left?"

"We do," promised Kim. "I'll fetch a couple. I'm not sure what cuts there are; do you mind which we have?"

"No preference. I've got some veggies of some sort and I do believe there's a bottle of that claret we liked."

Kim smiled. This was more like the Patrick he knew. "There might be a beer or two while we wait for the meat to warm up. Now – go shower! I can smell you from here - again."

-----//-----

A good meal and sleeping in his own bed did wonders for Patrick's outlook. He was almost bouncy the next morning. It may have been 'survivor relief' after such challenging events, but he tapped on the glass doors of the branch with something approaching joyful anticipation for the day.

"I heard they let you out," commented Joe.

"And you need some strong coffee," answered Patrick. He wasn't going to let Joe's customary doleful morning mood get him down.

"Hmmn."

Sara arrived right behind him and almost skipped along to greet Patrick. *"Oh, mefela hapi tumas blo' seeim yufela – e gud?"*

Patrick turned and gave her a big, wide smile. "Everything is fine, this morning, Sara, thank you. I have not enjoyed the past couple of days, though, I must admit."

"Mr Cutlass – he is not happy. He shouted at Marianne yesterday and…" she paused and her happy face disappeared. "Did you hear about Hone?"

"Oh - yes. I did. Kim told me last night. *Kastom* is serious, isn't it?"

Sara nodded.

"What will happen, Sara?"

She looked at her feet. "*Me no savvy.*"

"Should I talk to Marianne?"

"Yes. She needs help. Oh – *meforgettim* - there is a ship today." She turned towards a tottering stack of papers on Patrick's desk. Clearly nobody had taken over his duties while he was absent 'on holiday' in prison. She leafed through, pulling out several sheafs of documents and ran her finger down the master list of port arrivals. "No – there are two ships, not one."

Together they pored through the paperwork and figured out what had to be done. Checking his watch, Patrick said, "Right. I'd better get going. Thanks, Sara. I'll speak with Marianne when I get back."

Some part of Patrick's brain was hesitant to go down to the port. He'd be all too visible to Nguyen's men, but he wanted very much to be able to update the British Ambassador. Also to find out about the posting of bail money to release him. He spent a few valuable minutes telephoning the official Residence and found out that Florence had come into town to go to the market. He would attend to his port duties and hunt for her while he picked up some vegetables for himself and for Kim.

-----//-----

Strolling up and down the dock side, Patrick was acutely aware that others were staring at him. He told himself that he was being over-sensitive and tried to focus on the job in hand. One transaction required him to visit the Harbour Master. He climbed the steps to the man's hut overlooking the harbour and tapped on the door. Captain Brasted beckoned him in.

'Morning, Patrick. What do you need?" The captain's greeting was not as fulsome as normal.

"Good morning, Captain. I need a couple of stamps on these bills of lading." He opened and held the sheaf of paperwork at the requisite pages. The man duly obliged, but didn't bother paging through the rest of the documents.

"Are you alright, Captain?" asked Patrick. "Is there a problem?"

Brasted raised his head. "Nothing." The man paused. "I heard about your visit to prison and…" His voice tailed off. This wasn't like the bluff sea captain at all.

"What is it? How did you know about that?"

"After you enquired about those boxes you saw unloaded on to the Bon Plats truck, I asked around a bit – you know – officially. It's my job, you see."

"Yes," Patrick encouraged, perching himself on the other chair in the Harbour Master's hut. "Go on."

Brasted was silent for a bit. He seemed to be wrestling with some decision or other. He took a swig from his stained coffee cup.

"Look. If I tell you, promise you won't say anything. I might be in a spot of trouble."

"Of course – I promise. What is the matter?"

Glancing out of his window in case anyone was listening on the steps outside, the Captain lowered his voice. "Tai Nyuyen came to see me."

"Oh, yes?" Patrick sat forwards, making the chair creak. It wasn't used very often.

"He suggested I might be developing trouble with my sight and hadn't actually seen anything. That's arrant nonsense. And I said so. Always had 20/20 vision, me," he said, puffing out his chest. "But then Nguyen said I ought to look out for Mrs B. the next time I asked questions about things which 'don't concern me'." His direct and open gaze was telling.

This was fitting into an unpleasant pattern for Patrick, and he said so. "That's straight up intimidation, Captain. Can you involve the Police?" But as he said that, he also realised that a significant part of the Police force might be in the pay of this criminal.

The other shook his head. "I've got two years to go before I retire, Patrick. I don't want to make waves. But I also want to sleep at night. All this rebellion stuff we've had has been bad enough, but this…"

Patrick nodded sympathetically. Nguyen had spies who passed him information and also some sort of immunity from the authorities. At this local level, he was very,

very dangerous. Could his reach extend beyond the shores of the New Hebrides, too?

"Captain, I'm determined to do something about Nguyen and his men. I don't know what yet, but I saw those boxes being opened around at Forari Mine and there were guns in them."

"Guns?" A look of shock passed across Brasted's face. Discovering undeclared imports of spirits or other valuable goods was one thing. It was the main reason the government employed him, but guns were far, far worse. This was a different league of danger.

"It's become worse. That isn't all." Brasted looked him straight in the eye. "If you want to know, someone has kidnapped Sheila."

Now it was Patrick's turn to be horrified.

"I received a note telling me she is safe – at the moment – but she will be harmed if I don't cooperate."

"Oh, Captain…" This was escalating out of control. The man must be going out of his mind with worry. "I hope she will be alright. We have to do something. Will you let me know if there is any news?" He put his hand on the captain's shoulder, took his documents and opened the door to return to his car.

He trotted back along the dock. There was still time for a brief sortie into the market before he was due back at the bank. Now it was even more important to find Florence to update her.

-----//-----

He drew up opposite the covered market, where traders sold their produce from all over Efate and the outer islands. Most traders were women. They wore bright, coloured dresses and would sit on the ground with their bananas or coconuts or vegetables piled beside them. Some used folding tables, all the better to display their wares. They'd chatter together, calling across the market when they spotted a friend. Banana or pandanus leaves served to fan the produce (especially fruit) keeping flies at bay.

Of course, those selling meat or fish had to fan the hardest. Patrick had never plucked up the courage to buy either at this market for fear of acquiring some infection or other. But he and Kim figured that they could wash vegetables with care. And they would cook them all, except occasional salad greens, so would be safe enough.

His luck was in. Peeking along the rows, he saw Florence almost hidden behind an armful of leaves. As he approached, he saw the boatman who had brought her across carrying even more. She spotted him and waved. "Patrick! Lovely to see you. Are you alright?"

"I am, thanks. I do need to talk with your father soon, though. Do you think you could ask him for me?"

"Of course. I'm heading back right now..." The boatman, behind her, grinned and rolled his eyes. He was carrying an enormous volume of vegetation and could barely get his arms around it all.

"Um, would you like a hand with all this? I only need a few things myself but I'd be happy to carry some of the ...er, whatever these are." He gestured at the load in the boatman's arms.

"That's really sweet of you, Patrick, but Arnold is fine, aren't you, Arnold?"

"*E gud, Miss. E gud.*" Arnold rolled his eyes again. In truth, there wasn't much else he could move, he was so burdened.

"Well, if you are sure... Do let your father know that we met. The situation ...has *expanded* somewhat." He hoped she picked up the emphasis.

"I will – bye now."

Cabbages and yams or sweet potatoes were pretty reliable, Patrick had found. He saw some papayas which could ripen on the window sill of his flat. He also treated himself to a *lap lap* parcel. They were rolls made from manioc filled with chicken or sometimes pork, wrapped in a banana leaf both to cook and to keep warm until consumed. This local delicacy was something else which Dr Jessica might avoid, doubting the hygiene of the conditions in which it had been prepared. But Patrick had never had food poisoning and reckoned to have a strong stomach.

He ate it while sitting in his car. Then, feeling satisfied he had accomplished what he needed to do, he headed back to work.

-----//-----

"Andrew wants you upstairs – again." Joe informed him, as he pushed open the door of the branch. As the danger of admitting savage rebels from Santo had abated, they no longer posted someone by the locked door. Patrick had noticed little difference in activity at the market – life seemed to be going on as it always had.

Not for the first time, a sympathetic thought for Joe crossed his mind. Being the branch accountant was the worst job there. He was first in the firing line for managerial ire when something went awry. The accountant could expect at least a section of the junior staff to dislike him if he needed to discipline them. Patrick believed that Joe viewed this current posting as serving a kind of penance in exchange for a junior managerial job next. He hoped he wouldn't have to go through it. If he did well, he could jump two grades at a time and omit this unpleasant step.

His shoulders slumped, though, at the thought of trudging up to Cutlass' office again. The prospect of being ripped apart for something or wrongly accused of some infraction was deflating, to say the least. "I'll just put these down," he held up his shopping, "And then I'll go upstairs."

Patrick could have sworn he saw Joe refiling a diary card. Did he have cards to remind him to go to the toilet?

That silly thought cheered him a little and he made his way up the carpeted stairs.

"Hello, Gail. Is he in?"

"Hello, Patrick. Yes – hang on a moment."

307

She pressed the intercom and Andrew Cutlass told her to send Patrick in.

"Close the door, Patrick. What news?"

"It's all as well as might be expected, Andrew" he answered, a little cheekily.

"Yes. Well. About this crash that you caused." Patrick opened his mouth to protest his innocence, but Cutlass continued, unabashed. "I have been informed that proceedings against you will be dropped provided you leave the island within six months. Do you understand?"

Patrick pricked up his ears. This development might play into his and Kim's hands with regard to telling Inspection Department about what they'd uncovered.

"Not fully, Andrew, no, but I follow what you are saying. Where would I go next? Do I have to wait until then for my Long Leave? I remember it's supposed to be in a couple of months' time, and I ought to write to Staff Department to find out when they want me for interviews."

To his surprise, Cutlass didn't have immediate and ready answers as he hadn't expected the lad to react so promptly. So, for once, Cutlass didn't cover that shortcoming with loud bluster. When it came, his response was measured.

"I'll do that. I will have to line up a replacement for you as well. It's also time for your annual review, so I will have to consider what I write. I'm sure you understand that the grade of any future posting will depend quite heavily on that. You may wish to keep that in mind for the rest of your time here. That is all."

"Er, right. Thank you, Andrew." Patrick rose to leave, his head whirling with possibilities. Of course, all staff in these far-away postings were dependent upon the Chief Manager's reports about them. How else could Head Office form a view about their performance? But, thinking back over Cutlass' words and phrasing, was he reminding Patrick of the power he held? Or ...was he holding out the possibility of promotion in return for unspecified favours during Patrick's remaining time in the New Hebrides?

He remembered to thank the long-suffering Gail as he passed her desk. Then there was the walk down the stairs to the banking hall. Patrick reflected that the rush of events in the last few weeks had blown apart what before he would have considered 'normal' or 'reasonable'. As he sat at his desk, it occurred to him that all his friends in the UK would agree with this. They lived repetitive and comparatively stale lives. They played golf on Saturdays, went to the pub or a restaurant on Saturday night and washed the car on Sunday. This went on week after week after week. Rare exceptions would be when they went on holiday. To Spain, perhaps, or Cornwall, for a fortnight. They might not be able even to comprehend the breadth of experiences he had undergone in this land so far from the UK. They wouldn't think assisting in a birth, mounting a commando-style raid at night on another island or being shot at or imprisoned was 'normal'.

Yes. His horizons had not just been expanded but exploded. Could he now trust his own feelings when a situation was put to him? His 'gut' feelings? He remembered, years before, asking his father what it was like in the Second World War. The man had spent all those years in jungles and deserts, fighting the enemy. Never one to speak about such things, especially not in front of Patrick, his father had contented himself by saying, "Travel broadens the mind". And wouldn't say another word about it.

310

These thoughts made him laugh out loud, startling Sara and John-Marc, both bent over their work in deep concentration. He felt an unreasonable sense of achievement, of accomplishment – of success.

But Patrick realised that his behaviour must have looked and sounded very odd. He apologised and handed Sara the papers he'd brought back from the port. "I'll go to see Marianne now – I won't be long."

When he approached her desk, she had both elbows on it and was covering her face. "Marianne? *Wunem blo'yu fela*?"

She struggled to raise a smile for him, but didn't manage it. Her hands wiped hard across her eyes, puffy from recent crying. "Oh, Patrick. *Hone – hemi dead finis*." And the tears welled up again.

He crouched down beside her. He knew already that she considered all the cashiers and Mech Room staff to be her 'children'. She had none of her own and so they all meant a great deal to her. He put his arm across the back of her shoulders and stroked her hair to try to sooth her. Straightaway, she turned her face into his chest. She wept uncontrollably as though, for the first time, letting go a great weight of anguish. He thought later on that his action might not have been deemed very wise. Hugging a female member of local staff might support Andrew Cutlass' belief that he had made another young woman pregnant. But Marianne was so desperately sad that he couldn't bear to push her away.

-----//-----

Sara's telephone rang. "Ok, I will. Yes, Sir. Yes," she said. Then to Patrick, "The British Commissioner wants you – in his office!"

Patrick gently disengaged himself from Marianne and refocussed his head. "Gosh. Did they say when?"

"He said now!"

Patrick noticed Sara was sitting more upright in her chair than normal and her eyes were rather wide. "You said 'he'?"

She nodded furiously. "That was Mr …I mean *Commissioner* Stuart on the telephone. Himself. Personally."

A personal call from the British Resident Commissioner directly to a junior ex-pat member of bank staff? There were added dimensions to this whole thing. He said, "Thank you, Sara. I'd better head off. Um, do you think you could avoid letting anyone know where I've gone?"

Her eyes widened even further, if that was possible. It was a national characteristic that New Hebrideans told the truth in almost all things. Sometimes they knew the telling would create embarrassment or anger, and would cast their eyes downward. But, for the most part, they couldn't lie convincingly. Any student of human body language could tell immediately if they were attempting to say something untrue.

Sara realised that Patrick would not have asked her to take part in this venture were it not of importance. Yet, she was very concerned that she might have to say something untrue.

Patrick saw that right away. "If anybody asks, say you don't know. Is that ok?"

She said, "Yes. Alright …but…"

"Yes?"

"But I do know."

"I see. How about you say you are not sure – because even I don't know exactly where we will meet."

She brightened at that. "Alright, Patrick. *Tank yu tumas*."

"And I won't be away long. After all, there is a lot to do here."

-----//-----

Patrick knew Joe had seen him leave but hoped that nobody spotted him sprinting along the quayside towards the Commissioner's launch.

As before, he was driven up to the Residence and shown inside. This time Andrew Stuart himself opened his door and strode the few steps down the corridor to greet him.

"Patrick – welcome. Are you feeling alright, now?"

"Yes, thank you very much. Prison food wasn't up to much - nor was the level of conversation with the guards."

The Commissioner gave a short chuckle. "Quite so, quite so. Things have moved along since we last spoke. Certain events have revealed a number of key players have been playing two sets of cards, if you follow me."

Patrick didn't really. It was the second conversation recently containing enigmatic references to matters he knew little about.

"It appears some powerful individuals have been conducting criminal enterprises here for many years. No doubt they have profited greatly. But there is also evidence of

…how should I put it? *'State interference'*. More worrying, I am reaching the conclusion that this group of islands is being used as a conduit for transmission of significant sums of money by international terrorists."

He saw Patrick had opened his mouth at that. "Yes?"

"My colleague, Kim, has discovered worrying patterns of foreign exchange trading through our bank which are out of all proportion to the size of the company doing them."

Stuart nodded his head. "And have you or has he informed the relevant banking authorities of this?"

"Not yet. There are …internal difficulties which we would have to overcome."

"Hmmn. I see. Does Cutlass know you have come here?"

"No, Sir. At least, not yet, I don't think. I asked my secretary to try to avoid telling anyone where I am."

"Good man. Are you able to share with me the names of the companies you have identified who may be executing these …'exceptional transactions'?"

"The truth is that I don't know if I am permitted to do that. Just before arriving, I

315

passed my banking exams. The final one was Law Relating to Banking. The textbooks cited *Joachimson vs Swiss Bank Corporation 1921* as outlining the occasions when disclosure of customer details can be made. I don't think this was one of them. But – I usually buy my groceries at Bon Plats supermarket and I recommend you ask your staff to do the same."

"Mmmm," said Stuart with a wry smile on his face. "Is Cutlass aware of your concerns with this or any other customer?"

"Oh, no. Most definitely not. We were not going to tell him of our findings, but rather approach Inspection Department, in Head Office. You see, Mr Cutlass has behaved oddly in relation to my own recent adventures."

Stuart raised one eyebrow. "For example, I wrote out a witness statement and handed it to a Policeman – but he passed it to Andrew Cutlass. There's more, Commissioner. And it's bad."

The other eyebrow was raised, inviting more detail.

"The Harbour Master told me this morning that his wife has been kidnapped. She is being held hostage to ensure he does

316

not pursue his enquiries into certain cargo movements. Like those boxes I told you about, containing guns."

"Ah," said the British Resident Commissioner. "I begin to follow. This is serious, indeed. You'd better return to the branch before you are missed, but we should keep in more regular touch." He opened his desk diary and scanned across the pages. "Perhaps you and your colleague …'Kim', is it, could come to dinner one evening next week and we could discuss the …ah, *quality* of produce at that supermarket."

"I'm sure we would be delighted. Could Florence let me know when best suits you, Sir?"

# Chapter 13

# Blood Donation and an Escape

At a private dinner the next Wednesday evening, Patrick and Kim briefed the British Resident Commissioner more fully. Kim outlined the trading patterns they had uncovered. Stuart was sympathetic to hear of the intimidation attempted on Patrick and was curious about the exact location of the firearms exchange he had seen. There was no further news to impart of the Harbour Master's wife, Sheila.

In return, Andrew Stuart advised them to do their best to steer clear of trouble. He told them to keep extra copies of whatever paperwork would evidence their discoveries and to continue to relay information to him. He also suggested that, if Patrick was to be replaced by someone new, then he should take the materials with him upon departure. They could be given to Inspection Department when next Kim was due to go on the normal six-week period of Long Leave. They agreed this might protect Kim to some extent from immediate retribution in country. But, the

Commissioner admitted, he knew the network of criminality could reach either of them anywhere.

They made a plan to try to meet up or at least communicate every seven days from now onwards. And the following week, Patrick was glad to report that when he had visited the Harbour Master's office, Captain Lionel was greatly relieved.

"They brought Sheila back yesterday evening – I am so happy!" Under his beard, the wide smile and crinkly eyes had returned. But there was also a slight tremor in the man's voice. "Nguyen is very bad news, Patrick. Be careful with him."

Patrick contented himself by saying that, "The British authorities are aware of the generalities of this, Captain," He didn't want to alarm the old man, who was fearful of word leaking back to Nguyen. But he also wanted to let him know that he was not alone in his plight. "Is your wife alright, now she is at home?"

"She's a tough old bird, you know. She's been through difficult situations with me before. She was upset, of course and, she said, cross at letting herself be caught like that. But she is safe now."

"I'm very glad." And they went about their business as usual.

-----//-----

Andrew Cutlass must have written to Staff Department back in the UK. About a month later, Patrick received word that he was to present himself to Head Office in London on a particular day for interviews. He scrutinised the list of senior people whom he was to meet. Several were his ultimate line managers or senior people in Personnel. And there was the obligatory examination by the bank doctor to check he was still healthy. There were a couple of others whose names he did not recognise, but who worked for other geographic areas in the bank's overseas division. One was clearly Arabian and the other had an Anglo-Saxon name, but an address in New York. Was he supposed to go to New York for the meeting? It didn't say that. Perhaps the man was visiting London.

As the date for his departure grew nearer, Patrick and Kim sorted their copies of the records into order and drafted a brief explanatory memo. For the time being, they addressed this memo impersonally to 'Inspection Department, Royal Counties Bank, UK'. Their plan was that Patrick should leave this initial block of evidence at his parents' house for safekeeping. He could add to it when he departed the New Hebrides for the last time.

Patrick broke the news to Jess after dinner the next Sunday. "I'm going on long leave a week Thursday. There are interviews and meetings I have to attend and I plan to take my Mum and Dad up to the Lake District to go walking for a bit."

"That sounds nice, Patrick," she said. "I went to the Lakes once when I was small. The rain was constant – but I suppose that's how the Lakes stay as lakes. I'm sure it doesn't always rain, though. Where are you going to stay?"

"I haven't tried to book anywhere, yet. I expect we'll head for Keswick, in the north and take day trips out from there. It's a little while since I've visited too. I hope it hasn't changed too much. I'm looking forward to getting out onto the fells."

"How long will you be gone for?" she asked.

"Long leave is six weeks."

Her face fell. "Six? That's a long time. How come you have so much holiday?"

"All overseas staff have thirty days plus Christmas and Bank Holidays. We have to take it in one lump because the bank will only pay for one return trip per posting. I suppose it wouldn't be so bad if I worked in France or Greece. Then I could save up for some extra return trips and split it that way – but out here, it's rather a long distance and flights cost a great deal."

She frowned. "I only have four weeks and am not supposed to take it except between rotations. That's 'postings' to you. And I have to fit exams and revision and health checks and extra educational courses into those four weeks. It doesn't sound fair to me."

Patrick hadn't known that. He hadn't appreciated how fortunate he was. He tried making a joke of it. "Ah, but you don't get shot at from time to time!"

"And you don't stay up all night trying to keep someone alive with inadequate medical supplies because you are On Call, having already worked the whole day."

"Yes. That's true, Jess. Sorry. I suppose I've not thought about it before."

He hadn't expected her to be exactly joyful at his temporary departure, but he had no idea he would darken her mood like this and for the evening to descend into acrimony.

"Um, is there anything you'd like me to bring back for you? You know, anything you can't get easily here?"

"I'm fine, thank you."

"Well, the offer stands. If something occurs to you, just let me know."

"It's late. I ought to go. I have an early ward round because we have an operation lined up tomorrow late morning and I have a bunch of stuff to prepare first."

"Sure …but it's only 8 o'clock. Are you sure you want to go?"

"I'm sure."

"Ok. See you tomorrow?"

"Maybe. It depends how I feel."

Patrick waved her goodbye. That had not gone very well. He slumped onto his sofa when he went back into his flat. Perhaps he should have gone to the Aussie bankers' Barbeque instead. He checked his watch. It wasn't that late. A bit of cheerful company and a beer or two would lift his spirits.

He jumped into his car and headed round there.

-----//-----

"S'matter, Mate?" enquired Dave. "You're normally the first here. Can't afford steaks on Pommy wages?"

"I've eaten, thanks," Patrick said. "It's just that…"

"Ah. She said 'No'?"

"Something like that, Dave. Are there any beers left?"

"Blaady Norah, Mate – Is the Pope a Catholic?"

Someone thrust a Fosters oil can into his hand. "Wrap yer laughing gear 'round that".

Patrick began to relax a little. He drank steadily and joined in with the banter. Much later, he found himself at his front door with someone opening it for him and pushing him inside.

All too soon, the Monday morning light flooded in and burned his eyes. He tried to roll out of bed, but found there was a table in the way. Blinking didn't help. Not only did it fail to move the table leg out of the way, but each blink vibrated through his head as though hammering his skull.

No matter which way he rolled, he couldn't seem to get off the bed. And for some reason, there was carpet on his bed –

no, wait – the carpet was on the floor. So he must be on the floor, not the bed.

Dragging himself upright was more an act of will than desire. He still wore his clothes from yesterday. Even Patrick thought he smelled rank. Off they came and he headed for the shower, pausing only to set the kettle to boil for coffee.

Now and again, the walls moved in an unexpected fashion, but he found he could keep them still by leaning on them. 'Naughty walls', he thought. Now - was acidic coffee the best thing to put into his stomach? He admitted he felt a little delicate and so some bread would be a good idea first. And water. Yes…

Thirty minutes later he felt more human. If only he didn't have to go into work. But the radio noise next door stopped and he knew the mosquito screen door would soon bang shut as Kim left for the bank. Patrick ought to go too.

He'd changed into the usual long cotton trousers, shirt jack and polished shoes expected of ex-pat staff at the bank. He grabbed his keys and opened his front door. But where was his car?

Of course – it must still be around at the Aussi Mess. Fortuitously, Kim emerged right then.

"'Morning, Kim. Could you give me a lift around to the Aussi Mess? I left my car there last night."

"Sure. No problem. Hey, you don't look too well. Are you ok?"

"A big cup of Sara's Tanna coffee and twelve hours' sleep is what I need, but I don't think the sleep bit is on today's menu, somehow."

"Well, alright. If you're sure. Hop in."

Patrick was grateful that the trade finance section was right at the back of the banking hall, furthest from the front door. It was around the corner from wherever Andrew was likely to prowl. He told Sara he was '*sik tumas*' and requested warning if she spotted the Chief Manager heading their way.

Sara was familiar with the results of over-enthusiastic bouts of refreshment during the night before. She brewed the coffee extra strong. He noticed that from the very first sip and thanked her, earning a knowing smile in return.

Only half of the cup had gone before his telephone rang. It was Jess.

"Patrick? We have a bit of an emergency here at Vila Base. You said you have 'O' negative blood, yes?"

"That's right. What do you need?"

"Can you come in, right away, please. Ask for me at Reception. They'll get you scrubbed up." And with that somewhat terse request, she was gone.

Patrick's brain was, shall we say, a little fogged, still. But he turned to Sara. "I am needed at Vila Base Hospital quite urgently. I'm guessing they need my blood type for an operation they are doing. There's nothing especially urgent here this morning, is there? I should only be an hour or so."

She shook her head. "*Me chekim olgeta. E gud.*"

"Great," Patrick said. "I'll be back as soon as I can. Could you tell Joe where I've gone?"

And off he went.

-----//-----

Dr Jessica had been as good as her word. One of the staff at Vila Base Hospital Reception hurried him down a short corridor, scented with antiseptic, and into an ante-room. There were flimsy blue gowns hung on hooks. Opposite them, a pile of elasticated face masks stood ready on the shelf above several sinks with long tap handles.

"Are you on any medication, Patrick?"

"No."

She sat him down at a small table, pressed a box onto the top of his index finger and made it click. He recalled the process from when he had donated blood back in the UK before. It was to take a tiny sample to double-check his blood group. He always carried his donor card showing he was group 'O' Rhesus negative, but he supposed they had to check. All the same, it smarted a little.

"Undress, please and put these on," the nurse then instructed, handing over one of the gowns and a mask.

"But I thought I was only here to donate blood?"

"You are – in a manner of speaking. Come on – the operation is at a critical stage." She smiled, to encourage him.

He still resisted. "Is Dr Jessica here?"

"She is performing the operation. Here. Take these. I won't peek! I'll be outside checking your blood group. Scrub your hands and arms with that brush and the soap and call when you are ready."

Patrick began unbuttoning his shirt jack, somewhat reluctantly. There was a chair in the corner, so he tucked his shoes and socks under it and hung his trousers over the back and covered them with his shirt.

He discovered that the gown was one which tied loosely at the back, so he elected to keep his underpants on to retain a vestige of modesty and fiddled with the mask. "Ready," he called.

"Have you scrubbed up?" asked the nurse, coming back in.

"Er, no. Not yet."

"Right. Your hands and entire arms, up to the shoulder, please. With the brush, there. That's why it's called 'scrubbing up'."

Patrick obeyed while she watched. He rinsed off all the soap as best as he could and mopped most of the water away with paper towels. "Now what?"

"Follow me."

She backed up against another door opening into the operating theatre. The entire room gleamed: ceiling, walls and floor. There were many power points around the room and electrical machines on trolleys plugged into them. An enormous compound light array in the centre of the ceiling shone down upon a patient on the second of two gurneys. The figure was shrouded, head to foot, except for one arm, nearest to Patrick and a stray foot poking out of the end. Medical staff clustered around the middle of the patient, all masked up and with hair coverings. He thought he recognised Jess's hair and her fairer skin.

"Good morning, Patrick. Lie on this gurney, please, head at that end."

Yup. That was Jessica.

He hitched one buttock onto the paper covering of the gurney and braced himself with both hands to lever up and scoot down a little to align his head with the pillow.

Making himself comfortable, he realised the gurney had a small side extension where his arm could rest. The nearest nurse had pulled it out and was beginning to wipe the skin inside his elbow with a giant cotton bud with brown liquid on the end.

The nurse who had brought him in said, "I've confirmed 'O' negative, Doctor." She wrapped the tourniquet around his upper arm. "There will be a small scratch, Patrick."

It was odd, Patrick thought, that inserting the larger needle actually to take blood hurt less than pricking his finger with a mini-lancet.

331

Maybe there were fewer nerve endings in his elbow..?

"Lie back and relax, now," and the nurse released the tourniquet. "This may take a while."

"I thought giving a pint of blood would only be a few minutes."

"We will be going much more slowly than donation centres manage. Just relax and let me know if you start to feel funny. Now we need to hook up your leg."

"Excuse me?"

"The right leg, I think…" And the nurse hiked up the flimsy blue covering. "Oh, those will have to come off" as she revealed Patrick's underpants. "Don't move that arm. Raise your behind …yes, like that. Now – we need an artery - another small scratch on your leg – there."

Patrick found himself going along with this most unusual blood donation procedure because of the air of professionalism and sense that this was all matter-of-fact for everyone else in the theatre. But he'd never had to undress before when donating blood. All that was needed usually was to roll up his sleeve as high as it could go and to offer up the inside of his elbow. An unseen bag positioned below his sight line would harvest the precious pint or so and be whisked away for storage as soon as it was full. He had first donated blood at the 1975 Moorgate Tube disaster in London. The authorities had called all offices near the tube station to send as many of their staff as could be spared for an hour to donate blood. More than 40 people lost their lives when a driver failed to stop at the southern terminus of the Northern City line. Doctors and nurses from the nearby St Bartholomew's Hospital set up a make-shift Blood Donation Centre to treat the 74 seriously injured passengers. Patrick had given blood every year since.

This double connection to give blood was ...well, unusual to say the least. Maybe they did things differently out here.

Patrick lay back and closed his eyes. It didn't do much to diminish the bright light above him which penetrated his eyelids and made his pounding head ache even more. For a second, he contemplated saying that he felt quite bad after last night's beery evening. But then he reasoned that wasn't what the nurse had meant by 'feeling funny'. Instead, he thought he'd use the opportunity to go over in his head the disconnected threads of criminality he'd encountered in recent months. Were these all part of the same enterprise? Or was the New Hebrides a hot-bed of individual bad guys, all plying their trade and taking advantage of the financial freedom of such tax havens.

Now and again, Jessica muttering instructions. Her voice was soft, but she spoke with authority and clarity. An air of calmness pervaded the room. The occasional rattle of an instrument being returned to a plate and insistent beeping of a machine were annoying, though. If only the beeping was steady or, preferably, absent altogether, then he could catch up on sleep.

Perhaps he *had* fallen asleep – because the next thing Jess said was, "Ok. That's it. She has started again. Disconnect and close." The nurse came back to his side.

"There. All done. Thank you very much." He could swear she was smiling under her mask - her eyes were smiling, that was certain. She busied herself withdrawing the needles and covering the puncture wounds with a plaster. "Could you press down on that with your right hand …and that with your left?"

Patrick followed instructions. He swung his legs off the side of the gurney and sat up.

"You may feel a little woozy for a while. You should sit down outside and I'll bring you some tea."

"That would be great. Thank you. Any chance of a biscuit? Oh, and my underpants?"

"We'll see. Off you go - take care. I'll be out in a moment."

He turned back to wave goodbye to Jess, but she was still bent over the patient. 'I'll try to call her later', he thought and made his way gingerly out of the operating theatre.

The cup of tea brought to him was laced with lots of sugar. He didn't take sugar in tea or coffee as a rule, but didn't complain. It was delicious and the nurse had found a couple of Custard Cream biscuits too. He sat back and savoured them. These were not stocked by Bon Plats – the hospital must have imported them specially.

As he neared the bottom of his tea cup, he remembered he was supposed to be at work and checked his watch. Horrified, he found almost four hours had gone by since he had left the branch that morning. He dressed in haste, hung the gown back on the wall and threw the mask into a bin by the door.

He turned the handle. The nurse was sitting at a desk outside writing something. She looked up.

"Hello, Mr Patrick. Are you feeling alright, now?"

"I am, thanks, but I've just seen what time it is and I really have to get back to work. The Chief Manager will kill me."

She checked her watch. "Are you going to drive?"

He nodded. "Yes."

"Well, take it steady and if you begin to feel strange, pull over. Alright?"

"OK," he said. "I don't have far to go – the bank is beside the Rossi Hotel."

"Very well. Take care and thank you for coming in."

-----//-----

Patrick wasn't sure whether he was pleased or sorry that even Joe hadn't shouted for him as he came into the branch and walked around to the Trade Finance area. Sara and Jean-Marc smiled to welcome him back, though.

"Did anything happen while I was away?" Patrick asked them. Both shook their heads. He settled down at his desk and began to leaf through the folders and odd pieces of paper in his In-Tray. Only then did he realise that he felt utterly clear-headed. There was no trace of this morning's fuzziness and pounding headache. 'Must have been the tea and biscuits. I'll remember those as a hangover cure'.

One of the papers was a note from Andrew Cutlass informing him that he would be boarding a certain flight to return to the UK on long leave. Stapled to it was an envelope bulging with air tickets. He sorted through them. There were tickets for all the flights to the UK plus return tickets to come back to the New Hebrides six weeks afterwards for a hand-over. He made a note to himself to ask Joe for his passport the day before the flight.

-----//-----

Before leaving work that day, he put in a telephone call to the Hospital. To his great disappointment, Jess had gone straight home after the operation 'to sleep', the nurse said, with emphasis.

It crossed his mind to drive over to her house, but he hesitated. She had not received the news of such an extensive period of Long Leave very well. And now he would need to broach the topic of him departing the New

Hebrides altogether. Today was not the right day to do that.

Instead, Patrick began setting out the modest amount of clothing he'd take with him. He had ample clothes at his parents' house together with all the suits he would need to attend the obligatory interviews in London. It would feel odd, wearing a suit again. Kim told Joe that he'd drive Patrick out to the airport when the time came. This, of course would allow Kim to pass a thick dossier of duplicate papers to Patrick to smuggle away from the branch. He'd left lots of room in his carry-on bag for it. Joe was delighted at being relieved of the responsibility and didn't argue.

-----//-----

When Patrick popped into one of the Aussie banks to collect some documents the next day, someone told him they were not ready because Lionel Brasted had gone walkabout.

"Walkabout?" said Patrick. "Where's he gone? And isn't there anyone else who could sign instead? The ship is due in tomorrow and our customer won't want to be paying demurrage for failure to clear his goods."

"It's a mystery, Mate" opined the Aussie. "Someone said he got into a bit of bother."

This was distinctly alarming to Patrick. He had a vague idea where the Harbour Master lived and was pretty sure he could identify the house if he saw the man's car outside. Even if the car wasn't there, he could nip in and ask Mrs Brasted - Sheila - about him.

He took the unsigned documents with him and drove off to the jungle edge to try to find the Brasted's house. It wasn't hard. The fishing nets and floats with crossed oars adorning the driveway entrance pretty much gave it away. He turned into the drive. A firm knock on the front door wasn't answered. He supposed the house was not occupied. But to make sure, he walked around the back and spoke with their garden boy.

*"Me no savvy"* was all Patrick could extract from the lad, no matter how persuasive he tried to be.

The Brasted's Land Rover was parked at the side of the house under a lean-to roof. That confirmed it was the right one. It boasted port area admission stickers on the windscreen, so Patrick was certain it was theirs. He returned to the front and tried the handle of the door. It was unlocked. True, that wasn't unusual in the New Hebrides. Most people had little of any real value, and if a thief stole something, how far would they get with it? A guilty flash of memory pricked Patrick's conscience about the theft he'd reported to the local chief, with such appalling results.

He stepped inside, calling, "Hello? Captain Brasted? Mrs Brasted? Is anyone home?"

There was no answer. He walked through to the kitchen with its view across the cultivated area at the back. The garden boy was no longer visible. Patrick stood for a second, turning over in his mind what to do.

As he walked back along the short corridor, he glanced into a room at the side. Feeling like a cross between a snooper and a thief, he realised it was the Captain's study. Book shelves lined the walls, there was a sofa and a couple of ancient armchairs. His desk had – of course – a matching captain's chair drawn up to it. Actually, that was not accurate - the chair wasn't drawn up. It sat away from the desk at an angle, as though the sitter had risen hurriedly and not taken the trouble to tidy the chair back into position.

All else was …well, neat and shipshape. Patrick thought hard about previous times he had visited the Captain's office at the harbour. Everything had been orderly. His desk would have several piles of documents, but he would know exactly where to find any particular information. The chair was out of place. Was it too far-fetched to draw any sort of conclusion from it?

It wasn't much to go on. Patrick looked at the few documents on the desk top. They didn't offer too many clues, either. Several importers featured on them. There were two requests from visiting 'yachties' for temporary berths for their boats next month. There was also someone's birthday card he'd not mailed yet. It read, 'Happy Birthday, Justine – from Lionel and Sheila'.

Even a fevered imagination couldn't make much out of this, thought Patrick. But …why were documents on the desk at all? If the Captain had nipped to the kitchen to make a cup of coffee, he'd leave them there. But not if he was leaving the house. And the birthday card addressed to Justine, whoever she might be. Why not take it and post it if he was going out for a while? In short, the man Patrick knew would clear his desk. He'd file away anything official or personal if he was leaving for a period – *unless he didn't have time*.

None of this was adding up to anything substantive, but a worrying feeling was building in Patrick's belly. Something about it was wrong. When the Australian banker said Lionel had 'gone walkabout', Patrick took it that meant he wasn't in his office whenever they'd enquired.

But supposing he really had 'gone walkabout' for a longer spell? Mrs Brasted wasn't there either – had she been kidnapped again and the old man had gone after her?

He shook his head and tried to give himself a stern talking-to. 'Deal in facts, Patrick. Don't let your imagination run ahead. What do you actually know?'

The documents he needed to have stamped wouldn't start to be a problem until tomorrow when the ship docked. Even then, Royal Counties Bank might get away with a couple of days' grace before port storage charges were levied – so called 'demurrage'. By then, the captain might be back at his post and stamping away for all he was worth. Patrick considered that waiting until tomorrow would not do any harm. He could talk it over with Kim tonight.

So he returned to the bank, leaving the Brasted's house exactly as he found it.

"Kim?" he asked, when he had been re-admitted through the glass door, it being after closing time. "There are some things I want to run by you – tonight – are you going to be working late?"

"I ought to," Kim admitted, "But I'm at the 'Sod it' stage with a couple of these proposals and annual reviews." He sighed deeply. "No, I'll be leaving on time tonight – depending on what happens here." He gestured towards the cashiers, who were still tilling up an hour and a half after the final customer had been ushered out. There was lots of happy chat going backwards and forwards and the occasional peal of delighted laughter.

'Perhaps,' Kim thought, 'Their minds were not quite 100% on their jobs...?'

"Maybe a quick beer next door will help?"

"Several, more like it," amended Kim, turning back to his desk.

-----//-----

Happily, Andrew Cutlass had been invited to play cricket somewhere that

343

afternoon, so Joe was in charge. The mood throughout the branch, except for Joe's office, of course, was buoyant. Even Marianne, who had been so affected by Hone's death, occasionally laughed at something. On occasions like this, Patrick recollected later, he liked his job very much. It was another valuable lesson. People who bring stress and anger into the work place make life unpleasant for everyone. Also, the quality of work suffers, he was sure. Not an original thought, but he hadn't read many Management Textbooks at that stage. He was pleased at what he considered penetrating insight.

Jean-Marc came up to his desk. "Can we go now, Patrick?" He looked up at the clock on the wall. It read five minutes past five o'clock.

"I suppose so," Patrick began, and out of habit checked his own watch. It read four forty five. He frowned and held it to his ear. It was still ticking. "Sara? What's the time on the telex machine?"

She scooted her chair over to it. "Sixteen forty four, Patrick."

It was very noticeable that Jean-Marc was grinning from ear to ear and couldn't stand still. Patrick raised one eyebrow at him and went around the corner to Gilles. "*Mon ami. Quelle heure est-il?*"

"*Près de cinq heures. Er… cinq heures moins dix.*"

Patrick returned to where Jean-Marc was still standing, shuffling from foot to foot. "Jean-Marc? Three different instruments suggest the wall clock may not yet be correct." He narrowed his gaze, theatrically. "Did you help it along in its timekeeping?"

The youngster laughed at having been so easily found out. "*Wunman – me no savvy – 'e setim wrong.*" He shrugged his shoulders and pulled out a chair so he could reset the clock to more or less the correct time.

"Do you have an urgent appointment, Jean-Marc?"

"Yes." Jean-Marc couldn't keep still, trying to cover his embarrassment, but grinning as widely as ever.

It would be to meet a girl, Patrick reasoned. "Ok. Off you go – just this once, mind. Tell Joe I said it's ok."

Jean-Marc needed no second invitation and was gone in a flash. When Patrick turned back, Sara was nodding sagely. "That boy is very lucky, Patrick."

"Aren't we all, Sara? Aren't we all?"

-----//-----

Patrick tapped Kim's shoulder on his way out of the branch. "See you next door, shortly?"

"We are almost there. Marianne? What's the difference down to now?"

Poor May, the last of the cashiers, was surrounded by piles of vouchers. The money in her till had been counted, recounted and, Patrick guessed, counted again. Her face was flushed and she clutched at her hair. He remembered Kim saying the most common causes of being unable to reconcile the amount of money in the tills were under- or over-paying a customer. After that, reversing numbers when writing out the transaction vouchers and, sometimes, notes sticking together. Usually, when the last two had been double-checked by Marianne or Kim himself, and if the difference in book value and actual cash present in the till was modest, the amount would be written off. They'd use Sundry Payments or Sundry Losses accounts – the banking equivalent of petty cash. It was always worth wheeling the till itself out of its cabinet in case a note or two had slipped behind.

"Three francs short, Kim."

"Ok – fine. Let's write that off. May? Don't worry - these things happen. Just take your time when you open up tomorrow."

May smiled in relief and gathered everything together ready to wheel the till into the strong room.

"I'll pass the Sundry Losses vouchers, Kim," said Marianne.

"Thanks," Kim replied. And then, to Patrick, "I'll be right there – could you could get the order in?"

-----//-----

The waiter at the Rossi Bar next door brought a small dish of peanuts with the two Fosters beers and a couple of icy-cold glasses from the refrigerator. Patrick settled down at his favourite table, beyond a potted plant. They'd be out of sight of anyone coming into the Rossi Hotel unless they actually stepped into the bar area. There was still a stunning view, though, out towards the bay. Kim arrived as the waiter was departing.

"Could you bring us two more, please?" he asked. "I don't think these will wet the sides!"

Patrick knew that his friend wasn't given to the drinking excesses so beloved of their

Australian and Kiwi acquaintances. He must have had a torrid time indeed.

"How about we play 'My Day was Worse than Your Day?"

"You aren't in the same league, Patrick. You don't want to know."

Patrick grinned. "Cheers, then."

They drank deeply and gazed at the view for a minute or two while their brains slowed and the cares of the day began to slide away. A slight onshore breeze ruffled their hair. The wash of the waves on the shore almost at their feet was most soothing of all. The arrival of the waiter with two more cans of Fosters prompted both to drain their glasses. Patrick began to pour his second beer.

"When I went to the ANZ today they said Captain Brasted hasn't been around for a bit. I called there for some documents, but they hadn't been able to get his release stamps on them and told me we'd have to wait. I hope he is back tomorrow, 'cos the ship is due to dock in the afternoon. Since Sheila was kidnapped, he has been rather nervous."

He took a sip of his beer. "I went over to his house in case he was ill, but there was nobody home. Well, the garden boy was when I arrived, but he ran away. Oddly, their Land Rover was still parked around the side. The front door was unlocked too. No sign of the Captain or Sheila."

Kim said, "That doesn't sound all that strange. Suppose they went for a day-sail round the island? They'd not need their car. They'd take a few provisions with them – and one of the men at the port could rustle up the stamps you need."

"I'm probably getting too excited," Patrick admitted. "I went into the house and peeked into his study. I wanted to make quite sure they weren't there." He stopped, realising he hadn't conducted a proper search of the house. There were several rooms he hadn't inspected. Supposing one or both of them had been lying, hurt and unable to make a sound? "Ok, it wasn't a thorough check, but I did notice that there were papers on the desk …and a birthday card."

"What's your point?" Kim queried.

"Lionel Brasted is not one to leave documents lying about, especially in an unlocked house – have you ever visited his office at the harbour? And his chair was pushed back from the desk."

Even as he said it, Patrick began to think he was reading too much into what he'd seen.

"I reckon it's time you went back to the UK," Kim joked. "I can think of a dozen plausible explanations for what you saw and none of them involve Bad Stuff."

"Oh, maybe you are right. Anyway - that was what I wanted to run by you - your turn."

"Where to start? Andrew got wind that Inspection might be on their way here and he's like a cat on hot bricks. He wants every single account reviewed - like, yesterday. The entire contents of the strong room double-checked and the Quarterly Returns prepared a week in advance. Why do so many of our borrowing customers choose now to be late with repayments?"

"Golly. I suppose a Head Office visit was inevitable right after the attempted rebellion. I guess they'll start in Santo with the sub-branch...?"

"If the rumour is true – if – then I would expect them to base themselves here and fly up with a couple of the ex-pat staff. They'd assess damage to the building and work out what is missing. Andrew is very lucky that you recovered the Keys and Codes."

Patrick nodded and they drank in silence for a bit.

One or two others began filing into the bar as their working day came to an end. Now and again, Kim nodded to someone he knew – most as Royal Counties Bank customers. As the clock edged towards six o'clock, their self-appointed leaving time, Florence turned up, with her boyfriend, Alan in tow.

Alan nodded at Patrick and Kim. "Hey, guys. Dry white, Flo?"

"Ooh, yes please." As Alan hurried away to place his order, Florence went to Patrick and said, very quietly, "I need to talk to you – alone." She checked that Alan was still trying to choose a wine at the bar. "That is, my father wants to see you. We've had a development."

Patrick was all ears. It wasn't like Florence to bring Serious into any conversation. "Can you tell me what? Briefly?"

"The Harbour Master is hiding on Iririki Island …with us. Shush!" Alan was coming back, tinkling glasses as he walked.

"What's up with you lads?" opened Alan, pulling up a chair for Florence and settling himself on the next table along. "You look quite stunned, if I may say so. It must be the shock of seeing the lovely Florence, eh?"

"Um, yes. It must be, Alan. She does brighten any room, doesn't she?" Patrick winked at Florence. If only the man knew how she spoke about him when not in earshot. "Actually, Kim and I were about to go home – we nipped in here first to put the world to rights and we need to get some dinner on the go."

"Did you?"

"Sorry?"

"'Put the world to rights'?"

Patrick gave him a half-hearted smile. "Not completely. But the beers are beginning to help. Actually, it's good that you came in here – Kim had something he wanted to discuss with you – privately."

This caught both Kim and Alan by surprise. Patrick mugged frantically at his friend, hoping to convey that he wanted a few minutes' chat alone with Florence. "You know, Kim - about the company…"

"Oh, yes. Right. The …er, company. Yes. Could we, …um, step over there for a second, Alan? I wanted to run something by you."

Florence suppressed a giggle, not very successfully. When Kim had propelled Alan out of earshot, she giggled, "You are bad, Patrick Field. Poor Kim! Anyway, Lionel swum over to Iririki Island after he and Sheila were attacked along the dockside. Men came to threaten him at home and they both ran out the back into the jungle. They made their way down to the dock and he was trying to board their boat when these men caught them up and attacked."

"What happened next? Why were they attacked?"

"Lionel says it is to do with the man who ordered Sheila's kidnapping before. He warned Lionel off – well, told him not to do his job, basically. But then Lionel impounded a crate which fell during the unloading process and was damaged. It burst open on the ground."

"Go on…"

"At first, he thought it was full of flour. But it was some other white powder – some drug or other he said – and Tai Nguyen wants it back."

"Oh dear. Where is the crate now?"

"Locked in one of the sheds."

"I suppose I understand why the Harbour Master is hiding on your island – it's British sovereign territory, after all. But what happened to Sheila? Was she kidnapped again?"

A tear formed in Florence's eyes. "Patrick, they stabbed her with a knife or something and that is why Lionel jumped into the water to escape."

"Jesus, Florence, I knew Nguyen was powerful in this town and likely dangerous, but... this is much worse than I'd considered. Did Sheila die? Is she ok? What happened?"

"I'm told bystanders pushed a wad of cloth into the wound and stopped the bleeding. At least long enough to get her to Vila Base. I think it was Jess who did an emergency operation on her to repair the damage and keep her alive. She's ok from what I hear."

"When was this?" asked Patrick.

"Early Monday morning."

That jolted Patrick. He didn't know what to say. Was Sheila Brasted the patient on the other gurney when he went for his urgent blood donation?

-----//-----

Patrick realised Kim was waving his hands with desperation to illustrate something. It was obvious that he'd confused Alan who wasn't following him at all. High time to rescue his friend. But he bent his head closer to Florence and said, "Could I visit your father tomorrow? Actually, I also have some documents for the captain to sign, if he's up to it."

She nodded, vigorously. "I'll say you are ready to receive his call whenever he has a chance."

Using the few seconds it took to walk Alan across to the other side of the bar, Kim had tried to made up some flaky story. He pretended to seek accounting or legal advice about setting up an offshore company for trade finance purposes. He knew it was all rubbish as he was inventing it as he went along and was beginning to worry that Alan might cotton on.

Patrick got up and went over. "Sorry to interrupt, Kim, but we really must be setting off – all the best cuts at Bon Plats will have gone if we aren't quick. I must tear him away, Alan – have a good evening with Florence!"

"Maybe if you give me a call in the morning, Kim..?"

"Righto – thanks. 'Night…'"

Patrick and Kim strode out of the front of the Hotel towards their cars. "What the Hell was that about?" asked Kim. "Thank goodness Alan isn't the sharpest tack in the box. It was easy to send him on a wild goose chase of fictional 'What Ifs', but why did you need him out of the way?"

"All that stuff I was worrying about for Lionel Brasted? It's all true, and much worse. I'll fill you in at home. Come on. We can stop in at Bon Plats for some paté and veggies."

-----//-----

As they chopped, peeled and sliced food in Kim's flat for their dinner, Patrick filled him in with all the details Florence had relayed. Kim forgave him for the embarrassing episode with Alan before he got even halfway through.

"Jesus. So it's drugs and guns? What else is this man into?"

"If we are counting, add money-laundering to that list."

"You know you said you'd take the bank documents for Brasted to sign when you visit Iririki Island? Better not do that."

"Why not? We need his signature."

"Come on! I've had as much beer as you. If you get the Harbour Master's signature

356

on documents tomorrow, that means you know where he is." Patrick was still looking blank. "And other people *don't* know where he is – if you follow my drift?"

"Oh. Yes, ok. Hmmn. I'll take them and he can tell me what to do - maybe he has a colleague who can act in his stead."

"I'd be surprised if he is in the least bit worried about Royal Counties Bank documents, Patrick. He does have a couple of other pressing items bearing down on him right now."

"True. This is all turning a bit nasty, isn't it?"

It took several glasses of Glayva after dinner to make either of them sleepy enough to turn in.

-----//-----

Even before the bank was open the next morning, Patrick's phone rang. He answered right away and told the British Resident Commissioner it would be his pleasure to join them for dinner that night. A little later, he telephoned the hospital.

"Good morning? This is Patrick Field at Royal Counties Bank. I'm calling to enquire about the progress of Mrs Brasted?"

"Are you a relative, Sir?"

357

"Er, no. Merely a concerned friend. I was …present during her operation. Back on Monday, you know and… Well. I just want to find out if she is getting better."

"I see. Just a minute, Sir." He sensed he'd been put on hold as the telephone emitted only strange electronic noises.

"Patrick, this is Jessica."

"Jess! Am I pleased to talk to you! Is she going to be alright?"

"In view of the …situation, I can't confirm whether she is here still, but there is no need to worry now."

"Ah, right. I begin to follow. I've been putting two and two together and ending up with a lot more than four. I haven't seen you for ages. Are you alright? I'm flying the day after tomorrow and I really wanted to see you before I go."

"That might be difficult, Patrick. Sorry, but there it is. Perhaps we'd better say good bye now."

"Goodbye? I can't do that on the telephone. I know – can we meet tonight? Oh, wait. Dammit."

"Don't tell me. You are seeing Florence again?"

"As it happens, I am…"

"Goodbye, Patrick. I have to go now."

And she did.

Patrick threw his pen at the wall. Then he slumped back in his chair. This was so unfair. Fate was conspiring against him.

The smell of coffee made him turn his head. Sara was standing beside him, holding a full, steaming mug. "*Wunem blo'yufela*?"

A tear brimmed in his eyes at this simple gesture of kindness. He took the coffee, wordlessly. For an instant he held Sara's hand. Her face radiated sympathy. "*Arretuu, e gud.*"

Somehow, he managed to agree, "Yes, tomorrow all will be good."

-----//-----

Dinner on Iririki was abbreviated and not lavish. It was far more of an informal, working meal than the Silver Service Patrick had experienced before. He felt emotionally battered. He tried confessing something of that to Florence, her mother and to the British Resident Commissioner himself when he arrived at the official residence.

"This is my first overseas posting with Royal Counties Bank and I know it is coming to an end shortly. I seem to have fitted so much into my couple of years here. The UK was never like this! I think I shall be needing the whole of my six weeks' leave to catch up on sleep."

They made sympathetic noises walking to the Dining Room where Captain Brasted awaited them. "Patrick! Dear boy. How are you?" He had recovered a little of his general bonhomie, for the greeting, anyway.

"I'm fine, thanks, Captain. I was confessing to some emotional exhaustion and am looking forward to a spell of leave starting tomorrow. But, more importantly, how are you? I understand that Mrs Brasted is recovering, although the hospital wouldn't give me any details or even confirm where she is."

"She is being guarded by a small contingent of the British Royal Marines from 42 Commando who have been allowed to disembark – at last, eh?" He looked back at Andrew Stuart. The Commissioner acknowledged this with a grim smile. Unbeknownst to Patrick, Stuart's French counterpart, Inspector Robert, had expressly forbidden deployment of the Marines. He claimed that his own French paratroopers, flown in earlier from Noumea, could take care of the rebellion. In fact, Robert ordered them to stand aside and take no action, leaving Jimmy Stevens unchecked.

"I have my tickets back to the UK for long leave," Patrick said. He spoke mainly towards the Commissioner, "So Kim and I have worked out our plan to deliver the money laundering evidence to Royal Counties Bank's Inspection department."

"Good, good. Let's sit down and have some supper." Stuart led the way. "Lionel? Would you like to sit there, beside Florence? Patrick? Over here, I think."

There was an enormous quiche, some cut meats and a vast bowl of salad leaves. The butler brought in a large loaf of crusty bread too, still warm from the oven.

All the place settings boasted a wine glass as well as knives and forks and spoons. The Commissioner extended a bottle of white wine towards Patrick. "Some wine? Or would you prefer a beer?"

"A glass of wine would be lovely," Patrick affirmed. "Thank you. I am trying to learn more about wine by exploring La Cave du Gourmets. I need to expand my horizons."

"Well, there's nothing wrong with a pint of proper ale, in my view" opined the host. "But wine has its place too."

"Captain? You have a great deal on your mind right now, in terms of personal safety, but is there someone working at the port who can carry out your administrative duties *pro tem* until this Nguyen man can be constrained?" Patrick couldn't help asking, even though he had been persuaded by Kim to leave his shipping papers behind. In fact, the man was relieved to be able to discuss a work-related topic. The Captain gave him a name to seek out at the port on the understanding that he'd not reveal the source of the introduction.

They began to eat. The Commissioner set out evidence which he had acquired. It featured low-volume thievery and criminality but also large amounts of money laundering at a state level. This could not be tackled locally but had been passed, he said, to Interpol and MI-6 in London.

"I hope you don't mind, Patrick, but I included your name in my recent reports to London. It is important that they can distinguish the Bad Hats from others," said the Commissioner as they said their goodbyes on the steps of the residency at the end of the evening.

"Whatever I can do to help…" replied Patrick. "Goodbye, Commissioner; Mrs Stuart – I do hope I will see you again after my leave. And Florence? We should definitely catch up the month after next! Captain – please pass my regards to your wife with my wishes for a speedy recovery."

They all waved as he made his way towards the little dock where the Commissioner's launch waited to take him back to town.

-----//-----

At the airport, Patrick and Kim shook hands, surprising each other with such formality, never having done that before.

"Good luck with those. I'll keep my eyes open for more material. Have a good flight."

"Thanks, Kim. Take care, and give Florence a ring now and again, so she can keep her father up to date."

Kim nodded. "Bye, now."

Patrick went into the terminal building to check in for the first leg of his return journey to the UK. He had stuffed the copies of bank records which Kim had prepared into his overnight bag. They would stay with him all the time during the journey. 'I wouldn't want those lost with the rest of my luggage,' he thought.

# Chapter 14
# Long Leave

As was usual for Royal Counties Bank ex-patriate staff, Patrick was required to attend a series of interviews back in the UK. These were to assess his performance during his time in the New Hebrides. Both Group Economics department and senior line management would want to know the most up to date information about the islands. On this occasion, Patrick hoped for promotion into another job at the end of his posting. There might be meetings with potential new managers having job openings.

"What did you do well, Patrick? And what do you feel you fell short on while in the New Hebrides?" asked the Staff Manager in Human Resources department. The man had on his desk a copy of Patrick's annual appraisal which Andrew Cutlass had sent through. Patrick tried hard to read it upside down. In those days, staff were not allowed to know what managers had written about them. He expected the man to pick out a particular phrase, or mention some element of the report to discuss in depth. But he was in the dark about details on both ends of the performance spectrum.

"I do find it challenging to talk about myself in these terms," he began. "It's easy to think of a few isolated incidents where I reckon I did well. I'm afraid it's also easy to recall a couple of errors which might have cost the bank money if I or a colleague hadn't discovered them in good time."

"Go on," said the man.

"Well, when the Keys and Codes were left behind in Santo Branch, I suggested to Mr Cutlass that I could put together a group of volunteers, sail up there and recover them."

The man had raised his eyebrows.

"I also brought down all the cash in the cages, but not the cash in the tills. I judged there wasn't time, and we didn't want to encounter the rebels."

"There are some references here to that escapade." The man adjusted the glasses on his nose, the better to focus on the relevant sentence. "I understand you were part of the group assembled by Cutlass to carry out his plan. Is that not the case?"

Patrick's jaw dropped. Should he contradict his Chief Manager or should he go along with Cutlass' fabricated version of events?

"In so far as I report to Mr Cutlass and he authorised the idea, it is right to include him in the final success of the mission."

The Staff manager grunted. "Jolly good. Jolly good. Let's move on. I understand you underwent some short period incarcerated in the British Prison..?" The spectacles came off and he rested them on his thigh and sat back. "What, pray, was the reason for that?"

Patrick thought fast. He was not yet ready to talk about the money laundering he and Kim thought they had uncovered. And this Staff Department fellow was not the right person to receive that news, anyway. How to explain why he - a British subject, a banker, no less, was locked up for some days? He hadn't even been able to call for a lawyer or similar third-party help. At last, he said, "It was very unpleasant. A complete misunderstanding, I'm afraid. Mistaken identity or something. The legal system in the New Hebrides isn't sophisticated and I had witnessed a road accident. The complication was that others claimed I had caused it. The matter was all cleared up in the end, I'm pleased to say."

"All part of Life's Rich Pageant, eh? And what tasks do you feel you underperformed, Patrick?"

This question called for a serious face. He frowned a little in his effort to produce the appropriate demeanour. "One error I made which came to light was to permit a customer to overdraw their business account. It was only a small amount to clear documents for shipments which had arrived, but the customer did not have a formal overdraft arrangement. There was no loss for the bank. And I'm happy to say that the customer now does have that marked facility. I do accept that I granted a loan when I did not have authority to do so."

The man made another unintelligible noise which may or may not have been favourable. Patrick couldn't tell.

"Moving on, where do you see yourself in ten years' time?"

He was fast gathering the impression that this man had a list of a dozen rote questions. Likely he'd record some semblance of Patrick's answers and they would never again see the light of day.

"As Chief Manager of a large regional branch in America or Canada. Also the Far

East, if the branch had an active trade finance and dealing operation. I have a penchant for all those activities now and there will be other skills I can gather between now and then."

Patrick had rehearsed that answer on the train during his journey to the interview. It pleased him. It sounded better said out loud than it had when drafted in his diary. But how was it received?

The man scribbled on the back of the Cutlass annual appraisal while Patrick waited. Then he said, "You may get your chance sooner than you think. We have arranged interviews for you tomorrow with the International Banking Division in London. It has divisions operating in the U.S. and Middle and Far East areas as well as Europe and the Pacific. Can you report to Head Office in the City tomorrow at 9:00am?"

"Oh, yes. With pleasure," Patrick answered. The man handed over an itinerary. There were six people listed.

"After those interviews, and lunch with Regional Office, you should make your way to Harley Street so the Bank doctor can give you a check over. Alright?"

Patrick nodded. He'd have to make sure he didn't over-indulge at luncheon lest the doctor form an unfavourable opinion of his usual alcohol consumption.

"Very well. Do you have any questions for me?" This in a tone which suggested that he expected or desired no questions at all.

"No, no - that's all fine, thanks," replied Patrick.

"Excellent. I am pleased to advise that your notional UK salary will increase by 5%, starting from next month. Mr Cutlass has given you a most favourable report. You understand, of course, that, should your next posting be abroad, you will be paid again in local currency rather than in Pounds Sterling?"

"I do. Like I have been in the New Hebrides."

"Indeed. And should you be approved for a job in the UK at a higher grade, your notional UK salary will reflect that higher pay scale."

"I see," said Patrick. "Thank you."

"Right. That's all. Good luck." The reading glasses came off again.

Patrick rose and shook the man's hand. Why would Cutlass have given him such a favourable report? Patrick knew the fellow thought him an idiot. Was promotion elsewhere to get him out of Cutlass' hair? To shift the 'Patrick Field' problem onto someone else's desk?

Patrick spotted someone he knew as he walked down the corridor towards the exit. They exchanged a few pleasantries and the man hurried on his way. Patrick signed out at the main building reception. He wandered in the general direction of the railway station. There was plenty of time - some forty minutes - to kill before the next London-bound train pulled in. Close to the station, he found an old-fashioned pub, clad in olive and brown coloured tiling. The windows were somewhat dingy. But his breakfast was long ago and the sign over the doorway assured the visitor that they could sample 'Cask Ales and Good Food'. Feeling over-dressed in his suit, Patrick pushed on the swing door. Warm, beery, Essence of Pub enveloped him. He approached the bar and smiled to himself. The publican stood behind it in a classic poise - polishing glasses, almost as a default activity while he waited for custom.

"Are you serving food yet?"

"We are. Shepherd's Pie, Turkey Pie and Beef and Ale Pie. Or a sandwich," the barman finished, as though Real Men didn't eat sandwiches.

"Ooh. Shepherd's Pie and peas, please. No chips, thanks. What do you have on draft?"

The barman wrote out his order and passed it through the serving hatch behind him. "These are all local ales; there's Flowers from Stratford upon Avon and Youngs from London up that end."

"A pint of Youngs, please."

While the food was being heated, Patrick went and sat by the window to savour his pint. The small amount of sunlight which managed to get through the pub's windows refracted and danced through the foaming liquid. He brought it to his lips and inhaled its fragrance. Taking a first long pull at the drink, he decided that it was far more refreshing than his recent drink of choice, Fosters, had been. However, the thought of serving such a bitter beer in the warmth of the New Hebrides was not pleasant. 'Horses for courses', he concluded.

-----//-----

As was his habit, Patrick laid out his clothes for the London interviews the night before. It was important to make sure all the creases were in the right places. He checked for unwanted stains too. He had to look his best. The particular choices of shirt and tie were more readily made now instead of early in the morning. He might not be at his brightest then, worrying about how many minutes remained before the train left. Would cufflinks appear pretentious? Plain silver ones would be smart but not dressy. He inserted them into one side of the shirt cuffs, set his alarm and climbed into bed. Sleep came almost as soon as his head hit the pillow.

He planned to catch one train earlier than the timetable suggested would be adequate. Any delay or service cancellation might result in being late. He did not want to be accused of a lack of forward planning for an important interview. He'd bagged a seat when he boarded, but it was a close thing. In the short time that he'd been abroad, commuter numbers on this route had increased. By the time the train had called at a couple more stations, many passengers were standing in his carriage. He watched out of the window as the train progressed from station to station. The countryside of open fields and woods near to his parents' house was superseded by built-up streets of closely-packed terraced houses. Collections of office buildings soon replaced them and signalled arrival into London itself.

Patrick had forgotten how little conversation ever occurred on commuter trains like this - at least, those heading into London. Everyone either read their newspaper or a book or stared vacantly out of the window. What were they thinking? *Were* they thinking? He did not want his career to be like this. The idea of boarding the same carriage on the same train every morning for forty years was appalling. To sit in the same compartment, often in the same seat opposite the same people all reading the same newspaper. And nobody even spoke to each other! He now knew there was more to life.

Hopefully, one of these upcoming interviews would result in him avoiding the soulless intellectual desert of the morning commute on British Rail for a while longer.

Pulling out of London Bridge, the train rattled past Borough Market on its elevated track and in towards the terminus north of the River Thames. In the event, they pulled into Cannon Street station bang on time. Almost as soon as the train had left London Bridge, many had folded their newspapers and prepared to get up. Everybody was in a rush and he alone had time to spare. He sheltered his feet as best he could from the shuffling, platform-bound masses and remained seated for a minute or two. Letting others off first might save the shine on his polished shoes.

He presented his return ticket at the barrier and gave a cheerful, "Good morning!" to the ticket collector, startling the man. People didn't say hello in the mornings in London. They just didn't. Patrick checked his watch. There might be time for a quick coffee in the Italian café near Leadenhall Market.

-----//-----

His first interview was with an American Senior Vice President named Hank Bagnato. Hank ran the Financial Institution relationship management team out of New York. They covered U.S. money-centre and regional banks throughout north America. The London-based team responsible for Canadian banks also reported to him. This convoluted arrangement, Hank explained, was to take account of Canadian sensibilities. They didn't like having oversight from New York – London was much more acceptable.

Hank strode about the 5th floor interview room, peering out of the window at the City of

London skyline. He had a restless energy and spoke in clipped sentences. Patrick guessed this was how people were in New York. At one point, the man sat opposite him and produced a very large Bowie knife. He proceeded to clean his finger nails. Patrick found himself staring at the knife - it was very distracting. Hank peppered direct questions about his banking experience like a Gatling gun. How deep was his knowledge of foreign exchange dealing? How did the money markets work - and so on. It was altogether most unnerving.

"Where's Cable today?"

"Cable? Oh, Sterling / dollar rates… It's heading up towards 2.4 again. I reckon it'll get there by the year end. It was 2.35 when I last checked."

"What's market sentiment on that?"

"It's discounted: the market says the dollar will be below 2 by next summer."

"What do you think?"

"I don't have enough economic data to predict it and would rely on Royal Counties Bank's economists. I'd be advising my British corporate customers to lock in these rates by buying whatever dollars they can afford now, at Spot price."

Hank paused for a moment. "And how would you advise an American bank?"

"I wouldn't advise them one way or the other. They have their own economists and would be using the same data we do." Hank looked at him intently. "Instead, I'd try to suggest products we can offer them to hedge against whatever they fear most."

"Good answer." Hank stabbed the big knife downwards into the blotter on top of the desk. It sat there, quivering. "Are you afraid of flying?"

Patrick suppressed a laugh. His journeys to and from the New Hebrides had taken several days each way. Overnight hotel stays in some exotic locations separated each leg of the long journey. The aeroplanes he'd taken ranged from very large jets to a twin engine, 50-seater Fokker Friendship. So, no, he didn't think he was afraid of flying.

"Er, no. I'm not. Although the New Hebrides was my first overseas posting, I have been on a wide variety of aeroplanes from the very big to the very small."

"You'd have a 30% travel schedule – can you manage that?"

Patrick wasn't quite sure what that meant. He assumed Hank had in mind trips equating to one week in three spent visiting neighbouring states and cities. In the second or two he had to answer, he gave no thought to what that might mean for his social or home life. His world view right now was almost all to do with his job. Everything else would have to fit in around that.

"Sure I can."

Hank tugged his knife out of the blotter with some effort. Patrick thought he stabbed it with enough force to go through to the desk surface beneath, but kept quiet.

"Right. Time's up. Any questions for me?"

Patrick felt that Hank had explained the general parameters of the opening in New York. But he also reasoned he would need to boost his product knowledge beyond the basic trade finance instruments of his past experience.

"If accepted, I'd like to spend a little time in the dealing room. I have a passing familiarity with the common trading instruments. But if I am talking with other banks, I need to be as fluent as they are - especially so in products where Royal Counties Bank is a market maker. Would that be possible?"

"Yes."

Hank was on his feet again. "Gotta go. I have an appointment with a couple Canadians I haven't seen this year." He extended his hand to Patrick. Their handshake was brief but firm.

-----//-----

Patrick's next interview was with an Arabian gentleman. Balding, pigeon-toed and with the faintest suggestion of a stoop, the man was the polar opposite to the clipped and precise Hank Bagnato. Patrick never understood exactly what Elias Al Masri was in charge of. He spoke about a position based in Bahrain, in the Arabian Gulf. He himself did not work there and the Bahrain office did not report to him, although Patrick gathered the Cairo, Egypt office did – perhaps! The job sounded rather like Kim's job in the New Hebrides, although did not involve personal or retail banking. Patrick would have corporate customers and financial institution customers, ie. not just banks. Some might be quasi-governmental investment entities.

"What geographic area will I be looking after?" asked Patrick.

"The Gulf and MATEL. Maybe Turkey; it depends."

"MATEL? What is that?"

"Morocco, Algeria, Tunisia, Egypt and Libya."

"Ah - right." Patrick's mind was whirling. He knew nothing about the region. It was common knowledge that the economies depended on oil and gas, of which they had lots, and most were ridiculously rich. But he'd also seen photographs of very poor Arabs begging in the streets. Perhaps the economies and social organisation were not that developed after all.

"You referred to the Bahrain office as the 'O.B.U.' What is that?"

"Offshore Banking Unit. It's the dealing hub for the Middle East, trading in 273 currencies, 7 days per week."

"Seven?" queried Patrick. "Do they work at weekends, then?"

"Friday is the 'weekend' in the Arab world: it's the day for religious observance. The dealing room needs to stay open on Friday, of course, as the rest of the world trades then."

An obvious question occurred to Patrick. "How does the dealing room manage to quote rates on Saturdays and Sundays? Do they

380

adjust value dates and amend the rates with one or two days' extra interest?"

Elias returned Patrick's gaze from beneath hooded eyes which gave nothing away. After a short pause, he murmured, "Something like that, yes."

Had he but known, that answer was telling. In that last part of their brief exchange, Patrick had experienced his first characteristic interaction with an Arabian person. In later life, he would learn, from such answers, to glean a great deal of information about the person with whom he was negotiating. It would take many, many such lessons for him to begin to appreciate that Arabs prized the art of negotiation. With these responses to each other, Patrick had revealed to his potential boss that he was capable of thinking quickly. He had come up with a practical explanation for a situation he had not encountered before – banks trading on Saturdays and Sundays. By his reply, Elias Al Masri was revealing he had never thought to enquire how the Bahrain dealing room managed to juggle these unusual value dates. Or that he knew well how it was done, but chose not to reveal the method. In time, Patrick would learn that withholding information might, one day, give him an advantage.

But for now, Patrick saw none of this.

The rest of the interview explored Patrick's knowledge of various aspects of the job. He had no clue about investment management. Some about interest rate hedging techniques and plenty about Foreign exchange and trade finance. At the end, they shook hands and Al Masri promised to be in touch through Staff Department. Unlike the first job interview, Patrick could not divine whether he had done well or failed miserably. It had been all rather confusing. He had little more idea about what the job might include. The man had been vague and shied away from detail. Patrick took this to suggest that the job would encompass whatever he wanted to make of it – or, more likely, whatever was thrown at him.

A couple of contacts in the Head Office Trade Finance area had asked to see Patrick as well, so he walked down to the second floor to say, 'Hello'. It was always wise to maintain your contacts, he knew.

That evening, he met up with several friends from school. He happened to be looking out of his parent's front window when

James' Austin 1300 pulled up. James beeped the car's horn and kept the engine running.

"I'll try not to be too late – I've got a key." Patrick called up the stairs to his Mum as he closed the front door.

"Wow! What a tan!" James greeted him as they hugged. "Did you spend any time indoors?"

"Yeah, a little – enough to avoid getting into trouble." Patrick replied. He patted his trouser pocket to assure himself he had his wallet.

"Right. You are first, Alan will be next, then Paul in Sidcup and we're going to the Woodman in Ide Hill. Do you know it?" Patrick shook his head.

"I don't mind which pub – as long as it doesn't serve Fosters!"

James drove towards Orpington, to collect Alan, then along the Footscray Road to Sidcup. Patrick gave up the front seat to Paul to accommodate his 6 feet 4 inches height, south into the countryside.

-----//-----

"The first round is on me," announced Patrick as they climbed out of James' car.

The Woodman pub in Ide Hill overlooks Goathurst Common and dates from the early

19th Century. The lower storey and the gable walls consist of two colours of bricks laid in the traditional Kent and Sussex manner. Diamond patterns stand out with a purple hue from the background of burnt orange bricks. A deeply hipped roof compliments the dormer windows of the upper storey. The oldest parts of the structure have lower ceilings than the later additions. Patrick wondered whether Paul would remember to duck his head every time they moved towards an exposed beam. The owners had thoughtfully wrapped leather padding around the beams most likely to give trouble. They had chosen padding which matched the many horse brasses, Toby Jugs and assorted pewter drinking vessels adorning the walls. The whole effect made the pub roomier and brighter than it might sound because the beams had not been allowed to darken with age. The exposed brickwork was clean and the areas of plaster were a light creamy colour. Even the floor boards were a light shade of brown. 'Sanded and refinished', he thought.

To his delight, there was a varied selection of real ales on draft. He straight away chose a pint of Harveys Best Bitter. A lighter (4% by vol) beer would be better for a 'session'. Recently, Patrick had done some research on the brewery. They used Maris Otter malted barley. The brewery had been in the hands of the same family since the late 18th Century. And they'd used the same strain of top fermenting yeast since 1960. Quite a record. He remembered how refreshing he found this particular ale. Did any of his friends care about all that? Reciting all these facts might not impress them. Better to keep all that knowledge inside his head and not show off.

"What'll you have? I'm having Harveys." he asserted, before elbowing his way through the thirsty patrons towards the bar. James and Paul went along with Patrick's choice, but Alan asked, "What lagers do they have?"

Patrick made a show of curling his upper lip in affected disdain. "Lager? Listen, I've been forced to drink nothing but lager for the last two years… Oh, alright. I'll ask and we'll have to hope they don't throw us out."

Alan grinned and punched his arm. "Ow! You see? They'll be afraid we're lager louts."

Patrick excused his way up to the bar. "Three pints of Harveys Best, please and a pint of lager – if you have any."

As the barman began pulling the Harveys he said, "We've got Hoffmeister and Fosters."

"Ok, and a pint of Fosters, please."

"Just cans at the moment, I'm afraid."

"A can, then." Patrick handed over his fiver and scooped up the change. "Could I borrow a tray?" he asked the barman.

"They're all in use, I'm afraid."

At that moment, a young woman who had been standing beside Patrick at the bar turned to him and asked, "Would you like a hand with those? I'm still waiting for my friends so I don't mind losing my place at the bar."

She had such an open face that Patrick accepted the offer with alacrity. "That is so kind of you. I'd be afraid of dropping one or more of the glasses even if I had a tray. But there's one condition!"

"And what might that be?"

"That I buy you a drink to say 'thank you'." She beamed at him.

"Well, that is very kind of you! May I have a glass of red?"

Patrick raised his hand to attract the barman's attention.

"Is everything alright, Sir?"

"Oh yes. But I'd like to add one more drink to my order if that's ok."

"By all means, Sir. Another beer?"

"What red wines do you have?"

Patrick turned to the young woman. "Do you have a favourite or shall I choose for you?"

"Go ahead. You choose," she said.

"We've got a House red, a Bordeaux which we sell by the glass and some of the Beaujolais Nouveau."

This last was exciting for Patrick. He pricked up his ears. Recently, he and Kim had indulged in a couple of cases of that year's Nouveau and he vividly recalled its slight overtones of banana. He made up his mind.

"Could I have a bottle of the Nouveau and two glasses?" The barman went off to the wine rack at the far end of the bar and Patrick turned to the young woman. "Would you care to join my friends and I – at least until your friends appear?"

"I'd love to – thank you. Now I'll take those two and we can come back for the wine."

Patrick led the way. "This is James, that's Alan and Paul is the little chap at the end. My name is Patrick. I'd introduce you, but I don't know your name."

"I'm Penelope."

"Ok - Gents, meet Penelope. She has kindly offered to help me bring the drinks over."

Penelope leaned forward to shake everybody's hand in turn. Patrick had returned to the bar for the wine.

"Um, is this where we ask if you come here often?" James opened. She rewarded him with a shy smile.

"Something like that. I had wriggled all the way up to the bar to be ready to order as soon as my friends arrive. But then I saw Patrick was struggling with all your drinks so I took pity on him. I guess my friends are going to be late – again."

Patrick arrived with the bottle and the glasses and dragged a stool across from a neighbouring table. He stopped Alan reaching for his can of Fosters by warning everyone, "Watch out, chaps - that's not as cold as it ought to be. It's going to spray everywhere unless you give it the W.A. tap."

Alan paused, although his fingernail was already underneath the tab on the can. "The what?"

"It stands for 'West Australia'. Tell you what - give it here. I'll show you." Patrick reached over and tapped the top of the can twice, either side of the ring pull. "Now you can go ahead safely."

Alan smiled and shook his head. Patrick was either nutty or was showing off to this girl.

"You don't believe me, do you, Alan?"

"Nope. Can I open my beer now?"

"Sure. We won't have a problem now."

He operated the ring pull; there was a satisfying 'Phhiiitt' noise and Alan poured his beer into the glass.

"See?" said Patrick, pouring a glass of wine for Penelope.

She raised it and they all clinked glasses with murmurs of 'Cheers'. Patrick closed his eyes for a moment in pleasure at the taste of such excellent beer. He downed half of it in one draught. "That was …glorious," he opined. But then he remembered his manners and glanced at Penelope. For a second, he was transported back to the terrace outside his flat in the New Hebrides. That was where he and Kim had first tried that year's Beaujolais Nouveau. "Does it taste slightly of banana?" he enquired.

"Why, yes. It does. It's lovely, actually. How did you know?" She asked.

"I tried some while I was abroad. I returned very recently and so wanted to go out with these reprobates to find out what they've been up to all this time."

"How exciting," she exclaimed. "Could we play a little game – until my friends come along?"

Everybody nodded agreement. "Ok. How about I guess what you all do and you can tell me how close I am?"

"And then we guess what you do?" asked James.

"By all means. So – you first. You're James, right?"

"I am."

She leaned back and tilted her head as though trying to examine him from a different angle. "Hmmn. I'm thinking …'teacher', but not in a school. Am I close?"

James' parents had been teachers, but he wasn't. He worked in one of the domestic branches of Royal Counties Bank. "I have given some training classes at my office but my Mum and Dad were both teachers." Penelope smiled in partial triumph.

"Do I get half marks then? And may I suggest a change of career for you?" James laughed and took another pull at his beer to cover up his embarrassment. Somehow, she'd hit the nail on the head. He joined the Royal Counties Bank after school because he didn't know what else to do and in truth, he didn't like it one bit. He'd been thinking over and over how he could jump into something else. Having a monthly salary was nice, though; he and his girlfriend hoped to get married soon. Then there would be children... Not the time to be faffing around, unable to pick a career for the rest of his life. No – it was safer to stay where he was.

Penelope turned to Alan. "Engineer? Something methodical and requiring precision, I reckon. I saw the way you poured your Fosters – even without Patrick's help!"

"Wow. Spot on, actually. I'm training to be a structural engineer. I'm on attachment to a local firm at the moment as my 'Year in Industry'." He laughed, a little ruefully. "I haven't covered 'Fluid Dynamics yet."

"Paul, I am blanking on you completely. I saw some flour on your jacket, but you might have visited a doughnut shop on the way here. I admit defeat!"

Now it was Paul's turn to be amazed. His jaw sagged and he brushed his jacket self-consciously. "Gosh. You are observant, I must say. Actually, you should have gone with that idea. I'm working in my father's bakery at the moment and I hope to take it over from him when he retires next year."

Penelope raised her glass in his direction. "Well, I wish you good luck and good baking. May your dough always rise!"

Everybody chuckled.

"Now for you, Patrick."

She shifted around on her stool to see him better and brushed an imaginary lock of hair off her forehead. He began to think Penelope had rather a penetrating gaze. Instead of looking him up and down as she had the others, she was looking straight at his eyes, without blinking. After a few seconds, Patrick began to feel uncomfortable. He didn't want to be the one to break the eye contact, though. Instead, in his mind, he turned it into a competition. He refused to be the loser in a staring challenge.

As soon as he did that, though, Penelope said, "Now you are staring rather than looking at me."

That jolted Patrick. How did she know…?

His guilt at being found out must have communicated itself because she relaxed and broke the eye contact. "That's better. You, Patrick, are a banker. You work abroad – you have a tan – but it's deeper than you could get in Europe, and you know about the W.A. tap, so I'm thinking – somewhere in the Pacific?"

"Crikey. If I was wearing a hat, I'd remove it right now," admitted Patrick. "You are very observant indeed."

"Because I spotted you struggling with four drinks at the bar? I don't think so!"

"But now it's our turn," said Patrick. "Fair's fair. Any ideas, lads?" Alan and Paul shook their heads, fearful of suggesting a job which was way below Penelope's talents.

James was braver, though. "I think you might be one of those psychoanalysts the Police use when they are trying to work out what kind of person committed a crime."

Penelope giggled. "Oh, I must tell my boss when I see him. He'll like that. Patrick?" And she turned The Gaze back onto him.

Playing for time, he drained his beer, set it down and centred it with precision on the beer mat in front of him. "I reckoned James was on the right lines, but his suggestion was …too obvious. I am thinking Personnel Recruitment. Maybe a head hunter?"

Penelope pushed the empty second wine glass across to him and filled it about a third of the way up. She topped up her own glass too. Little creases formed beside her eyes as she fought to restrain her victory smile. She raised her glass to them and said, "Patrick and James, you are both right, in a way. James, I do work for the government, although I'm not a psychoanalyst. Patrick, you are closest - I do work in recruitment, at least for some of the time – so well done, both of you."

With the ice broken, Patrick asked, "Come on, you guys. What have you all been doing?"

"Oh, nothing much," said Alan. "You know: the usual. I broke 90 during a round of golf last month for the first time."

"Was that after the handicap was applied?" Paul joked.

"I'd like to see you do better," Alan retorted.

"How about next Saturday?"

"Done."

"Anyone got married? Robbed a bank? Been to Spain?" enquired Patrick.

"Spain in November?" James said. "Don't be daft. And I don't want my bank robbing activities to be public knowledge."

The banter continued in the same vein. But it revealed that the lives of Patrick's friends were repetitive. A staid round of golf on Saturday, wash the car on Sunday and curry night on Thursdays. A game of cards might follow afterwards. When it was Patrick's turn, he regaled them with some of his adventures. Snorkelling over reefs, barbeques with Australians, officiating in local politics and helping to name the new currency for the country. Their expressions were dull; their interest forced. His world was not understandable. They simply could not fathom a life which was so unsteady. His was filled with unexpected events, challenges and new, even dangerous situations.

Penelope, by contrast, was enthralled. She hung on his every word, asked for more and more detail and was obviously fascinated.

Paul got up soon to buy his round – James and Alan had already taken their turns, but Penelope said, "It should be my turn. My friends didn't show, so you have all kept me company. I'll get them in."

But James checked his watch and said, "Listen, Penelope, you are very kind, but it's getting a wee bit late. I, for one, have had enough – especially as I'm driving – a pint and a half is my limit." He looked around at the others. "How do you chaps feel? I could have a Coke or something if you fancy 'one for the road'."

Alan and Paul both muttered something about 'needing to work in the morning'. They started to push back their chairs.

"I don't have work tomorrow," Patrick crowed. "I'm on holiday – hooray! But it's been brilliant seeing you all again. I can get a taxi or something…" Then, directed at Penelope, "That is, if you are staying on for a bit?"

"I'd love to stay on too. We could share a cab at least part of the way. I'll get another bottle."

"Alright, that's settled, then. Bye, guys. See you again soon."

The others said goodbye to Penelope and how nice it had been to meet her. Paul bumped his head on a padded beam and staggered a bit, but leaned on Alan to keep his balance. And then they were gone.

"I'm not sure I'm comfortable with you buying the wine," Patrick started to rise to his feet.

"Ah, but I'm on expenses," Penelope reassured him, pressing his shoulder back down. Patrick wasn't wholly sure what that meant, as he had never been able to spend his employer's money like this. He subsided anyway. 'It's a good job Nouveau isn't strong', he mused as he waited for her to come back.

"You should call me 'Penny' - 'Penelope' sounds so formal – it's what my mother calls me when she disapproves of something."

Thus was amusing to Patrick. He'd thought of her immediately as a 'Penny' as soon as she had introduced herself. "Very well. From this day forward, I shall call you 'Penny'." He raised his recharged glass. "To 'Penny'."

"I'm enthralled by what you have been saying about the New Hebrides. It's so exciting to meet someone who lives there. I've heard that - as it's a tax shelter, being an Offshore Island - that lots of criminals launder their monies there. Is that true? I mean, you'd know about that stuff, being in the bank…?"

397

"I'm afraid you might be right, Penny. My colleague, Kim and I have been tracking certain transactions by one or two customers. None of them link to genuine commercial trading."

"So it's true, then." Patrick was aware that she had leaned forward towards him. Every so often, their knees touched under the table. Her hair was cut in a bob style so that the sides fell forward as she leaned, like curtains beside a stage. "And I believe some of the criminals also deal in drugs and gun running too. Did you come across any evidence of that?"

"As a matter of fact, I did happen upon what I think was an exchange of some guns. I saw men opening a large crate, unwrapping something and then one of them lifted out a rifle. This all took place in an abandoned mine and nobody was supposed to witness it – of course."

"But why did you go to Forari in the first place?" she asked.

So Patrick prattled on about wanting to go for a swim and being unable to go back into the water because of his leg wound. He explained that it was only during the drive back that he'd spotted through the trees a white truck belonging to the customer he suspected of money laundering. But he didn't register at first that *she* had been the first to mention the location of the abandoned Manganese mine.

"I didn't know how far the corruption in the financial sector might extend, so I reported all this to the British Resident Commissioner. I didn't want to use my local managerial line."

"I know," said Penny.

Later on, Patrick went over their conversation in his mind. He remembered taking this reply as meaning 'I would have reached the same conclusion' rather than claiming prior knowledge of his action.

"But what about you? You said you do recruiting or something and you work in the Government?"

"Yes, I do. Most big businesses use recruiters when they have a job to fill and the Government is no different – at least for some of the bigger jobs. These days they don't only hire from within. Is it like that with Royal Counties Bank as well?"

Patrick thought about that. When first he joined Royal Counties Bank, he gained the idea that you needed to wait for 'Dead Mens'

Shoes'. This was not an inspiring name for promotional opportunities but it was realistic. In other words, if your boss achieved promotion or retired, you might hope to be considered for his job. Rarely, a promising youngster might receive a promotion into another department, beyond his current line management. As Patrick had recently been accepted onto the Management Development Programme, this was the pattern of advancement he hoped he could achieve. More senior roles would call for experience in a wide range of the bank's functions, so he tried to keep his ear to the ground for suitable openings.

Yet it was also true that there had been new recruits to the bank from other institutions. Royal Counties Bank was keen on ex-Army people, especially at the most senior level. He said as much and outlined his own Game Plan. This was to make several sideways jumps gaining experience and general knowledge while still young.

"Someone has given you good advice."

"Well, not really. It's just a sensible thing to do. I must say, when I joined the bank, there was nothing on the job description about some of the things I've done in the last couple of years."

The barman rang the bell for Last Orders.

"Would you like anything else, Penny?"

"I'd better not, thanks. We have both had plenty to drink." She smiled and winked at him. "I'll order a taxi."

"Oh, no. I should do that. I'll ask the barman for a local firm."

"They'll take ages and most will be busy at closing time. My boss has an account with a regular firm who guarantee pickup for me within thirty minutes."

"Really?" Patrick queried, surprised again. This was another facet of other peoples' jobs with which he was unfamiliar. Expense accounts and now taxis which the firm would pay for.

"Well, if you are sure it will be ok. I feel a little guilty at catching a ride with you. Would you like a cup of coffee while you are waiting? I have no idea if it's drinkable here, although I suspect that most people don't care at this time of night."

"Coffee would be super. Black, please. I'll borrow their phone."

Patrick had to wait while the barman coped with his flurry of Last Orders for alcohol. Several of their fellow patrons could have done with switching to soft drinks at least an hour before. Many were swaying on their feet and spilled much of their final drinks as they found their tables again.

"Two black coffees, please."

They came with a tiny brown biscuit wrapped in cellophane. He took an exploratory sip before carrying them back to the table. When Penny returned, he pushed one towards her. "Here. The biscuit makes the flavour bearable."

Penny laughed as she sat down again. "The car will be here in five minutes - enough time to drink these." She too sipped at the hot, black liquid and wrinkled her mouth. "Ugh... Let's try with the biscuit. Hmmn... 'Bearable', as you said."

They sat in companionable silence, sipping until the coffees had gone.

"I expect he is outside, now. Come on." Penny got up and smoothed her skirt. "I hope your friends won't think I monopolised you."

"Oh, they'll be fine," Patrick responded. He hadn't given his friends another thought after their departure, what? Two hours ago?

This hadn't been the evening he'd expected when inviting them all.

"Thank you, kind sir," Penny acknowledged as he motioned for her to lead the way.

As they reached the door, a loutish bloke pushed his face in front of Patrick. His beery breath washed over them. "Yer in there, mate – go on - give 'er one." The group he was with started jeering encouragement. Right away, he sensed this wasn't the good-natured joshing he'd experienced with his Australian friends.

"I might – if you move out of my way."

Penny had reached the door and heard the exchange, but wasn't fazed or offended by it at all. Nowadays, any young woman walking past a building site could expect to be wolf-whistled at the very least. Often there would be coarse language to boot. She also knew that it was almost always just 'talk'. Lads showing off in front of their mates. She didn't hesitate, but reached around the man's head, pinched some hair in front of one ear and pulled him backwards towards the open door.

At first, Patrick didn't understand why his assailant was staggering backwards in obvious pain – he hadn't made contact with the man. But the drunken group saw what was happening and cheered what Penny was doing. The man's shoulder connected hard with the edge of the door as it began to swing closed. Although off balance, the big lad tried to regain his feet by bracing against it. He had to let go again as it made the pain in the side of his face even more excruciating when Penny pulled ever harder.

He yelled, "Ow! Ow – leggo. You bitch…!"

Of course, his backwards retreat out of the door left the way open for Patrick to follow. The door swung shut behind Patrick just as the stranger stumbled on something, falling towards Penny. It caused her fingers to lose their grip on his short, greasy hair. The lad regained his feet with surprising speed. Pausing to put one hand up to his sideboard, he found that it was now bleeding profusely. Penny had pulled some of the hairs out by the roots.

Patrick couldn't see his face, but he saw the lowered stance. The man had raised his arms before launching a frontal attack on the girl.

Maybe he could trip the fellow and subdue him once on the ground. But before any of that could be put into action, someone else in dark clothing came from the side. The flying kick knocked the lout sideways into a flower bed. Their rescuer knelt on his quarry, brought both of the man's arms around and used plastic cable ties to bind his hands together.

He looked up at Penny. "Are you alright, Miss?"

"I'm fine, Jonathan, thank you. I was about to take care of him myself, but you have saved me the trouble."

Leaving the semi-conscious man where he was, Jonathan opened the rear door of the car for Penny. "Will the young man be joining us, Miss?" he asked.

"As far as Petts Wood, I think. Is that right, Patrick?"

Patrick remembered to close his mouth, agape with astonishment at the rapid turn of events. "Um, that would be …very kind. Er, yes, please."

"If you'd like to get in the other side, Sir, I'll just take out the rubbish."

As Patrick extended one leg into the thick carpeting of the rear footwell of the

Jaguar XJ6, he turned his head to watch. Jonathan seized the drunken lout by his collar and pulled him to his feet. Though taller than Jonathan, the man allowed himself to be pushed towards the pub again and stood, still dazed, while the door was opened. The sound of the pub's bell rang out just then and the Barman shouted, "Time, ladies and gentleman, please." Jonathan planted a final kick on the fellow's backside to propel him inside towards his drunken friends. They roared approval and jeered. One threw the remains of his pint, adding a soaking shirt and jacket to the man's woes.

Patrick settled into the soft, sandy-coloured leather and pulled his door closed with a satisfying 'clunk'. Calm and relative silence and warmth were very welcome. He worried that his shoes would dirty the immaculate deep pile carpeting. Jonathan opened the driver's door, letting in the November chill, but the car's heater dispelled that as soon as he started the engine.

"Time, indeed." Penny smiled at Patrick. "You do seem to lead an interesting life."

"Me? Jonathan, I would like to say thank you for coming to our rescue."

"All part of the service, Sir."

"You …aren't a normal taxi service, are you?"

"No, Sir."

And that was almost the last thing that their driver said that evening. Patrick stared at the young woman with whom he had been talking and drinking. He had been happy to tell her all about some of his adventures. For whom he worked, about the criminal activities he thought he had seen, what he had tried to do about it. Yet he realised she had not reciprocated. She was 'in recruitment'. She 'worked for the government' – but what did that mean? How come she was collected in such a luxury car – she must have been dropped off in it too, because she hadn't worn a coat over her dress. She had deflected, evaded or dodged pretty much all his questions.

She finished wiping her fingers with a Kleenex from the box in the seat back pocket. There had been quite a bit of blood lost by her victim. She was now looking back with an amused expression on her face.

"What is it?"

"It's you - you work in recruitment for the government. You have a chauffeur who seems as much a body guard as a driver and you yourself are unafraid to tackle drunken louts weighing more than 200lbs. Are you a spy or something?"

Penny stretched back her head and laughed out loud. But didn't say anything.

"You have a lovely laugh," Patrick said. "You should do it more often."

Penny tried to put on a stern face. "I do laugh – lots, honestly. But maybe it's your stories which make me laugh."

Feeling giddy from the wine and the adrenaline rush of their attack, Patrick plucked up his courage: "Could I see you again?"

Penny addressed herself forwards and up at the interior mirror. "What do you think, Jonathan? Should I see Patrick again?"

"Your decision, Miss. Your decision."

She turned more towards him. "We should meet up again. Here's my card. Call me towards the end of this week if you want."

# Chapter 15

## The Next Posting

The next morning, Patrick felt a little guilty at having arranged to meet Penny again. He knew so little about her. He thought about Dr Jessica waiting for him in Port Vila. Their last couple of conversations hadn't gone well. In particular, there was the mix-up on his last night when he needed to meet with Florence. He had hoped to have a bit of a heart to heart with Jess, but ran out of time. He feared that telling her about meeting Penny might sound disloyal and could go the same way. 'Be realistic,' he told himself. 'Jessica's time in the New Hebrides might end in a few months and who knows where she will go next? She did say that her life was one long round of taking exams, learning new stuff and trying for advancement.'

Despite this spine-bracing self-lecture, he hadn't convinced himself. The feeling of being likely to hurt Jessica gnawed at his insides.

Later that week he took Penny's business card out of his wallet. It was very plain and printed in a simple typeface on high quality card. Its details were minimal too. It gave her name - Penny Baxter - her job title, 'Assistant' and a central London telephone number. There was no address, save for a P.O. Box for correspondence. There was no mention of the government department he assumed she worked in. He called the number. A woman answered on the first ring.

"Baxter."

"Oh, sorry, I would like to speak to Penny, please." Patrick completely forgot Baxter was the surname on her card. The assertive voice sounded at least twenty years older than the young woman he'd met.

"Is that Patrick? This is me – how are you?"

"I'm very well, thank you. I wanted to take you up on your offer to meet again, if that's alright."

"By all means. When did you have in mind?"

"I had interviews last week for a couple of possible new jobs and I will hear next week whether I succeeded. Would you be available on, say, Thursday?"

"Oh, yes. I'm sure I will be," she said. "What are the jobs?"

"The interviews were for a job in Bahrain and another based in New York. Both would be on promotion – I'm astonished that the New Hebrides Chief Manager gave me a good enough report!"

"Those sound great. Let's say Thursday and if you still don't know we can push it back or meet anyway. How does that sound?"

The call from his Staff Manager came the following Tuesday. His mother answered the telephone.

"Patrick? It's Staff Department calling for you." She waited by the phone, handing the receiver to him when he arrived.

"Patrick Field."

"Good afternoon, Patrick. This is Staff Department." He recognised the voice as the man who had conducted his interviews. How strange that he hadn't introduced himself with his name.

"Good afternoon."

"I'm calling to say that you have been offered the position in Bahrain. The New York job has been withdrawn for what they describe as 'budgetary reasons', so there is only that one on offer, I'm afraid. I'll be writing

411

to you tonight to confirm this and I will include the results of your medical examination."

"Very well," said Patrick. "Thank you. Are there any formalities I need to complete before going to Bahrain? Vaccinations? That kind of thing...?"

"Oh, no. All the jabs you received for the New Hebrides – or as they write it now, 'Vanuatu' - are still in date. The doctor says they will be ample protection for the Middle East."

"May I ask about my salary, please?"

"All in good time, laddie. All in good time. Your tickets will come through at the beginning of next month about a week before the flights, along with your Terms and Conditions letter."

"Very well. Thank you for calling."

"Goodbye."

He replaced the receiver and went to tell his parents. They were delighted for him. But didn't really understand why anyone would go to live in such hot and dusty places. They thought nobody would even speak English. But if that was what Patrick wanted to do, they'd support him in any way they could. Their own memories of going abroad had been coloured by the Second World War.

Both had served abroad, his mother in Europe and his father in some of those remote, hot and dusty places. Both had been hunted by the enemy back then and shot at, but had survived to tell the tale. Except, to Patrick's frustration, neither wanted ever to tell those tales.

"Oh, you don't want to know about that ancient history, Dear," his mother had objected when he enquired on one occasion. She changed the subject to what might he like for dinner?

His father was even more blunt. "There's nothing to tell. It's passed - it's gone and done with."

These replies only served to sharpen Patrick's interest. He knew that his father kept his Service pistol wrapped in cotton rags in a drawer beside the bed. One night, when Patrick was quite young, a burglar had tried to get into their house. The noises woke him up and he'd gone to his parents' bedroom to alert them. In the half light, he saw his father untie the string around the cotton package. The foreboding sound of a magazine being pushed home in the handle was as clear in his head now as it was back then. "Stay with your mother," his father instructed before padding along the corridor towards the sitting room. A shouted warning sent the burglar fleeing back through the window. There remained only a stale odour of sweat to mark the unwanted visitation.

Also, while clearing out part of the attic one year, he'd found a leather-bound notebook. It was very dusty and curiosity compelled him to undo the clasp. Most of the pages were full of his mother's handwriting - neat and clear sentences and notes written in pencil. They detailing the procedure for disassembling a Merlin aero engine. Every so often, there would be a page of line drawing displaying components blown apart. She had crammed engineering data like tolerances and torque wrench settings into the margins. When pressed for details, she acknowledged taking some 'aviation courses' during the War. But again, managed to switch the conversation onto some anodyne topic - such as the flavour of icing on the cake she was baking. 'Coffee or Chocolate, Dear?'

-----//-----

Patrick sat for a few minutes and reflected on the call from Staff Department. Just as he had before departing to the New Hebrides, he ought to do some research on

Bahrain and the Middle East in general. Chambers Encyclopaedia gave him basic facts and figures. He could borrow his mother's library card and visit the library tomorrow to find out more.

He remembered that Penny had been keen to learn where he was off to next. Before he dialled her number, though, he once again wrestled with those feelings of guilt as meeting up with her risked hurting Jess. It was bad enough that he would be leaving the New Hebrides (now 'Vanuatu'). But most of all by telling her he had gone out with another girl in the UK. Compounding this, his mind also took him forward to the next logical step. If Penny fancied him so wanted to keep in touch, maybe she was hoping he would not get an overseas job offer at all, but would stay in the UK. As things stood, by taking up the overseas posting, he was likely to disappoint not just one woman but two.

There was nothing for it. He put in a call to Penny.

"Patrick, that's fantastic news," she gushed. "I'm really, really pleased for you. I was so hoping you'd choose that one anyway because it will be more interesting. You'll earn more money too and you'll have a brilliant time."

There was nothing at all in her voice suggesting she was anything other than completely delighted with Patrick's news.

"So, you aren't disappointed, then?"

"Disappointed? You must be joking! This is the best thing, ever. I knew you were right for it and obviously Royal Counties Bank agrees. Come out for drinks with me – we must celebrate!"

"Alright – that would be great. Um, could you get out of work tomorrow around five o'clock?"

-----//-----

Patrick and Penny arrived at the Davy's Wine bar at the same time. She was radiating happiness and skipped forwards to award him a big hug. After a brief hesitation, he reciprocated, his nose burying itself in her hair. "Come on!" she said, taking his hand and leading him towards the door.

She turned to the right immediately after the entrance. There was a cosy corner close to the fire and beside the front window. "This is my favourite perch. Would you like wine? Champagne, perhaps?"

'Golly,' Patrick thought. 'Everything seems to be going so fast.' But he said, "I know we are celebrating, and should have champagne. But to be honest, I'd rather try to find something red and fruity. Would that be ok with you?"

"Champagne is generally over-done, isn't it? And they charge ridiculous prices for it in London. I'll get a wine list. Would you like some sandwiches too? You know - to soak up the alcohol."

"That sounds wise – I hadn't given it any thought, to be honest. I was going to invite you to have fish and chips afterwards. We'd have to get ourselves over to Whitecross Market near the Barbican."

"You can take me there next time. This is my local and my shout – no arguments – agreed?"

"You are a generous person, Penny. I place myself entirely in your hands."

"Steady, Tiger," she winked at him. "Not yet. Stay there."

Patrick obeyed and sat on the stool, trying to act as though he was reserving the corner for at least six people. It was hard to make her out. One moment she was brimming with enthusiasm for his promotion and imminent departure – puzzling in itself. The next, giving him a big hug like he was a long-lost cousin instead of someone she'd met by chance in a pub a week or so ago. Then dragging him into the wine bar, her 'local', no less. Buying wine and food. On top of it all, responding with a *double entendre* as though they'd be shedding their clothes together later that evening.

It was very flattering, but he couldn't understand why she might be quite so interested in him. He didn't want to find himself in a 'One Night Stand' situation, but then maybe he had this all wrong.

These musings ended with Penny's return to the table, brandishing a thick wine list. She settled onto the other stool and shuffled it towards Patrick. "That's better," she cooed. Patrick mumbled something about trying to take up more space so they wouldn't have other patrons falling over them later. But she waved away his explanation and added one of her own. "Being closer together means we don't have to shout at each other. You don't mind, do you?" This said with an amused eyebrow raised into her hairline.

"Of course not," Patrick affirmed. He cleared his throat in embarrassment and proved his point by scraping his stool a few millimetres closer to hers. In truth, he relished the intimacy - feeling the movements as she adjusted her position. Her subtle perfume washed over him.

"George is bringing over some sandwiches soon. Ham, cheese, some Coronation Chicken and rabbit food. Look here – the reds start with Beaujolais and get juicier as you go through."

"That sounds like you have dinner sorted too. Thank you." Patrick ran his finger down the page. He paused near the bottom.

Penny had been tracking his finger and she leaned a little closer. "I like that one too."

He'd found the Nuits St George, 1967. It was a wine he remembered his father ordering from the Wine Society, years before. The man had been furious that the Society restricted buyers to six bottles only, because of limited supplies. He had allowed young Patrick to sip a little. The recollection was rather pleasant, despite being unused to wines at such a tender age.

"This is a rare moment, son," his father had confided when there was a chance to open the first bottle. Patrick had watched, entranced, as the foil cutter revealed the cork.

Then an old-fashioned corkscrew was deployed and the cork itself eased from its home. His father held the cork under their noses and encouraged Patrick and his mother to note the absence of any untoward smell. There had been no leakage of air to spoil the wine. "You may never experience anything to rival this," he said, pouring small measures of the glistening, ruby liquid into three glasses.

His father demonstrated how to tilt the glass and swirl the wine to observe what he called its 'legs'. It was important too, to examine how light diffused through the turned-up edges of the wine. He then recorked the bottle and put it into the darkest, coolest place he could find in their dining room. It lasted over the next four nights and he kept that first bottle for years after it was empty. He reckoned to be able to conjure up the flavour in his head just by seeing the bottle.

Patrick read the description of the wine again, just to be sure. "Do you think they do have any or is this here to impress customers?"

"I can ask."

His eyes followed along the line and lit on the eye-watering price. "Oh, my God.

That's ridiculous. We may as well have a Jeroboam of champagne!"

"But we both like it and I'm paying, don't forget."

"Even so …I remember it as lovely wine but I'd feel terribly guilty."

"You worry about too many things, Patrick. I'll find out if George has a bottle; back in a ticcy."

Penny returned, bearing a tray piled high with sandwiches, smiling broadly. "We're in luck. He'll bring it over."

Patrick eyed the sandwich mountain. "Are all your friends joining us?" It was his turn to raise an eyebrow.

"Nope. All for us," she replied. "Ah, here's George."

-----//-----

When George placed the bottle on their table, Patrick noticed it had thrown a crust. He insisted upon pouring it himself, with great care. As the level fell, Penny's much older male colleague, Christopher, joined them for a spell. Christopher used to work in the Middle East, he said, spending most time in the Arabian Gulf, but North Africa too. He still had a trace of the tan he'd acquired over many years.

Penny fetched another clean glass for him and ordered a second bottle.

"If you will be covering the MATEL countries too, it would be wise to brush up your French. They often use French in Morocco, Algeria and particularly Tunisia as well as Arabic, but it comes in handy in Egypt too. I haven't needed it in Libya – yet."

Patrick watched as Christopher began to pour from the second bottle, large signet ring clinking against the side. He asserted that his French wasn't too bad. Occasional conversations in the New Hebrides had upgraded both his spoken and written language. Christopher also counselled beginning to learn some spoken Arabic. "Royal Counties Bank might offer or at least pay for some classes before you set off. You should read up on some of the cultural aspects to avoid offending anyone by mistake. It'll sound more complicated than it is, but a little foreknowledge will help you not to be too stiff."

"What do you mean, Christopher?"

"Arabs like to get to know your body language before negotiating with you. The more traditional ones prefer to meet in a social setting before getting down to business. If you seem comfortable in their presence, they'll be ready to trust you." Patrick nodded in agreement – it all sounded very sensible.

"I doubt you will run into any on Royal Counties Bank business, but there are some Bad Hats about." Patrick raised a querying eyebrow. "They suck you in until you cross the line. Then, they've got you – for life – or death."

"I have had brushes with some people like that in the New Hebrides – I mean, Vanuatu."

"Indeed", agreed Christopher. "And how is Andrew?"

"Andrew Stuart, the British Resident commissioner?"

"Yes. How is he doing, these days, hmmn?"

Maybe because of the excellent wine, Patrick flushed with embarrassment. He hadn't appreciated that this new acquaintance could move in the same exalted circles as the Resident Commissioner. "He was very well when last I went to Iririki Island."

"Good, good, good. A fine man", said Christopher. His face hardened. "Make sure you see him again before you leave Vanuatu for the final time. An up-to-date briefing will be jolly useful. Oh, my. Time flies – you young people must excuse me - I have a meeting at the FCO".

Penny saw Patrick's blank expression. "Foreign and Colonial Office, Patrick. Lord Carrington doesn't like to be kept waiting".

Patrick struggled to speed up his wine-befuddled brain. Was he being led along a particular path? His slow wits couldn't fathom which or why.

When the man had gone, Patrick asked, "Is Christopher your boss?"

"One of them. He's nice, isn't he?"

Patrick bit into another sandwich. 'Nice' wasn't the descriptor which came to mind. When he'd finished chewing, he said, "I couldn't help noticing his signet ring. It's engraved with a dot and then lower case 'B' and 'L'. with some swirly stuff around it. Do you know what that means?"

She shook her head. "Probably some family thing. He was knighted some time ago."

"Knighted? So he is *Sir* Christopher? I've never met a 'Sir' before. He knows a lot about the Middle East – did he work anywhere else?"

"Sir Christopher Sherrif. And he was there off and on, I think. Off and on."

"Thank you for introducing him to me." He wasn't quite sure why he'd said that, but it seemed the polite thing to do. Later, heading back to his parents' house on the train, he'd reflect that maybe he had been introduced to Sir Christopher rather than the other way around.

When next they looked, the second bottle was empty. Penny leaned back, steadied herself by holding Patrick's arm, and looked into his eyes. "I really want to see you again, Patrick, but I have to go now. You still have my card?"

Patrick said he did.

"I'll go and settle up with George." She stood up, collected her bag and leaned down a little to kiss him, holding one side of his face with her other hand. "Make sure you write. Bye!"

Patrick's head was whirling, his thoughts out of control. He realised he was blushing furiously, and although that might have been the wine, he didn't think it was. Her departing kiss had thrown him into a complete loop.

That night, as he removed his suit, he found another of her business cards in his top pocket. When did she manage that? And why give him another unless it was very important that he be able to keep in contact. He wrote the details into his address book for good measure and resolved to drop her a line every so often.

# Chapter 16

## Farewell

Before preparing his few belongings for the brief return to Port Vila, Patrick sorted through all the papers he and Kim had gathered. They would hand them to Inspection Department when it seemed safe to do so.

He had not written to Kim during his long leave. That morning, two days before he was to check in again at Heathrow airport, an Airmail letter arrived for him. His father spotted it on the door mat and brought it through to the breakfast table.

"They are missing you already, Patrick."

"Thanks, Dad." He took the envelope, saw Kim's handwriting on the outside and put it beside his plate. He'd read it later.

"Who's it from, Dear?" his mother asked, pouring tea for them all.

"From my colleague, Kim. I'll open it after breakfast."

Conversation turned to what they should have for dinner and what shopping needed to be done.

Afterwards, full of bacon and eggs and toast with marmalade, Patrick sat in his childhood bedroom. He opened the letter. Kim was saying that he would be going on long leave himself shortly after Patrick's final departure. He'd stay during Patrick's handover to his successor, whoever that might be. Kim wrote that he had been busy gathering 'yet more materials for a book' which he intended to write. Patrick took this to mean he'd set aside yet more evidence of the money laundering they believed they'd uncovered. Intriguingly, these materials concerned different characters. Maybe there were others beyond Tai Nguyen whose transactions were coming through Royal Counties Bank's books.

Patrick tucked the letter carefully into date order in the collection of incriminating evidence. He put it on his bookshelf.

The short time remaining before his flight sped by and soon he was bidding his parents farewell again and climbing into a taxi for the airport.

This time, when his flight approached Bahrain International airport on the island of Muharraq, he watched the scenery out of the window with greater interest. This was the first scheduled stop for refuelling. It was early evening, so he could discern little about the surrounding land mass. As the aeroplane descended, small ships dotted the surface of the sea. He'd read that the name for these was 'dhows' and they were used for both fishing and pearl-diving. Did men still harvest pearls by free-diving in the shallow waters around the islands? It sounded fascinating. He promised himself he'd investigate when his next posting began.

The sky glowed bright orange where it met the land creating an impression of brown everything. Brown houses, brown soil, even brown cars and trucks. By now, Patrick felt himself becoming a seasoned traveller. He was familiar with the apparent speeding up of the scenery whipping past the window as the aeroplane neared touchdown and the buildings by the airport became very close. Then, with a brief squeal of protest from the landing gear, they were down. The captain announced that refuelling would take an hour. Passengers were to disembark and wait in a sectioned-off Transit area. Although Patrick prepared for it, the sudden oven-like rush of hot, humid air admitted by the opening door still took his breath away. Long leave in the temperate UK had made him soft. How did aircrews cope with these frequent temperature changes as they flew around the world?

This time, he had brought a bottle of fresh water and a packet of sandwiches to see him through at least some part of his journey. He made sure to seek out more water, fruit and plain foods once he'd consumed those. As a result, he didn't feel quite so exhausted when Air Melanesia finally delivered him, with a bump, to the single runway of Bauerfield International Airport, Port Vila.

Kim was there to meet him.

They shook hands and walked through the cool airport building once again into the humidity and heat of the car park.

"How was the flight? Or should I say 'flights'?"

"Not bad. I'm tired, but not exhausted. It could be because it isn't my first time arriving here."

They got into Kim's car. As he started it, Kim then said, "There have been a couple of changes I ought to tell you about."

"Oh, yes?"

"I'm not sure it's the right time to tell you – straight after you landed – but - Jess has started seeing someone else."

Patrick slumped in his seat.

"Pat?"

"What?"

"Are you ok?"

"I suppose so." In truth, he had been very uncomfortable all through his period of leave about those last couple of conversations with Jessica. He wondered if he had said the wrong thing on too many occasions or been insensitive. Did this mean their relationship had run its course? All the same, he'd rather have learned it from her. Had he been 'dumped'?

"Anyone I know?"

"I don't think so. It's a guy called Max something or other. From what I know, he spends his time doing press-ups on the beach. That or rebuilding his Toyota – he rallies it and smashes it up most of the time."

"He sounds adorable. But what does Jess see in a person like that?"

431

"Search me. I'm hardly the world's expert on women."

At least that generated a brief smirk from Patrick. Kim caught it and was grateful that his friend was taking the news with some degree of equanimity.

"What's for dinner?"

Now it was Kim's turn to smile. If Patrick was thinking about his stomach, things couldn't be all that bad.

-----//-----

Patrick's phone rang shortly after the bank opened the following morning. He still felt some jet-lag, but Sara's coffee was working its usual magic.

"Patrick Field."

"Patrick, it's Jess."

"Hello, Jess," he said, cautiously. "I'm back ...well, obviously as you are talking to me..."

Never one to fuss around a topic, Jess came straight out with, "While you were away, I met someone else. You won't be back here for long and will be disappearing for good, so it's better we break it off now."

"Don't you want to see me any more, then?"

"Oh, we can meet up as friends – maybe at sailing – but I might be too busy."

Patrick couldn't help himself. "Who is it?"

"Max Foster."

Patrick hadn't heard of the man, but might know him by sight. "How did you meet?"

"Sailing. I have to go. I hope you get a good next posting, wherever it is. Goodbye, Patrick."

He opened his mouth to say 'goodbye', but was talking to a dead line.

-----//-----

Sara had listened to his side of the conversation. Marianne had briefed her already. As usual, Marianne knew everything about everyone's emotional lives – and she scooted her chair over to him. She asked, "*Olgeta gud, Patrick*?"

"Not really, Sara. Not really. But perhaps it's for the best." He tried to quash his riot of feelings. Not to be overcome by them, especially in front of Sara and the others. He knew his face was flushing and he struggled to keep his voice even in tone. "Some things come to a natural end, don't they?"

Conflicting emotions wrestled with each other. On one side was relief that he hadn't had to break up with Jessica. She had broken up with him first. On the other side was anger that some muscle-bound meat-head had lured her away in his absence. He searched Sara's concerned face for comfort.

To sooth him, she said, "*Afta - e gud tumas,*" and put a reassuring hand on his forearm.

He managed a thin smile. "Thank you. I'm sure you're right. I hope everything will be better after tomorrow."

"Oh," Sara said, smacking her head. "*Me forgettim wuntime*! Scottie from the ANZ and Dave Anstead left messages for you."

He picked up the message slips. He'd be calling Scottie later anyway about some documents, so called Dave first. The phone rang and rang ten times. Patrick figured Dave would be out attending to the cattle somewhere on his ranch. There was a loud repeater bell linked to the telephone on the roof of the shack which functioned as his office. So he would have heard, but Patrick guessed Dave was in the middle of something – he would try to call again later.

He dialled Scottie's number. "Morning, Scottie. How's it hanging?"

"Lower than yours mate! G'day, Patrick. Glad you're back. Waddya need?"

Patrick outlined details of the missing certificates of origin from one of the bundles of paperwork sent over from the ANZ Bank. Scottie promised a full-scale search to rectify matters. As it happened, Royal Counties Bank opened the letter of credit for Dave Anstead. The order was for new processing equipment to update his slaughter-house. The goods arrived on the dock the day before Patrick returned. Patrick had specified the certificates of origin to help make sure his customer received what he was paying for. But Dave would not be able to clear the equipment until the documentation was complete.

This must have been why the man was chasing him. He determined to sort out the paperwork before returning the call again.

But before he could work out what to do next, Dave Anstead's girlfriend, Diana telephoned. "Good morning, Mr Field, this is Diana, Dave Anstead's partner."

"Hello, Diana." Why was she being so formal? "How are you?"

"Dave asked me to call to say he is happy to pay for the new equipment even though you don't have the certificates of origin."

This was very odd. Letters of credit enable buyers and sellers to do business with each other, even if they have never done so before.

They remove any doubts about honesty and credit-worthiness. In this case, Patrick had opened the letter of credit for Dave in favour of a manufacturer in Sydney, Australia. The specified certificates of origin were essential to ensure that the machines sent to Port Vila would be the ones Dave wanted. Normal procedure was that Royal Counties Bank would pay the amount contracted for against sight of complete and correct documents. Patrick could then issue a clearance certificate so Dave could collect his goods from the dock.

Three factors were alarming - first, Diana was not authorised to sign on Dave's account, so if he was strict, she could not vary the terms of the letter of credit. Second, Scottie's bank was usually very correct in the way it handled documentation. He would know that his bank was liable for port charges arising from delayed clearance due to their mishandling of the documentation. But it was not unknown for document bundles to come unstapled. Patrick had every expectation that

Scottie would discover the papers miss-filed somewhere. But third, and this most of all set his internal alarm bells going, why would Diana call him 'Mr Field'? She knew him well, having first got to know him when she made him an enormous breakfast after he set his first Hash Run. Also, they'd met socially every so often.

He replied, "I expect ANZ Bank will find the certificates later today. But if they don't, Dave will have to sign to agree to accept the goods despite the disparity. Could you ask him to pop into the bank in the morning?"

"No, no." She sounded agitated. "It's very important that we clear the goods today."

"I see," said Patrick, not seeing at all. "Um, is everything alright?"

Diana gave a strained laugh. "Oh yes. Everything is completely normal. It's just that we have asked Mr Nguyen if he would collect the machinery for us and he can only do it today. Dave's a bit …tied up right now."

Now he was getting very concerned. The machinery Dave had ordered would need a large truck to collect it – like the truck used when he moved his cattle or took carcasses to market. Tai Nguyen did not own such a vehicle, as far as he knew. All the Bon Plats imports were collected in the supermarket's white Toyota pickup – which wasn't big enough for this job. A nasty suspicion was starting to form in Patrick's mind.

"Well, ok, if you are sure. I tell you what - if Dave can't come in, I'll leave the bank early this afternoon and come over to you. I'll bring the documents you'll need with me so he can sign. How does that sound?"

"You are very kind, Mr Field. That would do the job. One other thought – I remember this has to be done under what you called 'Dual Control' so I'll expect you and a colleague about three o'clock – ok, bye for now."

And she rang off without letting him ask what she meant.

Patrick sat back, very puzzled. The number of odd things were accumulating at a rate of knots. Diana was behaving in a strange way. Why couldn't Dave sign the release papers and what was the big hurry, anyway? And what was all that stuff about 'Dual Control'? And saying 'everything was completely normal'. The Diana he knew would use a phrase like 'it's peachy'. It was nonsense. Unless …she was trying to tell him he would need another member of staff with him when he visited – for safety?

He especially didn't like finding out that Tai Nguyen was anything at all to do with this. Was it possible that Diana was being forced to make the telephone call to him?

He called Scottie at the ANZ Bank again. "G'day, mate. To what do I owe this unexpected pleasure? Twice in one day?"

"Sorry to chase for this, Scottie, but there's a bit of a hurry to clear these goods. I don't suppose you've had a chance to search for those missing certificates of origin?"

"Blaady Norah – you're keener than a dingo on a Saturday night. Give a bloke a chance!"

"Yeah, ok, Scottie. I just thought I'd ask before getting the customer to sign a documentary waiver."

"I'll keep looking, mate. No worries."

Patrick thanked him and rang off.

"Kim?" He walked over to his friend and colleague. "Any chance you could come with me over to Dave and Diana right after work?"

Kim brightened. It had been one of those days. "Sure. It'd be great to get together. But isn't it our turn to host?"

"I don't think this is a social call." He retold the very odd conversation he'd had with Diana. He finished with his understanding why she was trying to tell him not to come alone.

"Will this never end?" Kim remarked. "That man Nguyen – again!"

"I know. Could you come with me?"

Kim told him to get all his papers ready and agreed to come too. He also said that they should take both their cars. "I'll hang back in the trees by their driveway in case I need to get help."

"Good idea. You might want to turn your car around in case you need to skedaddle fast."

The remaining hours of the day dragged. At long last the wall clock showed 2:30pm, this time without any help from Jean-Marc. Patrick packed up his desk, put the letter of clearance into an envelope and told Sara where he was going. Kim saw him heading for the door and nodded that all was ok. He too had cleared his desk and just had to put his piles of loan applications into the safe. A few minutes later, he joined Patrick outside.

-----//-----

As Patrick reached the top of the dusty track which wound through the coconut trees to Dave and Diana's house, he paused for Kim to catch up. It had been a good idea to hang back in reserve, in case something bad was going on.

"Ok?" He asked, as Kim pulled up.

"Yup. I'll reverse into those bushes over there. Good luck."

Patrick waited until Kim's beige-coloured Starlet had merged into the scenery. 'Thank goodness he hadn't cleaned it,' he thought.

He'd left his own engine running and now engaged first gear and drove slowly along the track. He went by the hidden car and around the bend, swinging the steering back and forth to skirt the enormous potholes Dave hadn't bothered to fill.

He switched off the ignition and listened.

A gentle breeze off the sea rustled the drying leaves on the coconut trees. A bird called in the distance. He eased the car door closed and advanced to their front door. It was ajar.

He pressed it with two fingers and it swung open. He stopped it before it hit the wall and took a step inside. None of this felt right. But it could all be in his imagination. The

441

Boogie Man which you can't see in the cupboard is always more scary than if you open the door.

He called out. "Dave? Diana? It's Patrick - Patrick Field."

There was no answer. He guessed they were outside.

Most likely, they'd be through in the slaughter house itself and wouldn't have heard him. He didn't feel comfortable walking into their house like this, uninvited. So he went back through the door and around the front.

But then stopped in his tracks. Ahead he saw Diana standing halfway down the path. Over her shoulder was Tai Nguyen, holding a gun to her head.

Seeing Patrick, Nguyen smiled. "Did you bring the release document as Diana asked?"

Patrick nodded his head and held up the envelope. "I did …but it needs Dave Anstead's signature as he is the Accreditor of Record."

"That might be a problem. Dave is …not here right now."

Diana started to say, "He ran away…" but Nguyen shoved the gun further into her neck and silenced her.

Patrick calculated what were his choices. If he let Nguyen think Diana was of no use to him, he might kill her. But if Nguyen thought she could be bait to bring back Dave, wherever he'd gone, there was a chance.

"I do need Dave's signature, though, otherwise it wouldn't be a proper release. Perhaps Diana could help us find him?"

"Where did he go? Tell me!"

Nguyen emphasised his words by jabbing the gun into Diana's neck again. For a moment Patrick feared that she was going to scream that she didn't know and the situation would escalate fast. But Patrick's arrival had given her hope. She remained calm.

"There's a place… We often sit there watching the sunset," she said. "It's on the other side of the field."

Tai Nguyen stared at Patrick for a moment, while he worked out if this was some trick. Patrick was hoping he hadn't brought any of his men. But the man's ego had made him confident he could shake down Dave Anstead by himself.

"Alright." Nguyen consented. "Patrick – you walk in front. And you, my dear, follow close behind him. Don't try anything stupid."

Patrick hoped that Kim was seeing all this and even more that the conversation could be overheard. He would have to shout loud and clear if he spoke again. The trouble was that they had moved to the seaward side of the house. Kim needed to have crept forwards in the trees to know what was happening.

As Patrick began to walk towards Diana and Nguyen, she winked at him. His heart leapt – Nguyen hadn't seen this gesture, of course. He should not have doubted her. She was no weak-willed fragile girl after all! But did she have a plan? He had to avoid getting in the way, whatever it might be.

He kept walking past them. The trio moved together to the back of the small formal garden. They arrived at a hefty farm gate beyond which was pasture where the couple's cattle grazed. Patrick remembered picking a route through Dave Anstead's land for his Hash Run. Prominent in his mind was the main hazard of twisting an ankle on fallen coconuts.

Every so often he encountered a cowpat. Most were dry because of the searing sunshine. A few were disconcertingly fresh, though. "I don't like cows," he called out. "I'm afraid of them."

"Keep walking," instructed Nguyen.

There was a slight offshore breeze on their backs. It took their scent forwards towards some of the animals. One cow mooed its displeasure at the disturbance. Keeping one eye on the coconut-strewn ground, Patrick stepped around a palm tree. And then, he could see it as well as hear and smell it – no, them. Five or six cows lumbered to the side and away from their path. As he kept walking, a dozen more trotted from the right, trying to catch up with the others. There were more disgruntled noises from the herd.

The three continued forward, Patrick in front, then Diana with Nguyen keeping his gun barrel poked into her neck right behind. Soon, they came to the perimeter of the coconut tree plantation. A barbed-wire fence across the cliff edge marked the limit of Dave's land. Beyond it, sun reflected off the ocean.

"I don't think we can go much further," he called over his shoulder, as loudly as he dared. "We are right at the fence."

445

Stopping some five yards back from the rusted barbed wire, Patrick half turned towards their attacker. "What now?"

Nguyen pushed Diana towards Patrick. "Stand together, you two. I hope you were right, claiming Dave will be hiding here somewhere. Call out for him, if his signature is really needed. You'd better shout loud if you want to live."

Diana and Patrick began to yell for Dave Anstead. This disturbed the cows even more. They milled around, snorting, mooing and lowing to each other. Why were these humans making so much noise?

"Dave?" Diane hollered at the top of her voice.

"Where are you, Dave? We need your signature." Patrick joined in.

Now the sun was behind their backs, Patrick realised that Tai Nguyen couldn't discern exactly where they were focussing. Their eyes were in shade while he had the full glare of the sun to deal with. Nguyen had narrowed his gaze to watch for any unexpected movement on their part. This left him unaware of another cow standing a little way behind him, very still. Very quiet. Unmoved by the intrusion.

This cow had horns. Plus, it was twice as big as the others. It pawed the sandy ground. Maybe it wasn't unmoved after all.

Diana gave up calling for Dave and instead yelled, "Oscar!"

Nguyen tensed, levelled the gun at her and crouched. He knew something was up. Why weren't they both still yelling for Dave? Their lives depended on his reappearance. Behind him, the huge animal began to move forwards and gathered speed with startling acceleration.

Nguyen demanded, "Who is Oscar?" At that very moment, around one ton of angry bull hit the backs of his legs and vaulted him up and into the air. He soared clean over Patrick and Diana. The gun went off and he cried out in pain and surprise.

He landed on his side with an audible thump beyond the barbed wire right on the cliff edge. For a moment, his free hand grasped a tuft of browning grass, but as he brought his gun to bear on them again, the grass roots gave up the unequal struggle. He disappeared over the edge.

The bull had pulled up short of the barbed wire. It looked around, searching for further danger. The animal glowered and snorted at Patrick. He knew Diana, but who was this other human? She stepped between them making soothing and cooing noises. The huge animal allowed her to blow in its nostrils. To Patrick's enormous relief, the animal relaxed and soon Diana took its nose ring in her hand. She led Oscar away and back towards his herd of cows.

Dave Anstead hopped out from behind a rock in front of them wearing a grin from ear to ear. "Well, would you look at that?" he laughed. "I reckoned Oscar might help you out a bit."

"You have no idea how scary that... I mean, I thought..." Patrick's mouth opened and closed without making another sound for a bit. He recovered enough to ask, "You let the bull out on purpose?"

"Yeah. Thought you could do with a bit of muscle to even the odds. He's soft as butter, Oscar is." Dave gazed with evident fondness towards the retreating backside of the bull, as he strode, unhurried, towards his harem of ladies. Out here, Oscar was king of all he surveyed.

Diana gave Patrick a big hug – for which he was grateful as he was afraid his legs were about to give way. As his pulse returned to somewhere near normality, Kim arrived, puffing. "Is everything alright? I heard a shot. Hello, Diana – Dave. Are you all ok?"

"No worries, mate," drawled Dave. "*Tru yah*?" He lapsed into Bislama to add a splash of colour to his otherwise dry comment.

"I saw Tai Nguyen." Kim said. "Where did he go?"

"Oscar thought he fancied a swim," Diana explained. "He won't be back."

Kim glanced around. "I guess Oscar left too?"

"Kim, I'm not sure you would believe me when I tell you what has happened, but let's just say Mr Nguyen may not be around anymore. I don't know how steep or high this cliff is, but that bull over there punted him clean over the fence." Alarm flickered across Kim's face at mention of the word 'bull' and he turned to look – he was as nervous as Patrick around cows too, especially boy cows.

Patrick said to Dave, "I take it that Nguyen's 'offer' to collect your machinery was not an optional arrangement?" Dave gave a short laugh and agreed that there had been little practical choice. Nguyen's demand was that he had to pay for a shipment which he would never actually receive. If he didn't, either Nguyen's men would use Dave's cattle for target practice or they'd kidnap Diana.

"I asked Nguyen if I could choose between those two options."

Patrick saw that a mischievous smile was still lurking around the man's mouth.

"Oh! You pig!" Diana thumped him, hard, when understanding dawned of what he had implied. Poor Dave staggered backwards, roaring with mirth, tinged with pain: for a small woman, Diana packed a solid punch.

"Ah," Patrick said. "Now I understand why the exporter couldn't get certificates of origin from the manufacturer. The company hadn't shipped the goods. So any money we paid on your behalf would go to some other beneficiary – for more guns or drugs or ...who knows what?"

"Why don't we go down to visit Captain Brasted all together and decide what's to be done?" asked Kim.

"Good idea. I'm up for that," affirmed Patrick. "What about you two?"

Dave and Diana looked at each other. "Sure," Dave agreed. "Let's do it."

-----//-----

Dave and Diana jumped into Patrick's car and they followed Kim's trail of dust

450

towards the port. "I must admit I'm glad I'm no longer in the same field as the cows," Patrick told them. "I don't know why, but they make me very nervous. It's their size, I reckon."

"You prefer them on your plate, I take it," Dave observed. He won a relieved smile in return.

The captain was tidying up his desk as they all arrived, taking the short steps up to his hut two at a time.

"Woah, there! A deputation! Is this important or can it wait for the morning?"

"We won't keep you long, Captain," assured Patrick. "At least, I hope not. I expect we can leave practicalities for tomorrow, but we wanted to alert you to some murky goings on. We want to find out if our suspicions are right. Five minutes would do it."

"Very well, young man. Five minutes it is – I'm taking Mrs Brasted out for dinner tonight as she is much better - largely thanks to you, Patrick, I understand..? Sorry this office is small, but do step inside, everyone."

"Uh... What we wanted to set out for you is this. Dave Anstead here has ordered some machinery for his slaughter house. He runs the cattle ranch up in Numba Tu district." The two men nodded at each other. "The goods have already arrived, but when ANZ Bank sent me the documents, they did not include certificates of origin. Dave can waive that clause if he wants. But when I found out that Tai Nguyen would be delivering his goods to the farm, I was reluctant to let him do that."

The captain had stiffened at the mention of Nguyen. "I can see that."

"I also know that Bon Plats does not have a truck big enough to move such machinery. I don't suppose you could let us see the crates corresponding to these documents?"

The captain scratched his beard. "Mrs Brasted can wait a little while. She won't mind a bit, I'm sure. Follow me."

The captain was portly and his office tiny, so squeezing past everyone wasn't practical. In the end, Patrick's party retreated down the steps in the order they had ascended. Captain Brasted locked the door behind himself.

"This way, I do believe."

For once, there was little cargo awaiting collection. The five stout boxes stood by themselves in the open. They had the same appearance as those Patrick had spotted months ago being opened at the Forari mine.

"No way is my machinery in those little boxes," remarked Dave. "I don't know what they are, but processing beef can't be done with whatever is inside."

Brasted bent down and checked the reference numbers on the crates against the documentation Patrick held out to him. "The numbers match. I'd have released them if you gave me the release certificate, Patrick."

"You are sure these cannot be your machinery, Dave?" Patrick asked.

"No way, mate. No bloody way."

"Alright. Tomorrow, when the bank opens, I'll reject the documents. The exporter will have to recover his machinery himself, if he can find it. And Dave? You might want to alert the Police. I don't think Nguyen can get out of this one."

Dave and Diana both chuckled. She said, "You didn't check over the cliff edge, did you? I don't believe Mr Nguyen has anything to worry about, ever again."

Kim didn't follow. Patrick was rather afraid that he understood exactly what Diana had meant, but he chose not to comment.

-----//-----

Patrick's replacement, Kevin, flew in the next day. Patrick thought him a decent lad, if a bit wet behind the ears. Much like himself, two years earlier, really. Over beers in the Rossi hotel, having fetched Kevin from the airport, Patrick asked Kim for the 'materials for his book'.

"Oh yes. They're already in a folder waiting for you. Remind me when we go home tonight," Kim said. "We now have some more exciting news for Andrew Stuart, as well, though."

"We do. I'll give Florence a call in the morning to arrange when we could visit."

Florence was delighted to hear from Patrick. He was envious of her uncrushable upbeat attitude to life. Even when the news or topic of discussion was bad or depressing, somehow, she could jump past this given the tiniest glimmer of hope to grab.

"Patrick! It's lovely of you to call. We have all missed you while you were away – even Daddy!"

"You are very kind, Flo, but I doubt that. Anyway, Kim and I have some updating to give him – some quite important good news for a change."

"Oh, super. Can you come on Wednesday? I'm sure it'll be alright with Mummy and Daddy." And then in a less buoyant tone, "I expect it'll be Quiche and salad again. Sorry…"

He couldn't help smiling at her innocent truthfulness. "That's quite alright, Flo – actually, both Kim and I like Quiche very much. It makes a healthy change from our normal carnivorous diets. But do check with them about Wednesday – we don't want to put them out at all."

"Ok, I promise. See you soon. Byeee!"

Later that day, Mrs Brasted came into the bank and walked down the banking hall to Patrick. She was looking well. He said as much after they had shaken hands.

"Thank you for saying so. It has been a prolonged recovery, but the reason I came in was to thank you for donating blood during my operation. The hospital didn't have any stocks of my blood type and I was losing a lot during the operation. They needed what the doctor called 'Universal Donor' blood – that's your type, she said. So I wanted to say 'thank you."

"Gosh, you are very welcome, of course. I'd have come in for anybody, but am very glad I could help you."

"There was one strange thing, though," she went on. "I expected to feel a bit woozy from the anaesthetic. Maybe there would be some pain from the operation site itself, but when I woke up - oh my! I had the mother and father of all hangovers! It was as though I'd drunk a dozen beers all by myself the night before!"

Patrick recalled, with a stab of guilt, how delicate he had felt that Monday morning following the Sunday evening ANZ barbeque. Now he was ashamed of his delight at how clear-headed he became after the blood transfusion. "Hmmn. Very odd, I do agree. Still, the main thing is that you are better now. The captain said he was taking you out to dinner last night – did you have a good time?"

"Oh, yes. It was lovely. We had my favourite - coconut crab." She put her hands on her still swollen tummy. "I ate too much, but it was a real treat."

They shook hands again and parted. Patrick thought he would enjoy relating this unlikely story to Kim later.

-----//-----

The British Resident Commissioner was indeed pleased to see and hear from Patrick and Kim. His daughter had told him that they'd be bringing news of some positive developments. His personal mood improved further with the prospect of chocolate cake to follow the Quiche. He debated for a moment whether to share it with the two young bankers. As an experienced diplomat, he decided to put off the decision until they had conveyed their news. 'Letting the dog see the rabbit', he thought.

At dinner, Patrick was explaining the intricacies of Letters of Credit, and why exactly he needed Dave Anstead's signature. "I kept telling Diana that I couldn't take her instructions. She isn't a signatory on the account, you see. But afterwards, I realised that, with Tai Nguyen involved, there might also be something fishy going on."

"Yes, yes. But why take Kim with you?"

"It was Diana's odd suggestion that the signature needed to be 'under dual control'. We use the phrase 'dual control' a lot in banking, but having a customer sign something doesn't need two witnesses. It doesn't need any witnesses at all, usually. That's why we have a specimen signature on file to compare the instruction document."

"Sorry to hurry you, but you are losing me. Why did you ask Kim to come along too?"

"Oh yes. Diana knows what I just explained. Everyone does who uses trade

457

finance instruments like LCs. Under pressure, she hoped Nguyen didn't. The more I thought about it, the more I felt that her voice had sounded strained. She called me 'Mr Field' – and saying 'dual control' was her coded way of calling for extra help."

"In the end," Kim interrupted, "I wasn't actually needed. But I might have been, and I could have driven off to fetch more help."

"Tell me about this man, Oscar," asked the Commissioner. "He seems like a particularly good egg."

With a broad grin, Patrick explained that Dave Anstead had been hiding in the coconut trees. He'd seen Patrick and Diana forced to walk across the field at gun point. He took the opportunity to untie his bull, knowing it would create a major distraction. The calculation was that Nguyen might kill or injure the bull, but the viability of his business was under threat anyway, so it was worth the risk.

"The bull is named 'Oscar'?"

"He is. Dave and Diana love him dearly and with them, he is tame. But with intruders – like Nguyen – he is very protective of his 'ladies'."

"We believe Nguyen may well be dead," put in Kim. "Oscar punted him over the cliff edge. Not only was he hit at full speed, but it's a pretty big drop down to the rocks below. Have you heard any news about him in the last day or two?"

"As a matter of fact, there was talk about him going away for a long time." Andrew Stuart cocked one eyebrow. "I took it to mean he was up to some distasteful business which he would bring back to Vanuatu in due course. Would Mr and Mrs Anstead object to a low-key visit from a British official?"

"Sir, I don't think they are actually married. But both are Australian and are very welcoming and personable. And you might consider giving them a modest order for beef – as their produce is top quality!" Patrick added, cheekily.

So, for the time remaining that Commissioner and Mrs Stuart resided in Vanuatu, Dave Anstead brought his pickup down to the dock every week. He would unload a consignment of selected cuts of beef to be transported across to Iririki Island.

-----//-----

It was obvious to Kim that, when he wasn't busy or engaged in something exciting, Patrick was still moping around and feeling rejected by Jessica. These moods

459

usually emerged after dinner. Their consumption of Glayva liqueur increased to the point that Kim began to worry about his friend. At last, he raised the subject. He blurted it out, hoping to cut through his friend's descending pall of misery.

"You know Jessica has moved on – she didn't want to be hurt or tied down as the recipient of your news of imminent departure, so took action. Ok, it's painful right now, but you need to move on too."

"I know," acknowledged Patrick. "And you are right, of course." He shook his head. "For her to take up with this meathead character, Max Whatever he's called. I'm more concerned for her than I am for myself. Does that make sense?"

"Oh, didn't you hear? He's history. Seems he's been 'playing away' with some yachtie girl and Jessica found out."

That was news to Patrick. "What happened?"

"She fell off a balcony as they were …um. You know…"

"What? But how did Jess find out?"

"The girl broke her arm or leg or something so Max had to take her into hospital. While there, she told the doctor who set her limb how it happened."

"And that doctor was Jessica, of course?"

Kim nodded.

"Poor Jess. I'd better call her and check she's ok."

Kim was doubtful. "Are you sure that's a good idea?"

"Positive. I'll call her tomorrow morning."

-----//-----

Soon the day came for his final departure from Vila. Most of Patrick's possessions were already in a crate and would travel by sea back to the UK to his parents' address. He had his air tickets and passport and enough cash and travellers' cheques to last for his three-day journey.

He checked in his hold baggage and went back to the little gaggle of well-wishers there to wave him goodbye. In the end, Jessica had come to the airport with Kim and Florence. Dave and Diana were there as well.

He shook hands with everyone. Florence gave him a hug and said her mother and father would miss him too. Just before he went through to Departures – an open-air waiting area beyond the Immigration Hall -

Jessica hugged and kissed him and made him promise to write now and again. He turned back to give them all a final wave before boarding the Air Melanesia Fokker Friendship for the last time.

The acceleration down the runway pressed him back into his seat. Tears welled up and streaked his face. He didn't bother to try to wipe them away because nobody was sitting beside him. He could let the tears flow without embarrassment.

The aeroplane's nose came up as it began to climb into the sky. Patrick couldn't bear to look out of the window at the receding country that he realised he had come to love so much. He fixed his gaze on the back of the pilot's head. Then spent the next few minutes unfocussed, but with his brain swirling and a steady stream of tears soaking his shirt front. He was still clutching his passport. He tried to tuck it into his inside jacket pocket, but there was something stopping it.

He stretched two fingers down to the bottom of the pocket and extracted a folded piece of paper. It was the most recent letter from Penelope.

His tears stopped then. He closed his eyes and began to think about Bahrain.

*Cover Design by James, GoOnWrite.com*

# About the Author

Richard Sexton joined a British commercial bank at the tender age of sixteen and retired as a director of its investment bank after twenty-eight years of service. He was lucky to live in many countries to which access these days is barred or at least is deemed unwise.

He knows that living in a culture which is not your own is a remarkable privilege. He met many amazing characters, good and bad. Elements of some of them are included in this story and in the subsequent stories in this series.

# Also by Richard Sexton

## 'Saved from the Desert'

After Long Leave in the UK, Royal Counties Bank posts Patrick to Bahrain. He is quickly tracked by *Al Sharika* which found him in Vanuatu and they redouble efforts to compromise and blackmail him into assisting their funding. He may have dodged their kidnap attempts but now he risks arrest by the Religious Police in Saudi Arabia. How can he survive capture and get back to Bahrain? Will he ever see his doctor girlfriend again? Can Penny and his friends protect him?

## 'Saved by the Gris-gris'

Royal Counties Bank closes the Bahrain Branch. Patrick transfers to their Wall Street, New York office. His first investment banking success in New Orleans brings him into direct conflict with the America arm of the ancient organisation again. Fraudulent trading patterns reveal *Al Sharika* activity as Penny in MI-6 had predicted. His girlfriend, Dr Jessica, has landed a job in New York as well, so they are together at last, but for how long? A chance meeting with a Voodoo priest in New Orleans may help him, but a Mafia godfather offers more practical assistance.

## 'Saved by the Colonel'

Patrick has been offered a more senior job in Royal Counties Bank in London which would involve travelling to the Middle East. Now his beloved Bahrain dealing room has been closed, close liaison with his former Arab and North African customers is vital. He leaves his fiancée, Dr Jessica, in New York for a short project in the UK. But he feels that his career has lost its way. A chance meeting with a head hunter introduces him to an entrepreneur starting a manufacturing business. His excitement at the new opportunity is blunted because agents of *Al Sharika* find him again. He is drawn into a web of financial intrigue and new dangers from organised crime in Turkey. His friend Penny says MI-6 has been infiltrated and she fears for her safety as well as his. He cannot live like this and determines to unmask the head of *Al Sharika*. He comes face to face with the current leader in a startling climax. Who will prevail?

www.ingramcontent.com/pod-product-compliance
Lightning Source LLC
Chambersburg PA
CBHW060241030726
47493CB00024B/1460